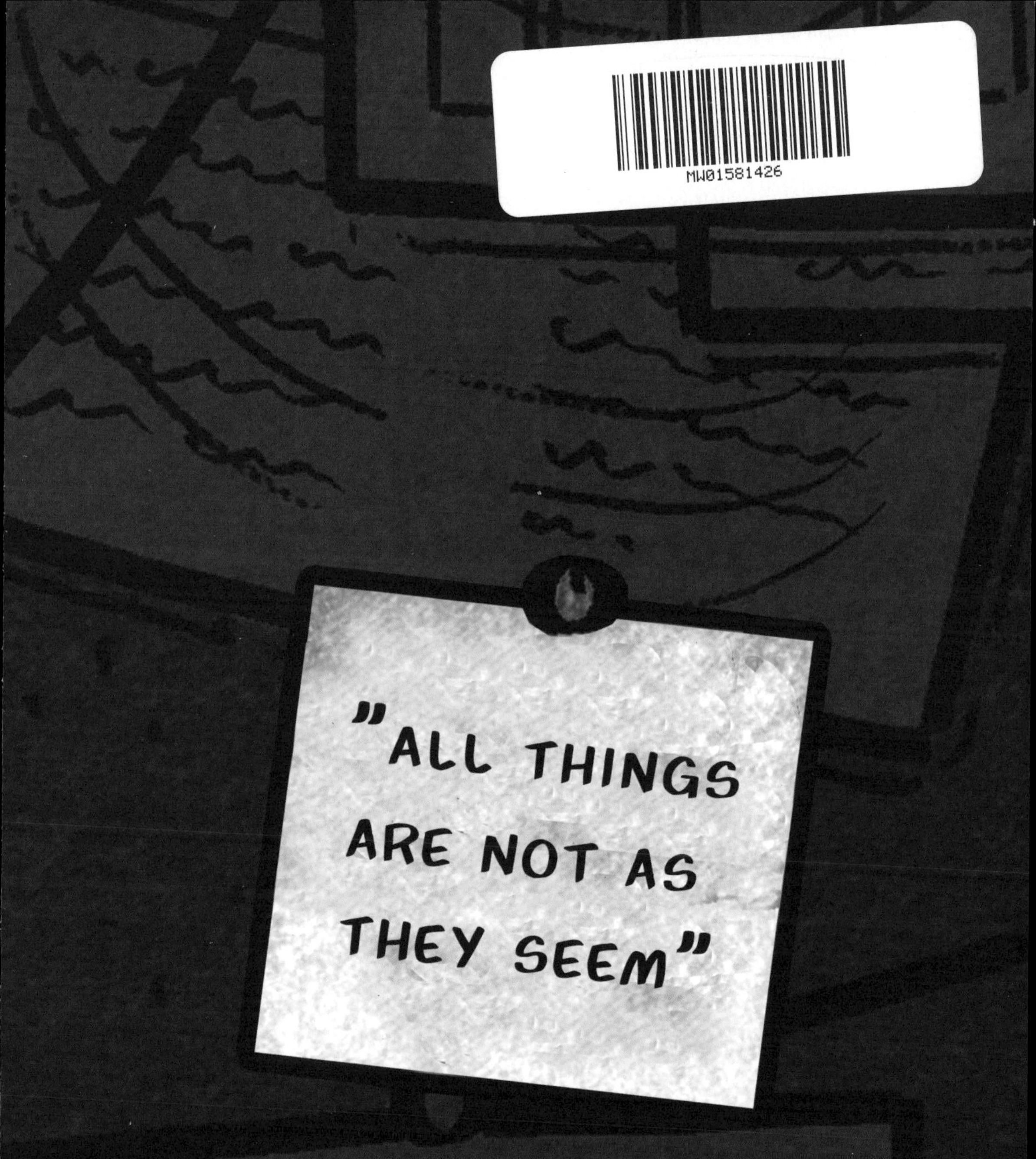
"ALL THINGS
ARE NOT AS
THEY SEEM"

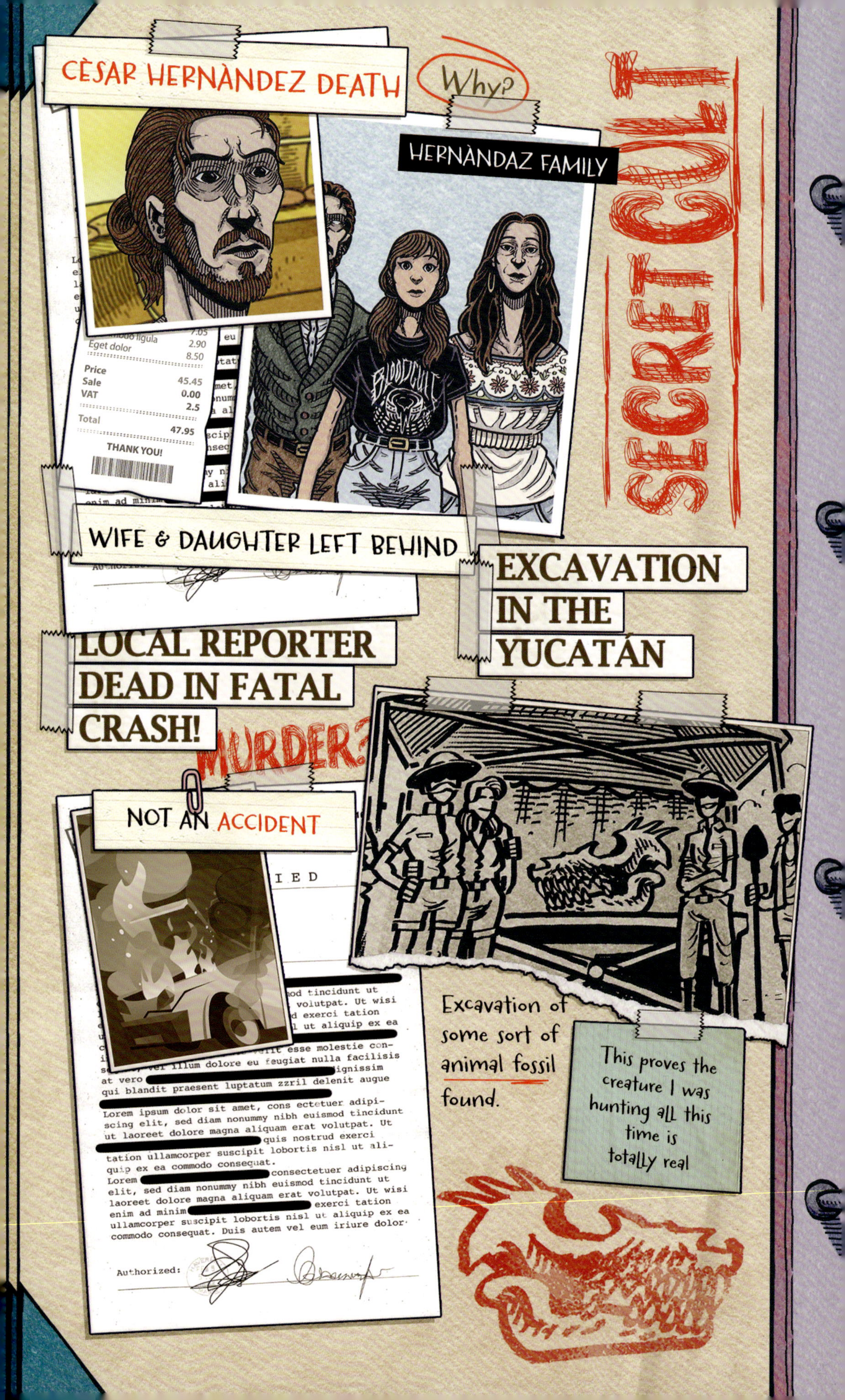
CÈSAR HERNÀNDEZ DEATH
Why?
HERNÀNDAZ FAMILY
SECRET CULT
Eget dolor 2.90
8.50
Price
Sale 45.45
VAT 0.00
2.5
Total 47.95
THANK YOU!
WIFE & DAUGHTER LEFT BEHIND
EXCAVATION
IN THE
YUCATÁN
LOCAL REPORTER
DEAD IN FATAL
CRASH!
MURDER?
NOT AN ACCIDENT
Excavation of some sort of animal fossil found.
This proves the creature I was hunting all this time is totally real
Authorized:

Tales of Blood and Ink

CHUPACABRA

Creators
Matthew Medney

Written by
Matthew Medney

Story by
Matthew Medney
Eric Bromberg
Fernando Rodriguez-Vila

Cover Artist
Lip Wei Chang

Alternative Cover Artist
Vincenzo Riccardi

Pencils, Inks, Colors
Kyle Faehnrich
(aka) Goons & Goblins

Letters
Dave Sharpe

Editorial & Title Design
Voodoo Bownz
Mohamed Samah

Produced by
Exile Content Studio
Gungnir Entertainment
Herø Projects

Executive Producer
Matthew Medney
Eric Bromberg
Fernando Rodriguez-Vila

Senior Production Designer
Mohamed Samah

CULT LEADER
IMMORTAL??
STONEHART
BLOOD FUSION
SACRIFICING HUMANS AND DRAINING THEIR BLOOD FOR THE CULT RITUAL.

GUNGNIR
TALES FROM THE ALL-FATHER

Founder
Matthew Medney

Executive Editor
Steve Orlando

Editor In Chief
Jim Krueger

Marketing
Paul Reed

Publishing & Production
Frazier Dodek

Publicity
Tracey Daniels

First Edition

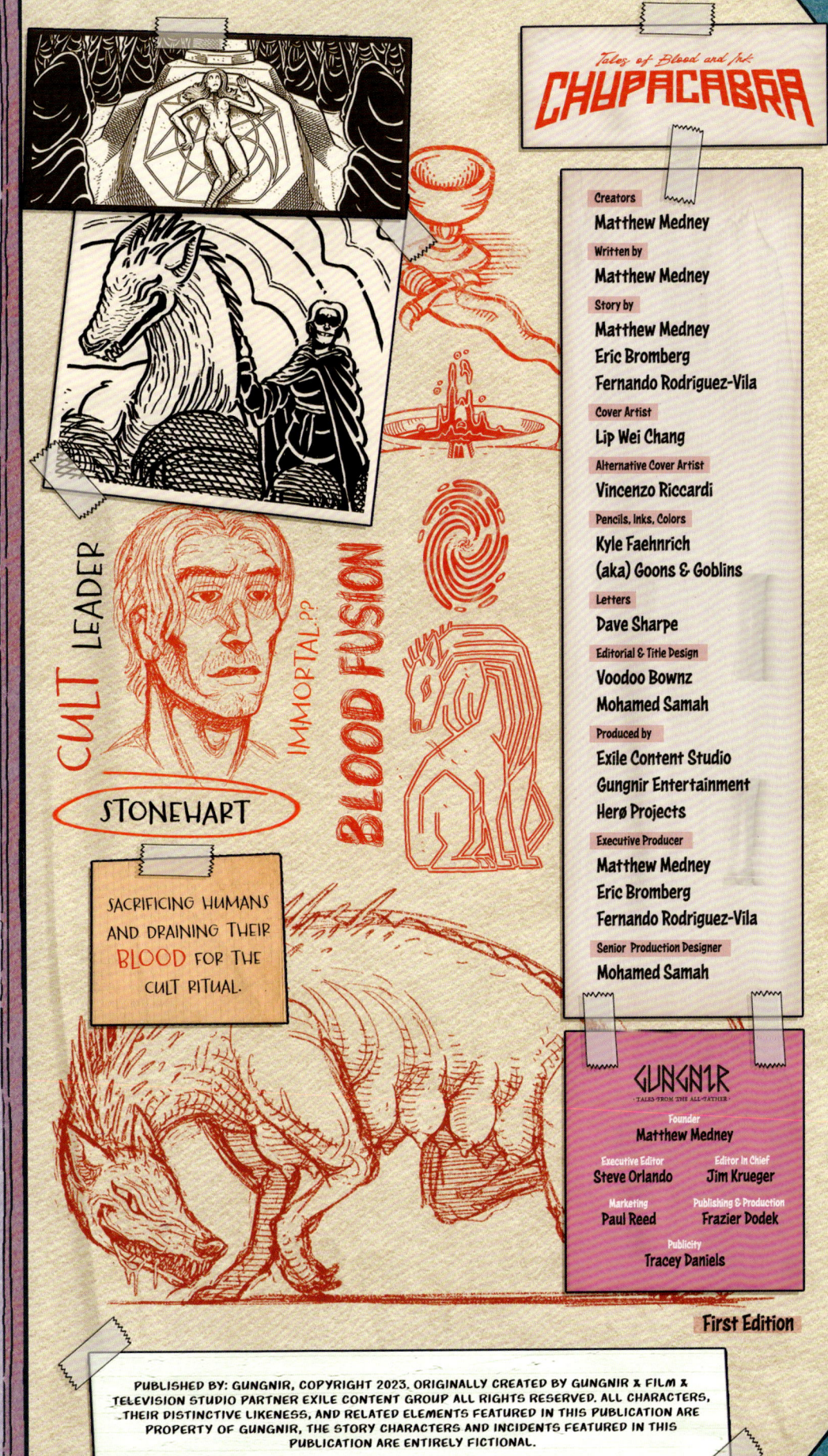

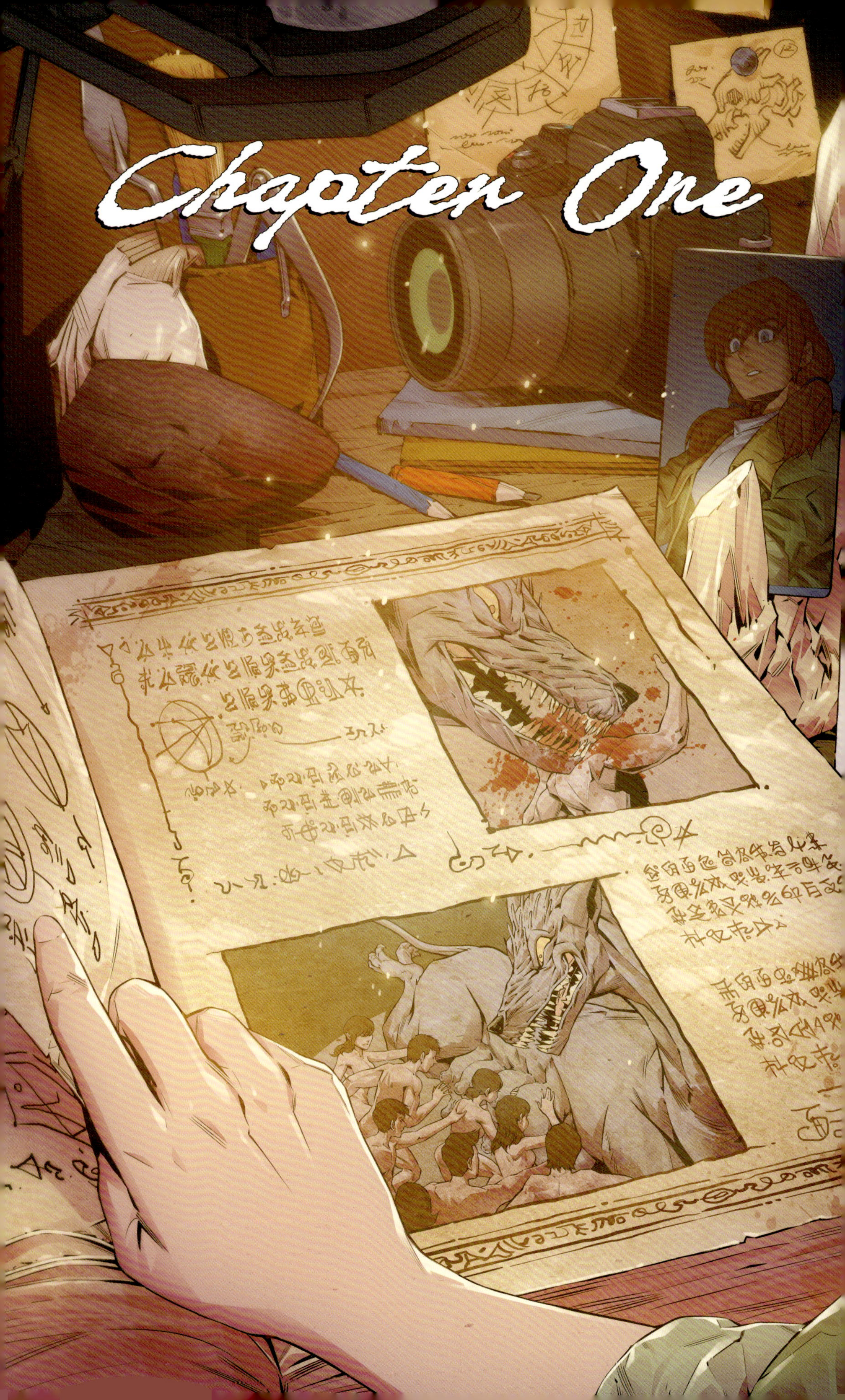
Chapter One

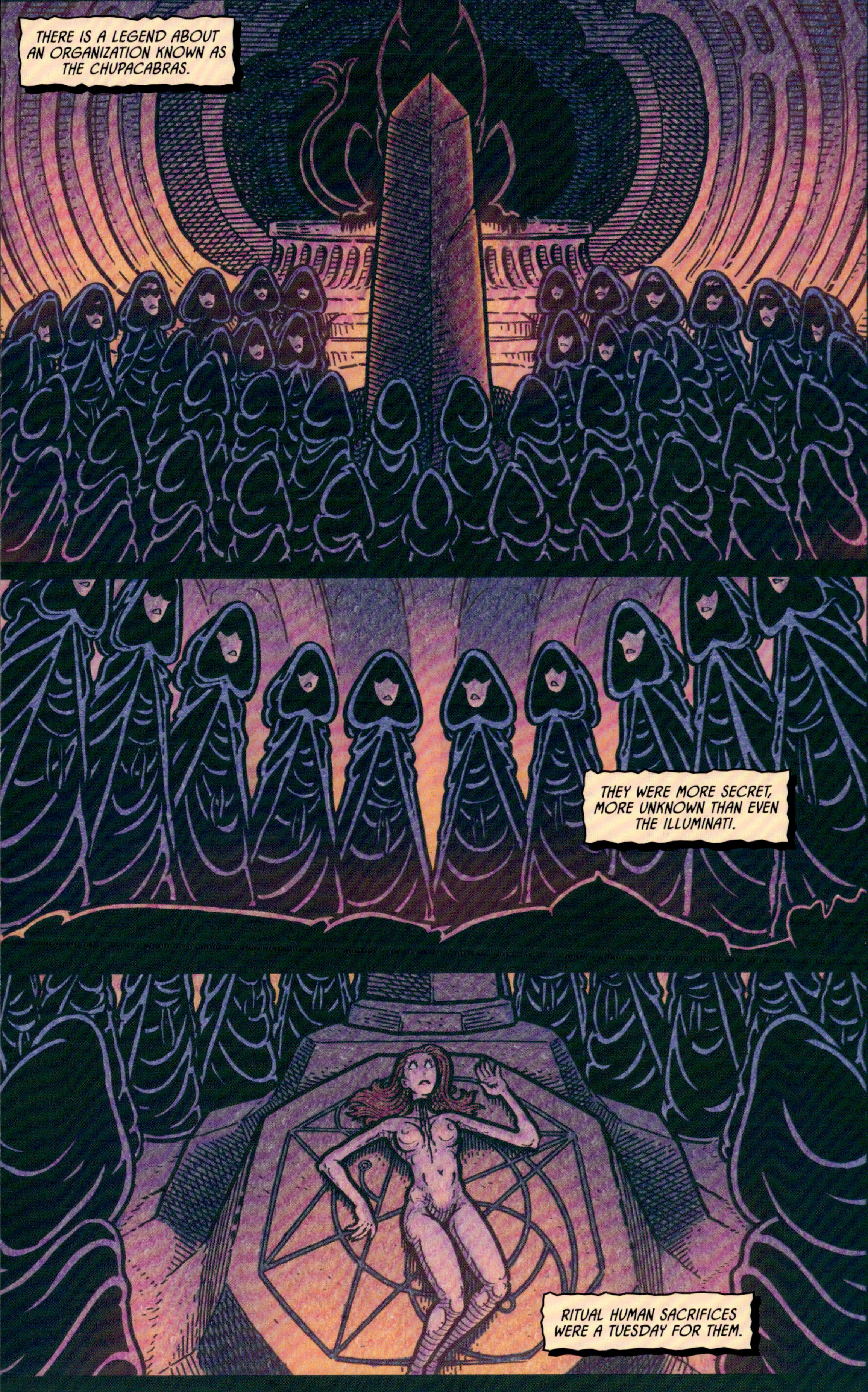
THERE IS A LEGEND ABOUT AN ORGANIZATION KNOWN AS THE CHUPACABRAS.
THEY WERE MORE SECRET, MORE UNKNOWN THAN EVEN THE ILLUMINATI.
RITUAL HUMAN SACRIFICES WERE A TUESDAY FOR THEM.

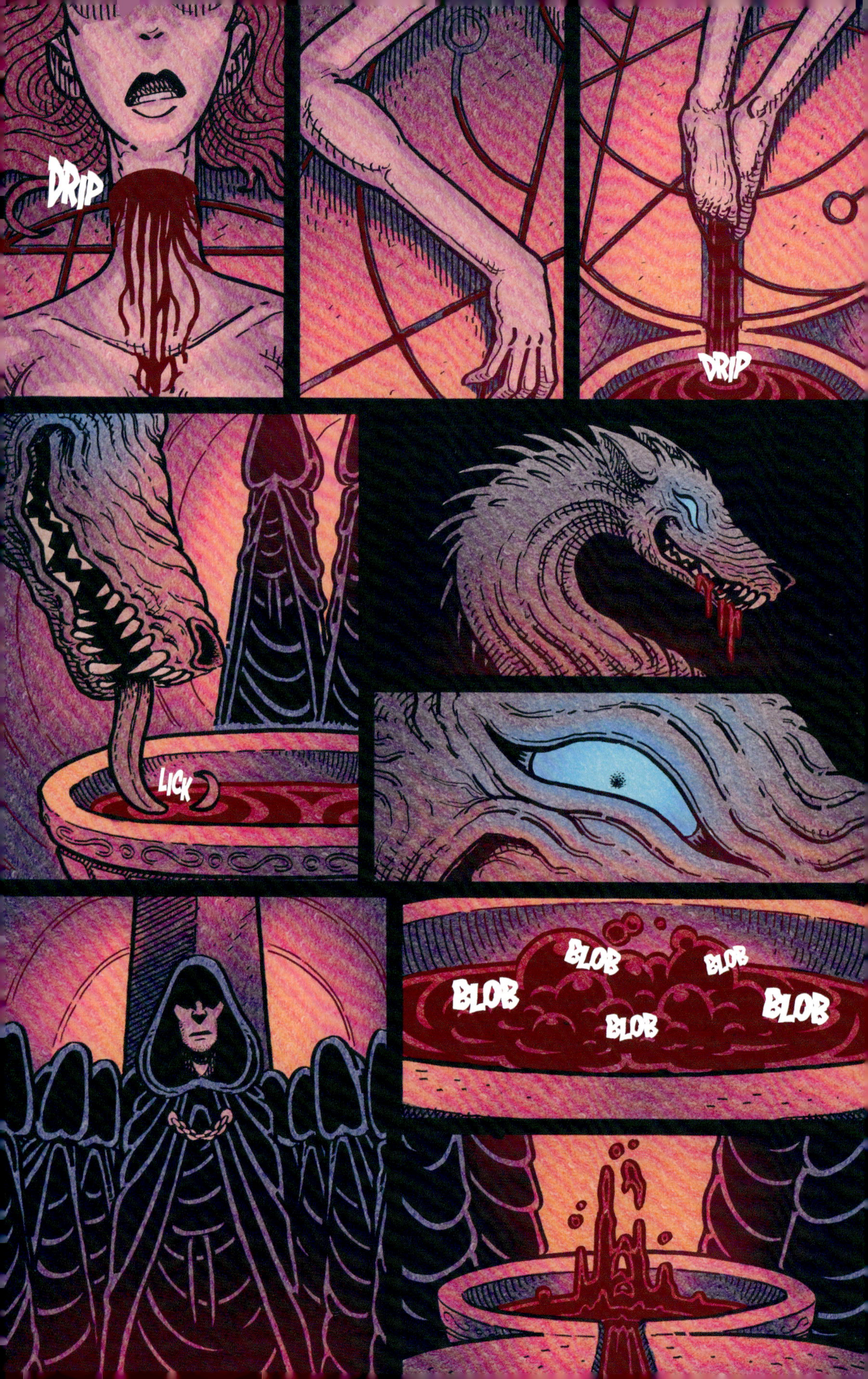
DRIP
DRIP
LICK
BLOB
BLOB
BLOB
BLOB
BLOB

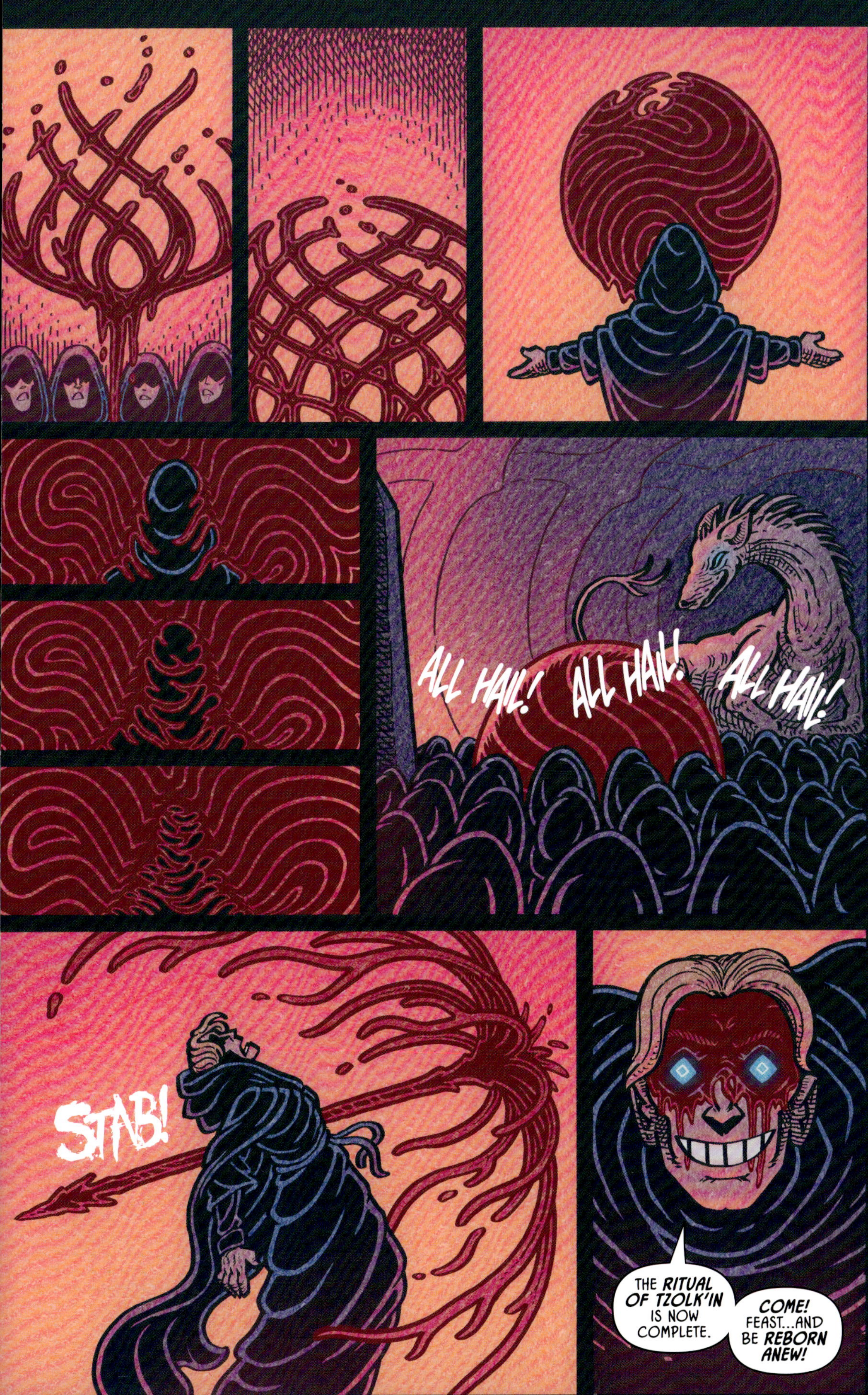
ALL HAIL!
ALL HAIL!
ALL HAIL!
STAB!
THE RITUAL OF TZOLK'IN IS NOW COMPLETE.
COME! FEAST...AND BE REBORN ANEW!

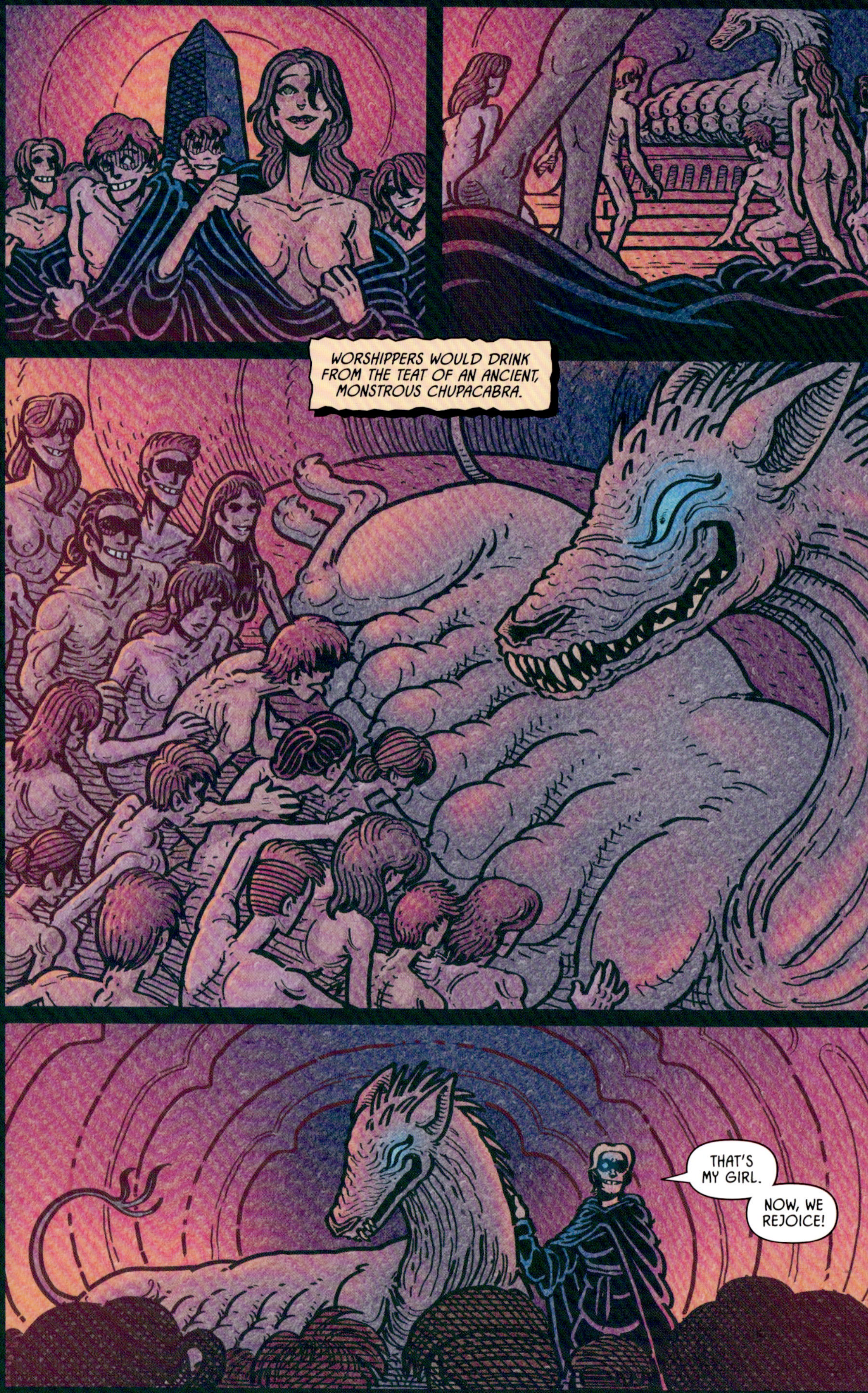
WORSHIPPERS WOULD DRINK FROM THE TEAT OF AN ANCIENT, MONSTROUS CHUPACABRA.
THAT'S MY GIRL.
NOW, WE REJOICE!

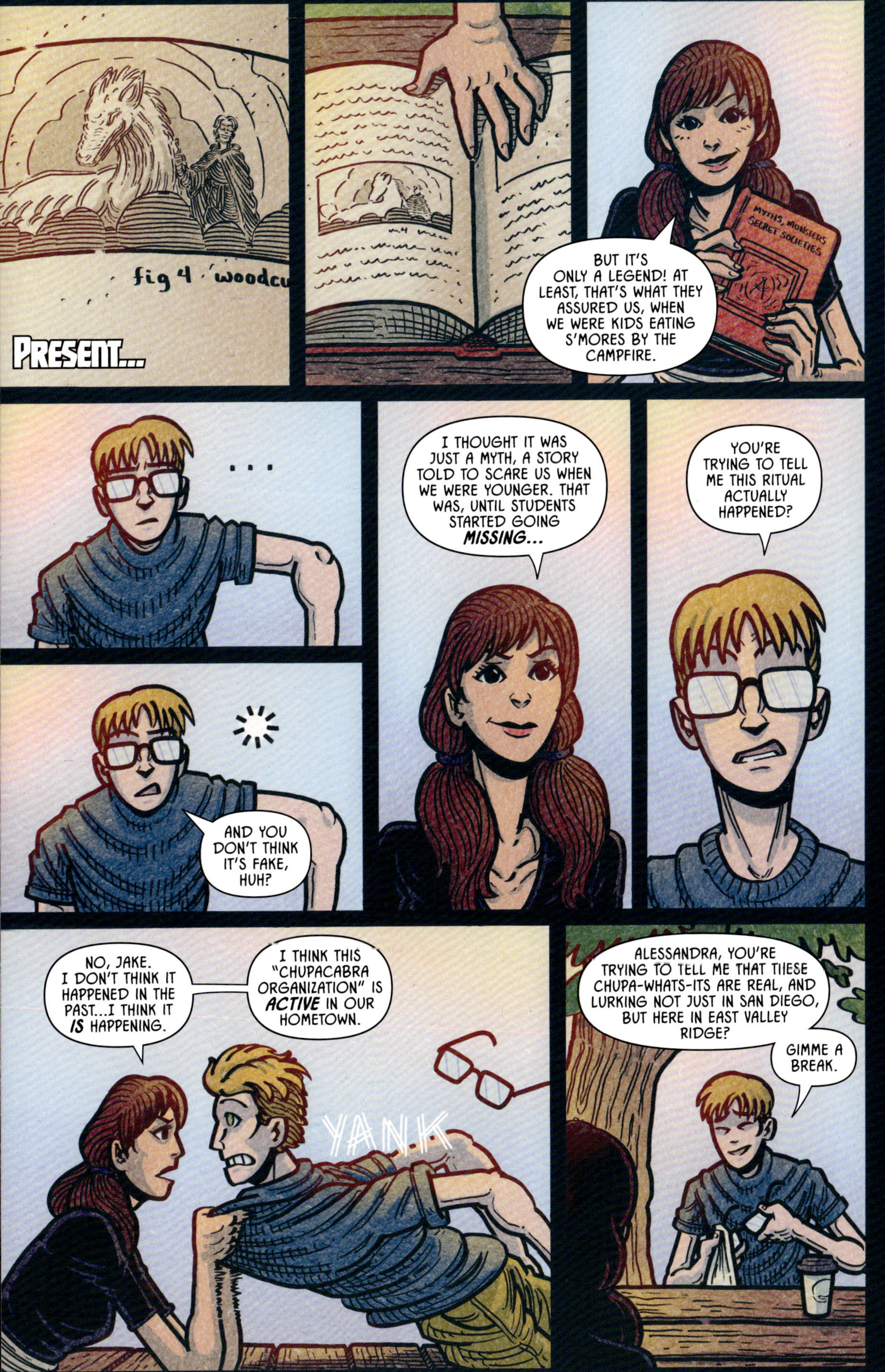
fig 4 'woodcu
PRESENT...
BUT IT'S ONLY A LEGEND! AT LEAST, THAT'S WHAT THEY ASSURED US, WHEN WE WERE KIDS EATING S'MORES BY THE CAMPFIRE.
MYTHS, MONSTERS SECRET SOCIETIES
...
I THOUGHT IT WAS JUST A MYTH, A STORY TOLD TO SCARE US WHEN WE WERE YOUNGER. THAT WAS, UNTIL STUDENTS STARTED GOING MISSING...
YOU'RE TRYING TO TELL ME THIS RITUAL ACTUALLY HAPPENED?
AND YOU DON'T THINK IT'S FAKE, HUH?
NO, JAKE. I DON'T THINK IT HAPPENED IN THE PAST...I THINK IT IS HAPPENING.
I THINK THIS "CHUPACABRA ORGANIZATION" IS ACTIVE IN OUR HOMETOWN.
YANK
ALESSANDRA, YOU'RE TRYING TO TELL ME THAT THESE CHUPA-WHATS-ITS ARE REAL, AND LURKING NOT JUST IN SAN DIEGO, BUT HERE IN EAST VALLEY RIDGE?
GIMME A BREAK.

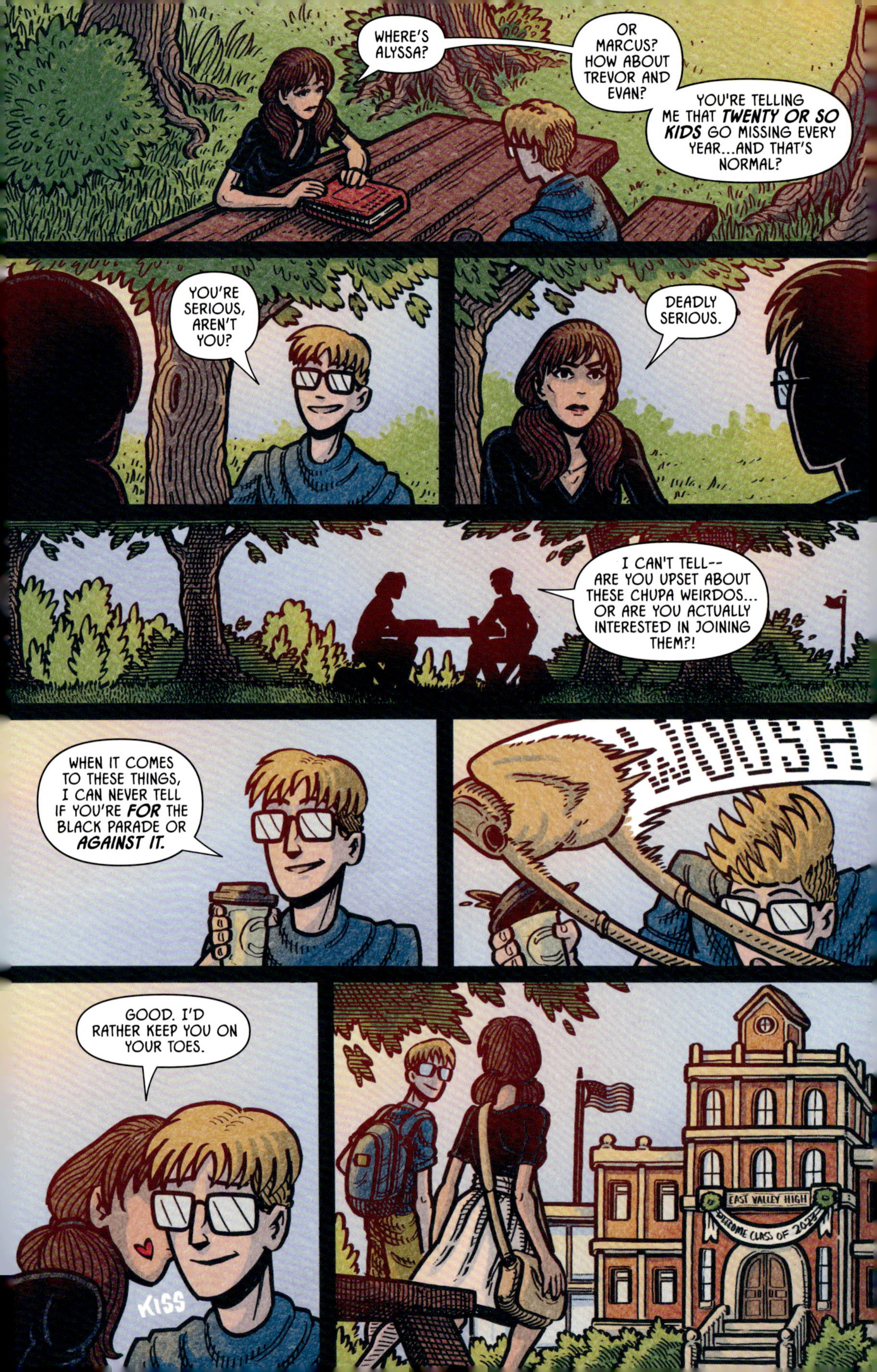

WHERE'S ALYSSA?
OR MARCUS? HOW ABOUT TREVOR AND EVAN?
YOU'RE TELLING ME THAT **TWENTY OR SO KIDS** GO MISSING EVERY YEAR...AND THAT'S NORMAL?
YOU'RE SERIOUS, AREN'T YOU?
DEADLY SERIOUS.
I CAN'T TELL-- ARE YOU UPSET ABOUT THESE CHUPA WEIRDOS... OR ARE YOU ACTUALLY INTERESTED IN JOINING THEM?!
WHEN IT COMES TO THESE THINGS, I CAN NEVER TELL IF YOU'RE **FOR** THE BLACK PARADE OR **AGAINST IT.**
WOOSH
GOOD. I'D RATHER KEEP YOU ON YOUR TOES.
KISS
EAST VALLEY HIGH
WELCOME CLASS OF 2023

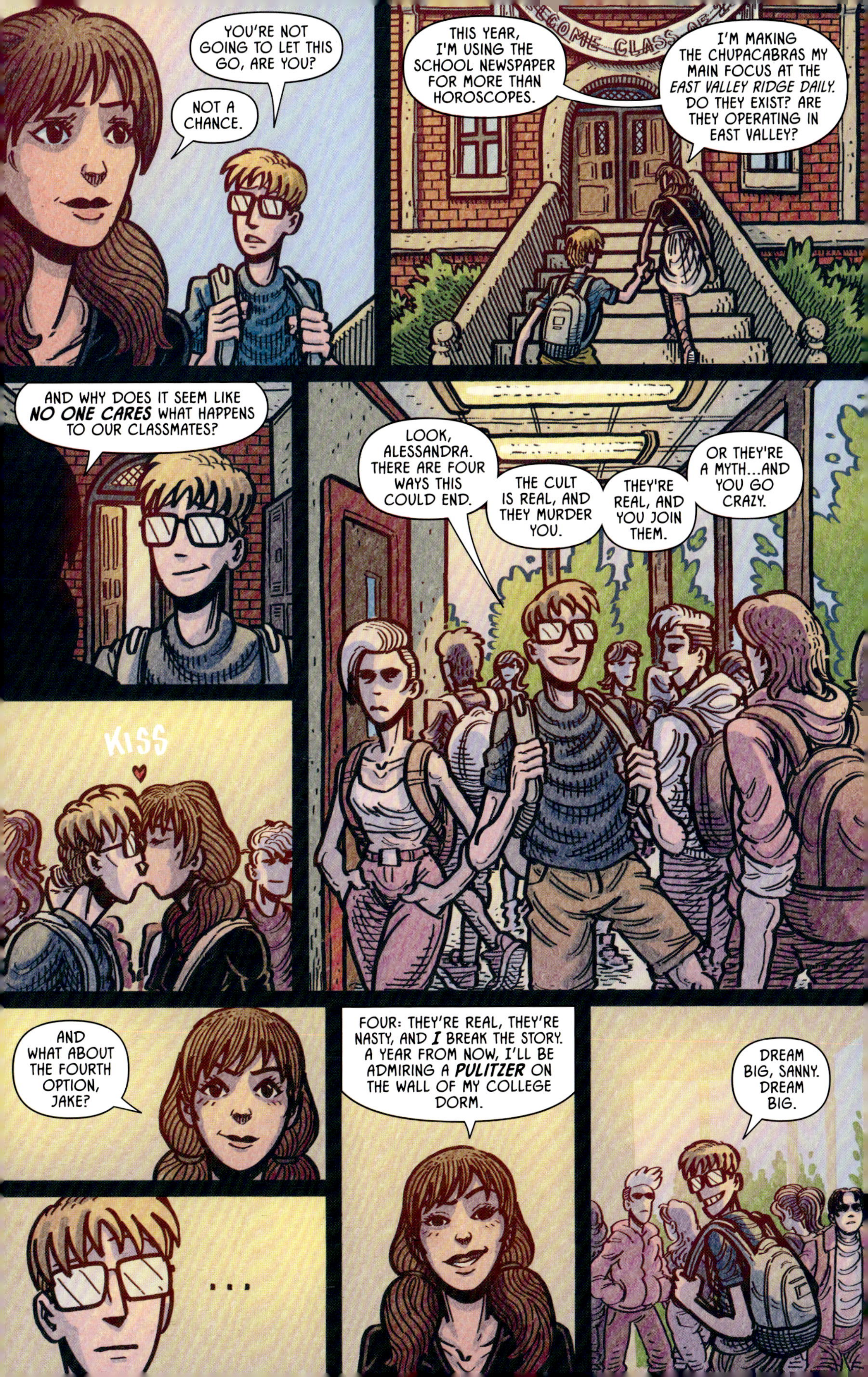
YOU'RE NOT GOING TO LET THIS GO, ARE YOU?
NOT A CHANCE.
THIS YEAR, I'M USING THE SCHOOL NEWSPAPER FOR MORE THAN HOROSCOPES.
I'M MAKING THE CHUPACABRAS MY MAIN FOCUS AT THE *EAST VALLEY RIDGE DAILY.* DO THEY EXIST? ARE THEY OPERATING IN EAST VALLEY?
AND WHY DOES IT SEEM LIKE **NO ONE CARES** WHAT HAPPENS TO OUR CLASSMATES?
LOOK, ALESSANDRA. THERE ARE FOUR WAYS THIS COULD END.
THE CULT IS REAL, AND THEY MURDER YOU.
THEY'RE REAL, AND YOU JOIN THEM.
OR THEY'RE A MYTH...AND YOU GO CRAZY.
KISS
AND WHAT ABOUT THE FOURTH OPTION, JAKE?
...
FOUR: THEY'RE REAL, THEY'RE NASTY, AND ***I*** BREAK THE STORY. A YEAR FROM NOW, I'LL BE ADMIRING A ***PULITZER*** ON THE WALL OF MY COLLEGE DORM.
DREAM BIG, SANNY. DREAM BIG.

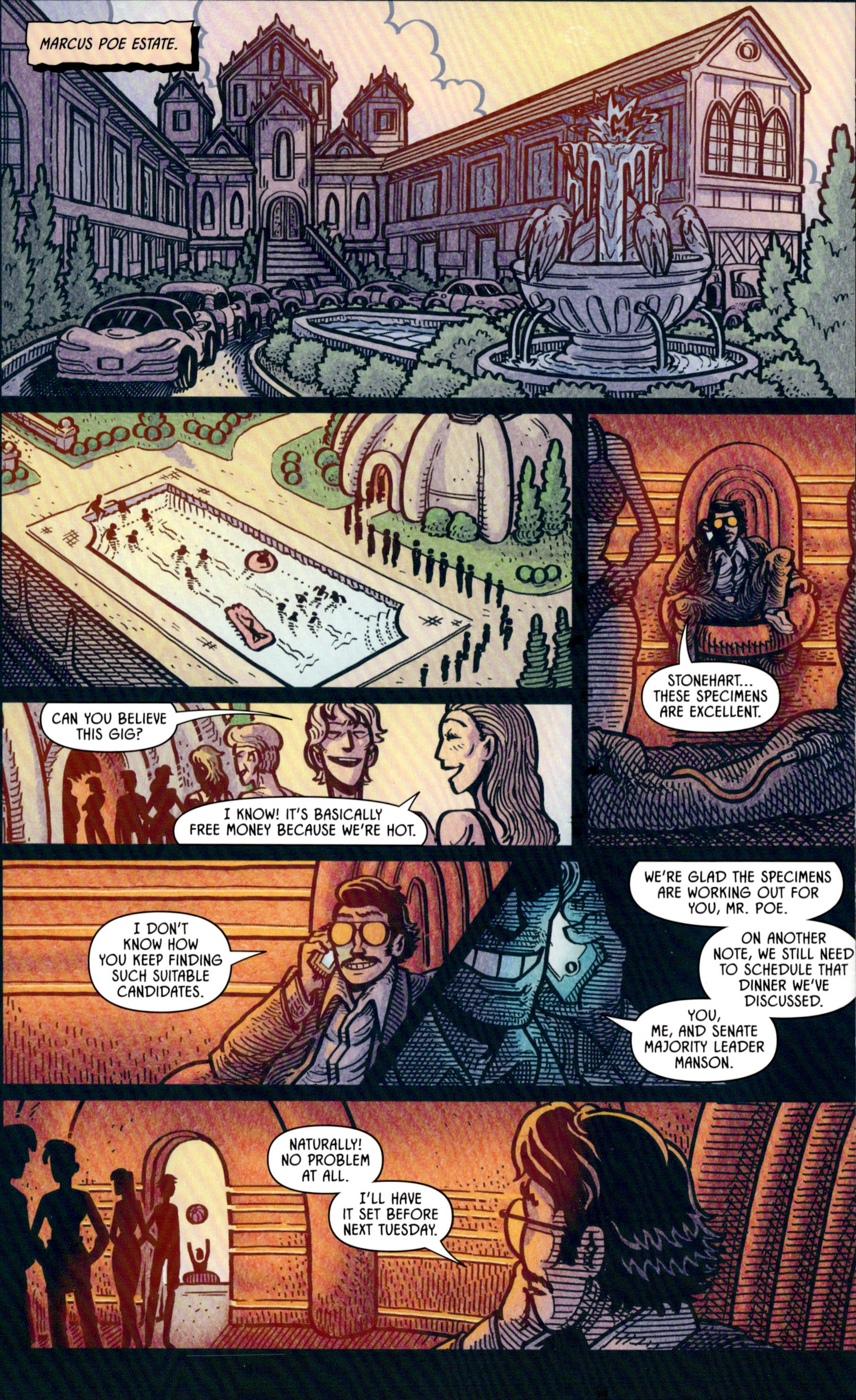
MARCUS POE ESTATE.
STONEHART... THESE SPECIMENS ARE EXCELLENT.
CAN YOU BELIEVE THIS GIG?
I KNOW! IT'S BASICALLY FREE MONEY BECAUSE WE'RE HOT.
I DON'T KNOW HOW YOU KEEP FINDING SUCH SUITABLE CANDIDATES.
WE'RE GLAD THE SPECIMENS ARE WORKING OUT FOR YOU, MR. POE.
ON ANOTHER NOTE, WE STILL NEED TO SCHEDULE THAT DINNER WE'VE DISCUSSED.
YOU, ME, AND SENATE MAJORITY LEADER MANSON.
NATURALLY! NO PROBLEM AT ALL.
I'LL HAVE IT SET BEFORE NEXT TUESDAY.

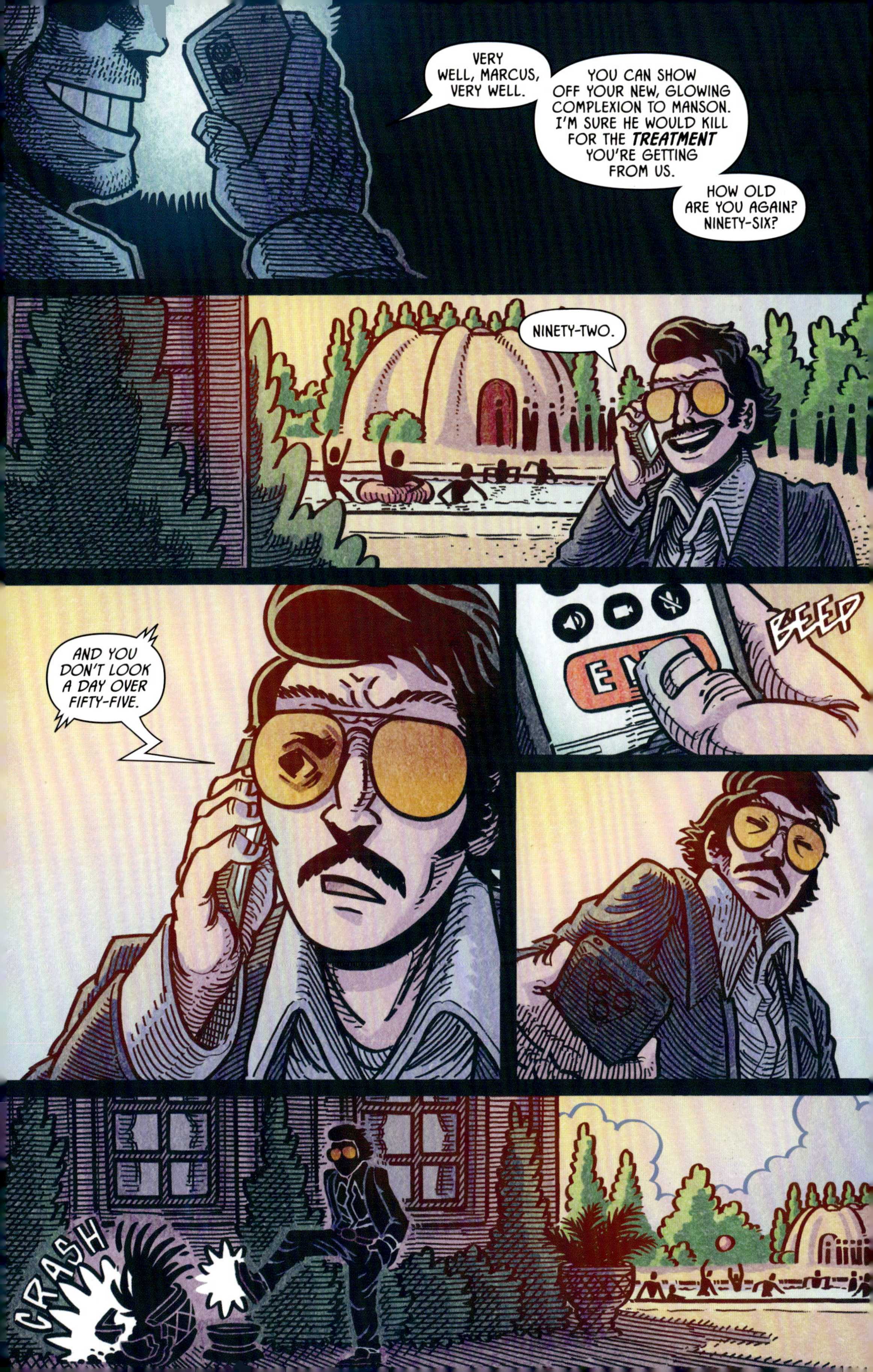
VERY WELL, MARCUS, VERY WELL.
YOU CAN SHOW OFF YOUR NEW, GLOWING COMPLEXION TO MANSON. I'M SURE HE WOULD KILL FOR THE TREATMENT YOU'RE GETTING FROM US.
HOW OLD ARE YOU AGAIN? NINETY-SIX?
NINETY-TWO.
AND YOU DON'T LOOK A DAY OVER FIFTY-FIVE.
BEEP
CRASH

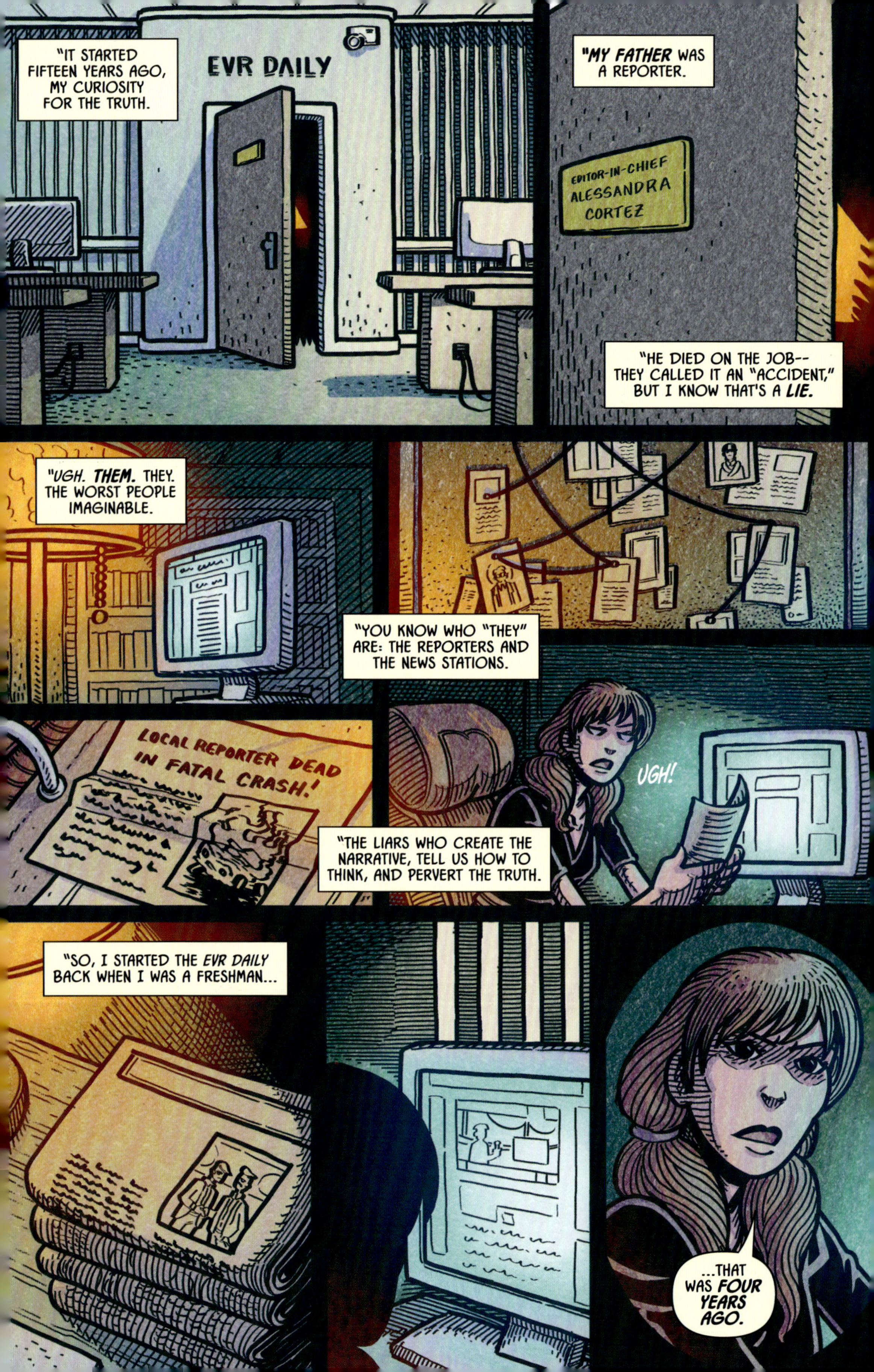
"IT STARTED FIFTEEN YEARS AGO, MY CURIOSITY FOR THE TRUTH.
EVR DAILY
"*MY FATHER* WAS A REPORTER.
EDITOR-IN-CHIEF ALESSANDRA CORTEZ
"HE DIED ON THE JOB-- THEY CALLED IT AN "ACCIDENT," BUT I KNOW THAT'S A *LIE.*
"*UGH.* ***THEM.*** THEY. THE WORST PEOPLE IMAGINABLE.
"YOU KNOW WHO "THEY" ARE: THE REPORTERS AND THE NEWS STATIONS.
LOCAL REPORTER DEAD IN FATAL CRASH!
UGH!
"THE LIARS WHO CREATE THE NARRATIVE, TELL US HOW TO THINK, AND PERVERT THE TRUTH.
"SO, I STARTED THE *EVR DAILY* BACK WHEN I WAS A FRESHMAN...
...THAT WAS ***FOUR YEARS AGO.***

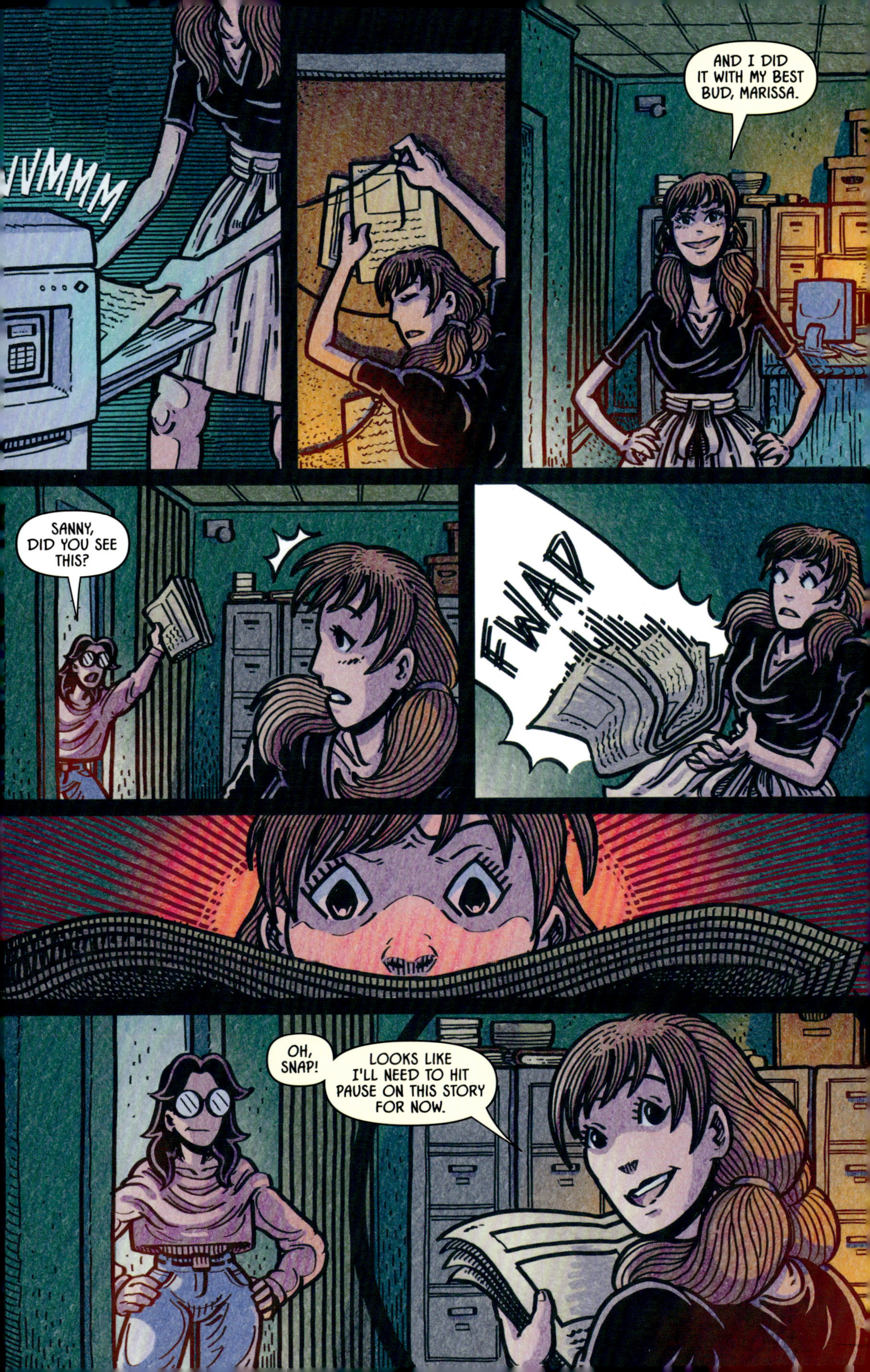

VVMMM
AND I DID IT WITH MY BEST BUD, MARISSA.
SANNY, DID YOU SEE THIS?
FWAP
OH, SNAP!
LOOKS LIKE I'LL NEED TO HIT PAUSE ON THIS STORY FOR NOW.

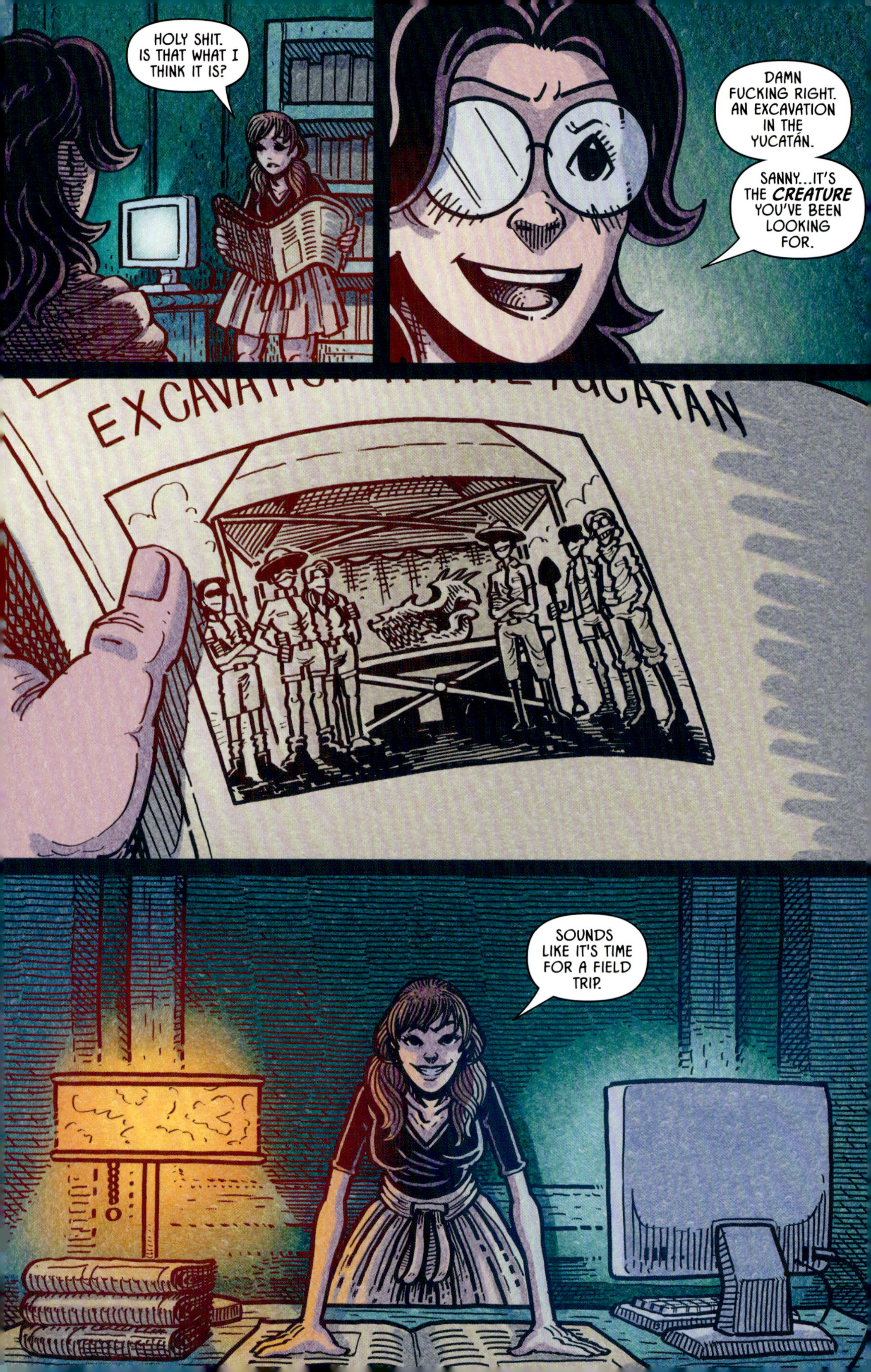
HOLY SHIT. IS THAT WHAT I THINK IT IS?
DAMN FUCKING RIGHT. AN EXCAVATION IN THE YUCATÁN.
SANNY...IT'S THE **CREATURE** YOU'VE BEEN LOOKING FOR.
EXCAVATION IN THE YUCATAN
SOUNDS LIKE IT'S TIME FOR A FIELD TRIP.

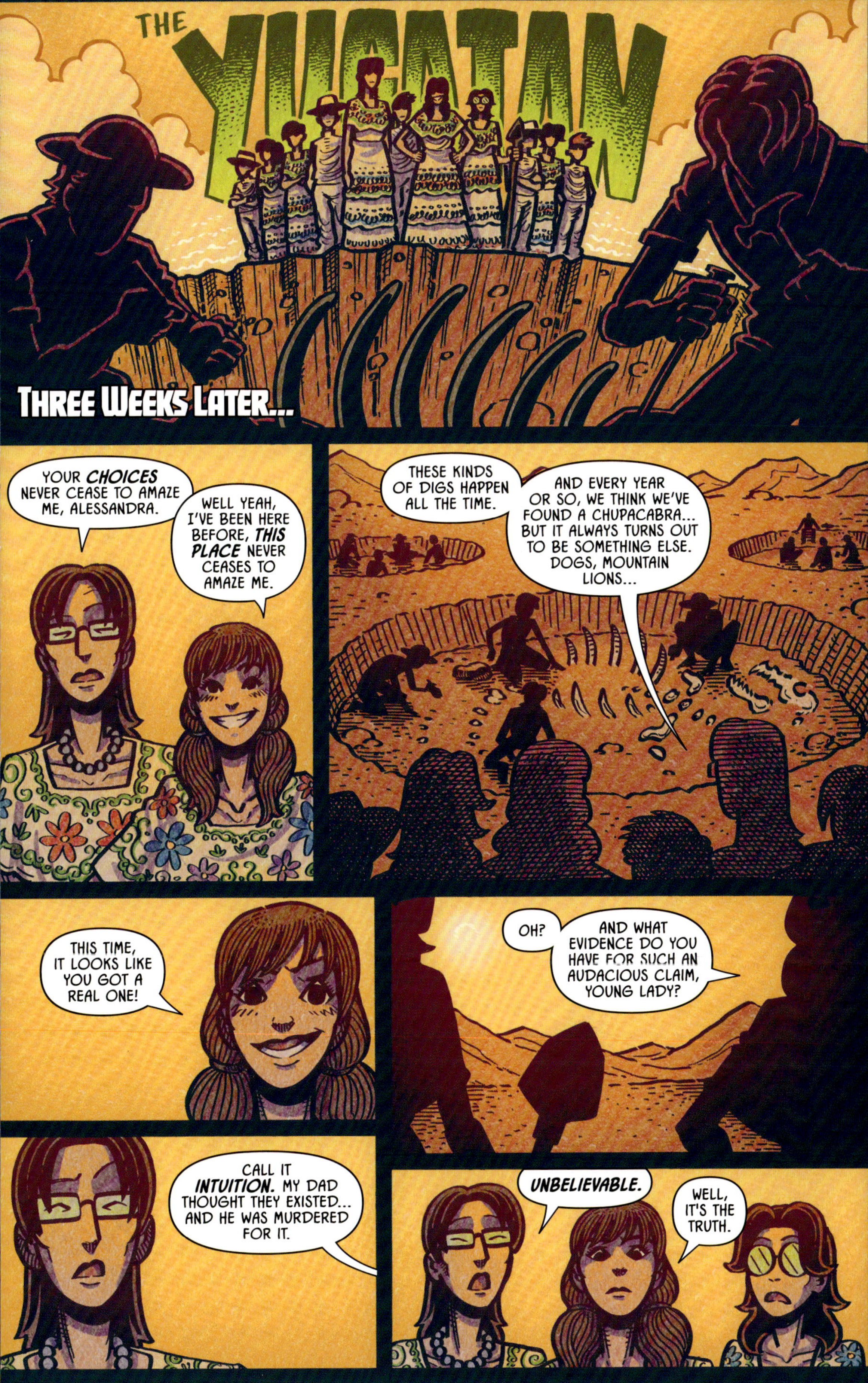
THE YUCATAN
THREE WEEKS LATER...
YOUR CHOICES NEVER CEASE TO AMAZE ME, ALESSANDRA.
WELL YEAH, I'VE BEEN HERE BEFORE, THIS PLACE NEVER CEASES TO AMAZE ME.
THESE KINDS OF DIGS HAPPEN ALL THE TIME.
AND EVERY YEAR OR SO, WE THINK WE'VE FOUND A CHUPACABRA... BUT IT ALWAYS TURNS OUT TO BE SOMETHING ELSE. DOGS, MOUNTAIN LIONS...
THIS TIME, IT LOOKS LIKE YOU GOT A REAL ONE!
OH?
AND WHAT EVIDENCE DO YOU HAVE FOR SUCH AN AUDACIOUS CLAIM, YOUNG LADY?
CALL IT INTUITION. MY DAD THOUGHT THEY EXISTED... AND HE WAS MURDERED FOR IT.
UNBELIEVABLE.
WELL, IT'S THE TRUTH.

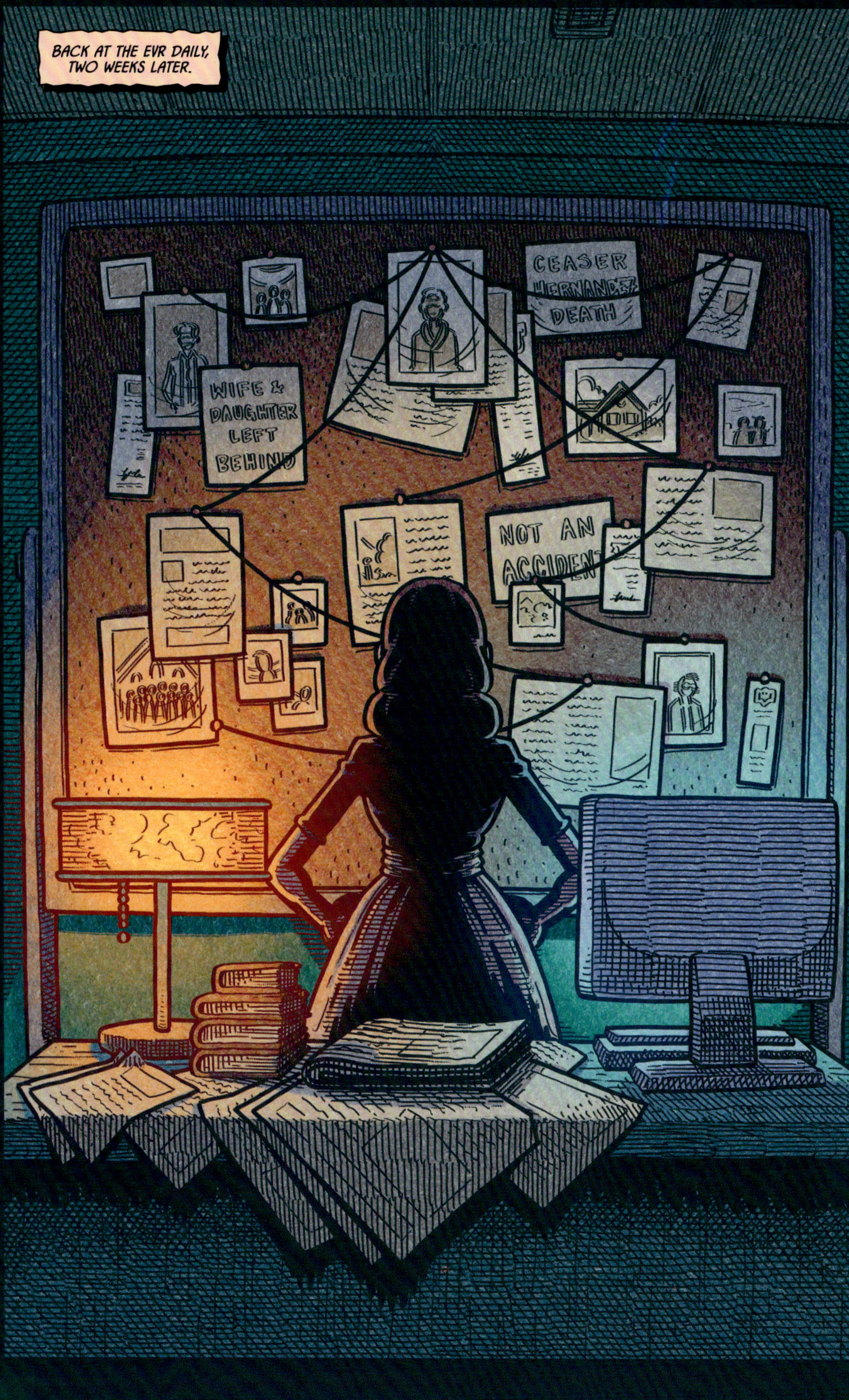
BACK AT THE EVR DAILY, TWO WEEKS LATER.
CEASER HERNANDEZ DEATH
WIFE & DAUGHTER LEFT BEHIND
NOT AN ACCIDENT

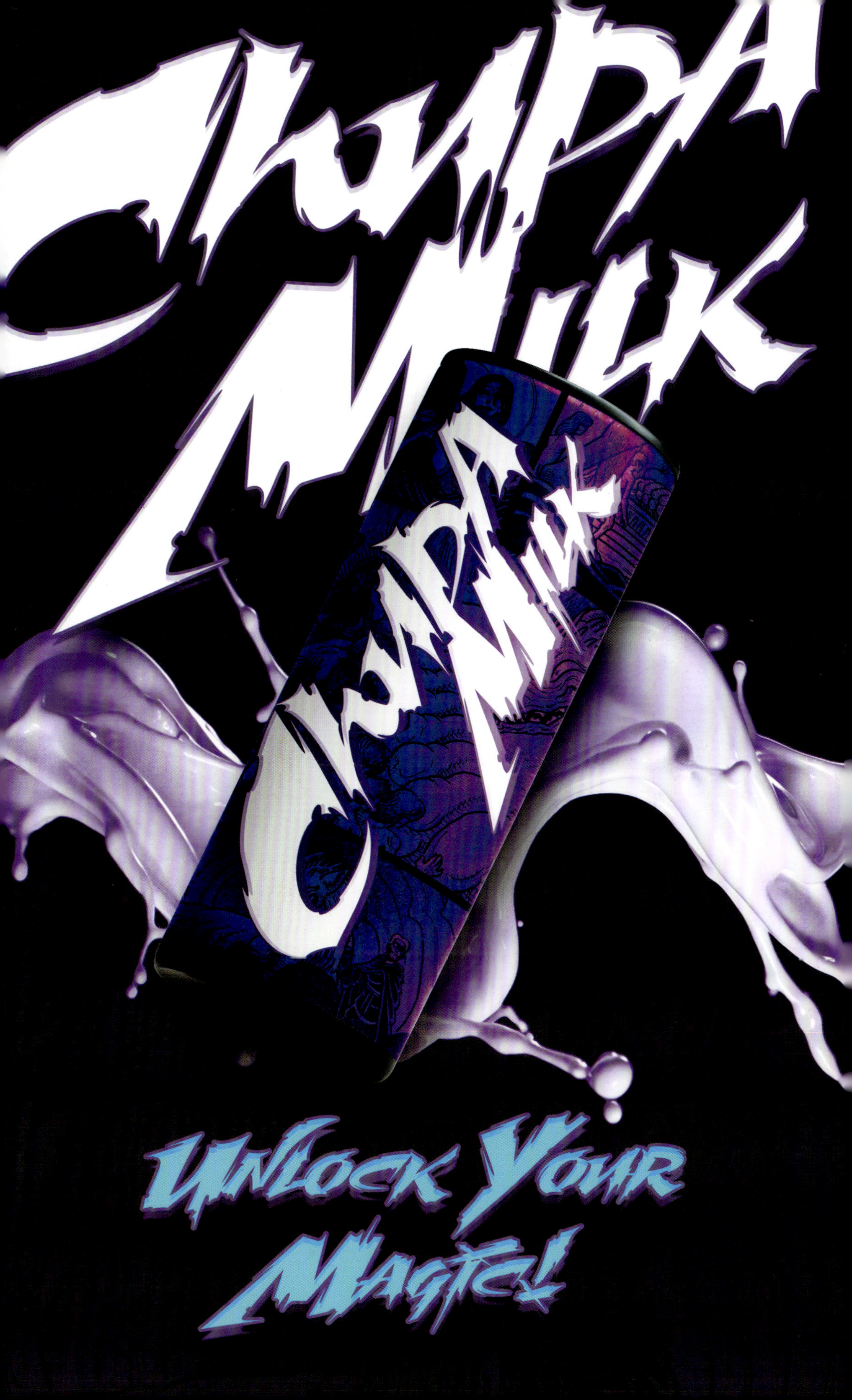
Chapa Milk
Unlock Your Magic!

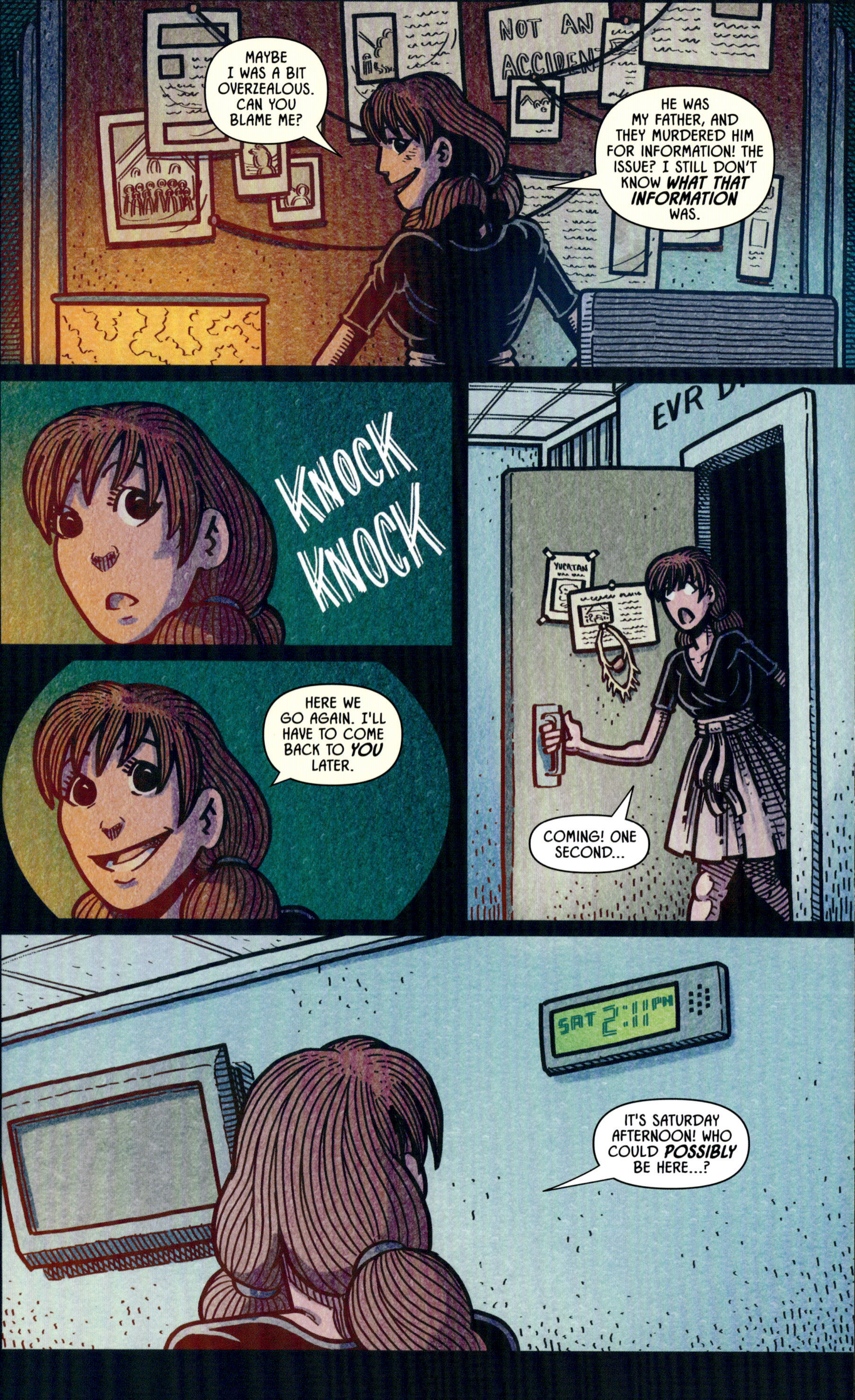
NOT AN ACCIDENT
MAYBE I WAS A BIT OVERZEALOUS. CAN YOU BLAME ME?
HE WAS MY FATHER, AND THEY MURDERED HIM FOR INFORMATION! THE ISSUE? I STILL DON'T KNOW ***WHAT THAT INFORMATION*** WAS.
KNOCK KNOCK
HERE WE GO AGAIN. I'LL HAVE TO COME BACK TO ***YOU*** LATER.
EVR
COMING! ONE SECOND...
SAT 2:11PM
IT'S SATURDAY AFTERNOON! WHO COULD ***POSSIBLY*** BE HERE...?

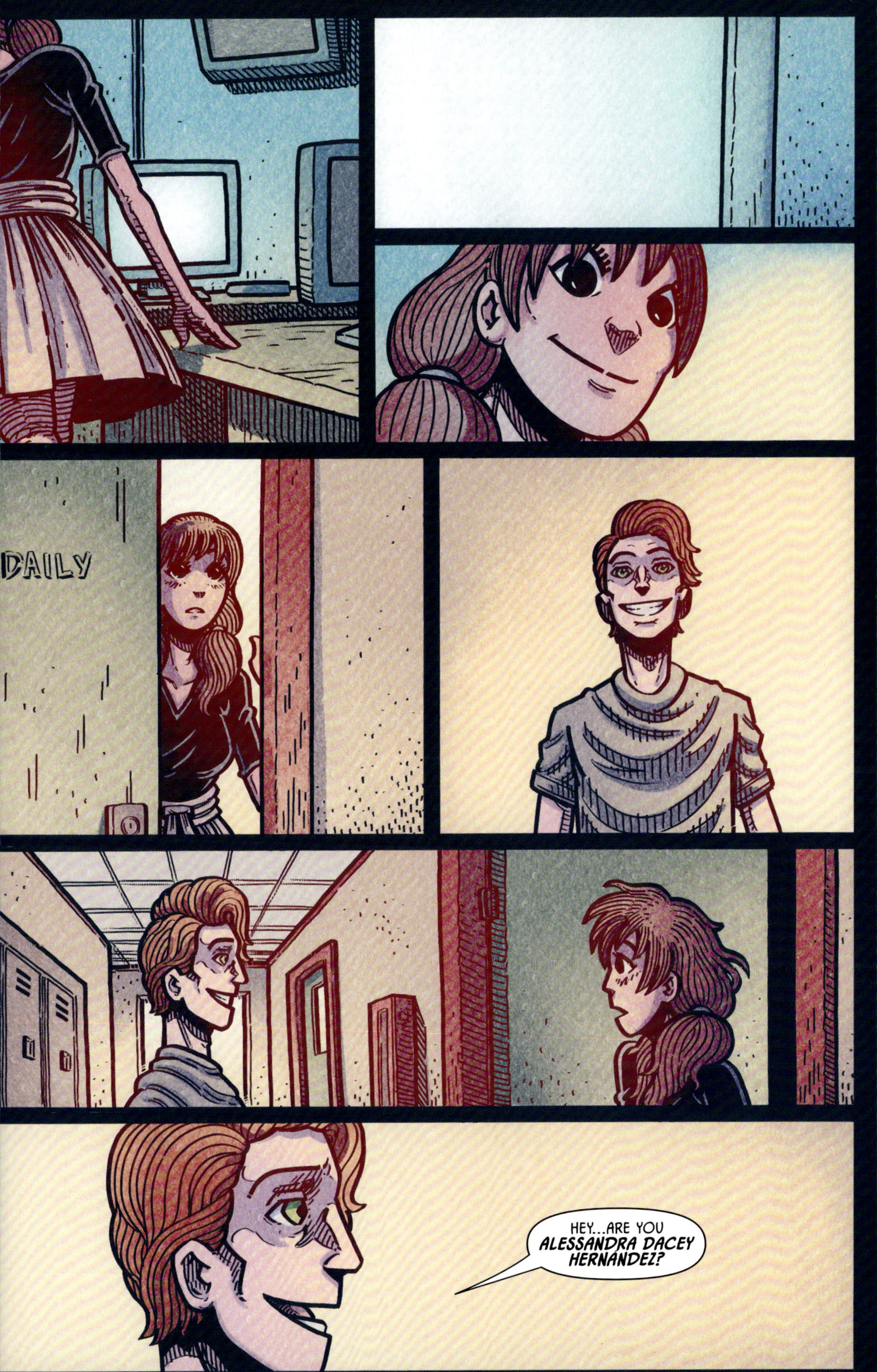
DAILY
HEY...ARE YOU *ALESSANDRA DACEY HERNANDEZ?*

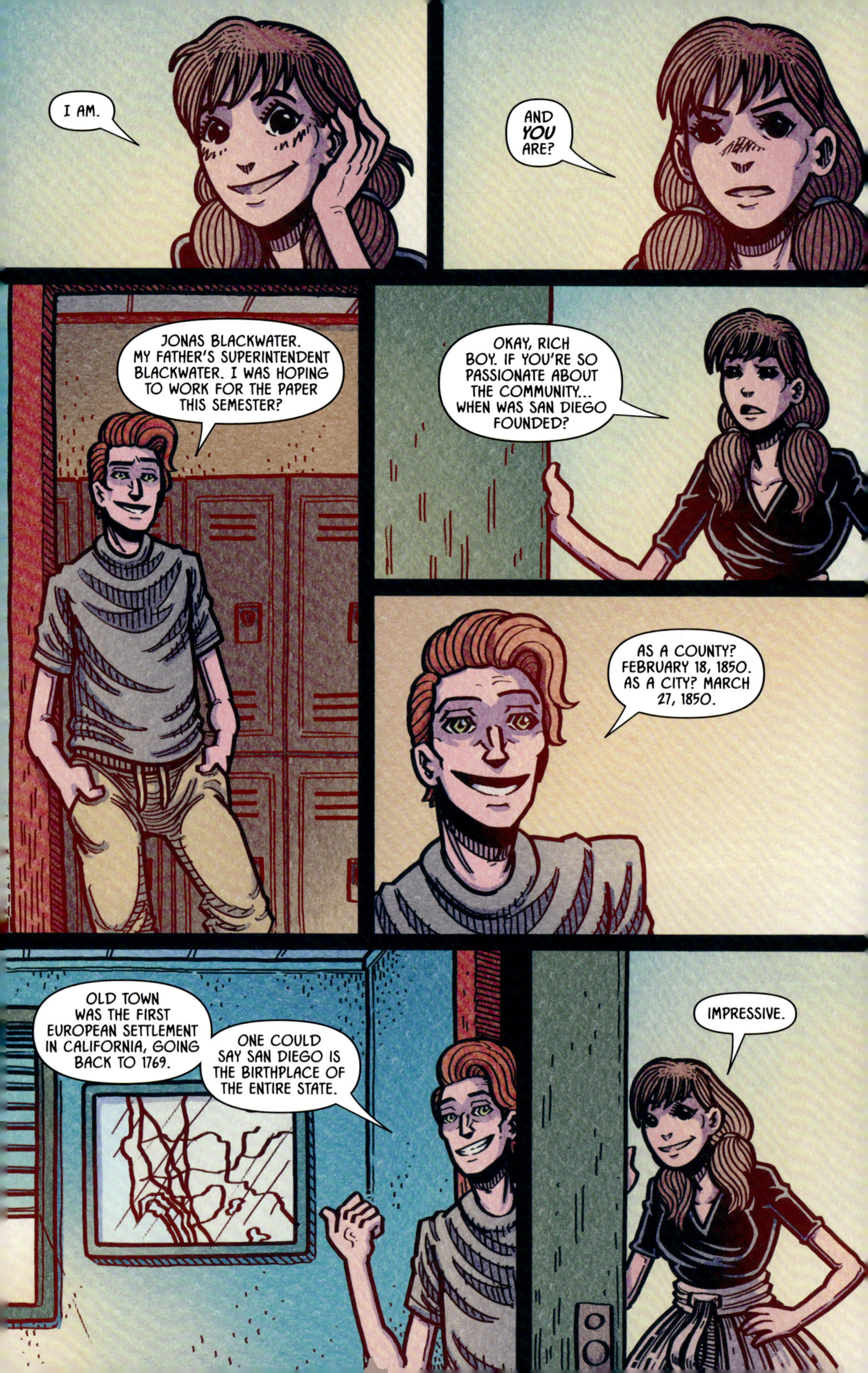
I AM.
AND *YOU* ARE?
JONAS BLACKWATER. MY FATHER'S SUPERINTENDENT BLACKWATER. I WAS HOPING TO WORK FOR THE PAPER THIS SEMESTER?
OKAY, RICH BOY. IF YOU'RE SO PASSIONATE ABOUT THE COMMUNITY... WHEN WAS SAN DIEGO FOUNDED?
AS A COUNTY? FEBRUARY 18, 1850. AS A CITY? MARCH 27, 1850.
OLD TOWN WAS THE FIRST EUROPEAN SETTLEMENT IN CALIFORNIA, GOING BACK TO 1769.
ONE COULD SAY SAN DIEGO IS THE BIRTHPLACE OF THE ENTIRE STATE.
IMPRESSIVE.

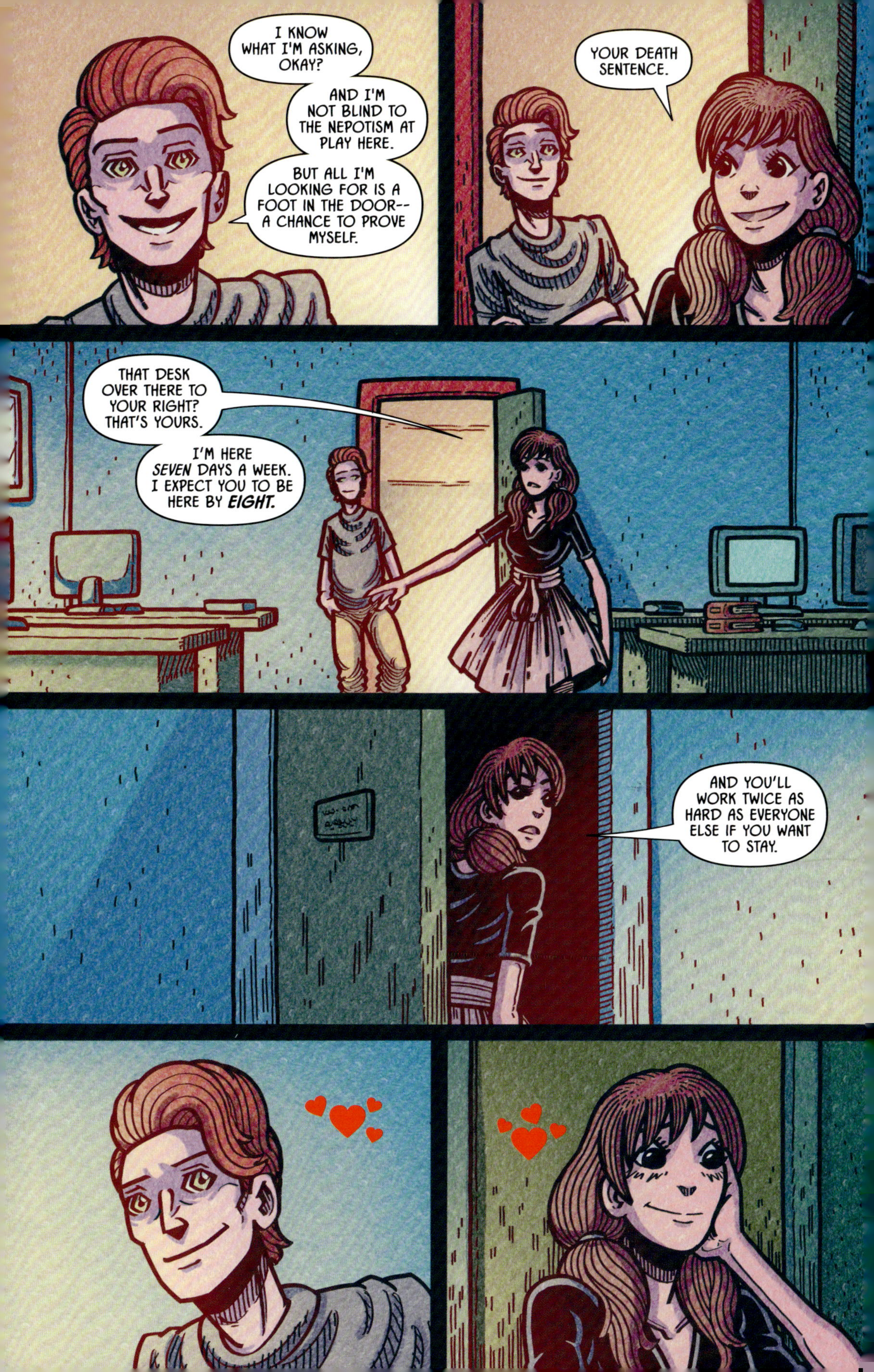
I KNOW WHAT I'M ASKING, OKAY?
AND I'M NOT BLIND TO THE NEPOTISM AT PLAY HERE.
BUT ALL I'M LOOKING FOR IS A FOOT IN THE DOOR-- A CHANCE TO PROVE MYSELF.
YOUR DEATH SENTENCE.
THAT DESK OVER THERE TO YOUR RIGHT? THAT'S YOURS.
I'M HERE *SEVEN* DAYS A WEEK. I EXPECT YOU TO BE HERE BY ***EIGHT.***
AND YOU'LL WORK TWICE AS HARD AS EVERYONE ELSE IF YOU WANT TO STAY.

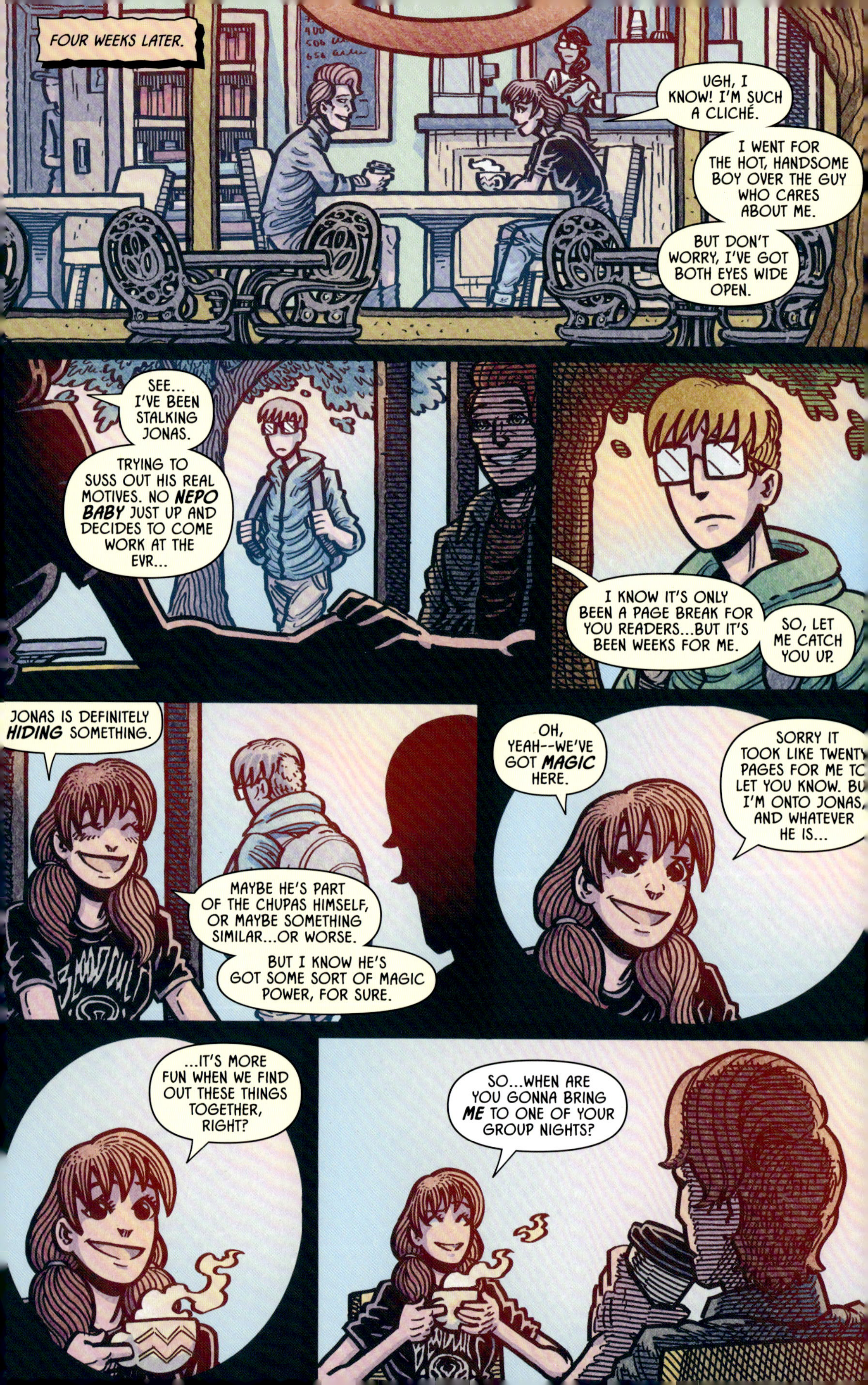
FOUR WEEKS LATER.
UGH, I KNOW! I'M SUCH A CLICHÉ.
I WENT FOR THE HOT, HANDSOME BOY OVER THE GUY WHO CARES ABOUT ME.
BUT DON'T WORRY, I'VE GOT BOTH EYES WIDE OPEN.
SEE... I'VE BEEN STALKING JONAS.
TRYING TO SUSS OUT HIS REAL MOTIVES. NO NEPO BABY JUST UP AND DECIDES TO COME WORK AT THE EVR...
I KNOW IT'S ONLY BEEN A PAGE BREAK FOR YOU READERS...BUT IT'S BEEN WEEKS FOR ME.
SO, LET ME CATCH YOU UP.
JONAS IS DEFINITELY HIDING SOMETHING.
MAYBE HE'S PART OF THE CHUPAS HIMSELF, OR MAYBE SOMETHING SIMILAR...OR WORSE.
BUT I KNOW HE'S GOT SOME SORT OF MAGIC POWER, FOR SURE.
OH, YEAH--WE'VE GOT MAGIC HERE.
SORRY IT TOOK LIKE TWENTY PAGES FOR ME TO LET YOU KNOW. BUT I'M ONTO JONAS, AND WHATEVER HE IS...
...IT'S MORE FUN WHEN WE FIND OUT THESE THINGS TOGETHER, RIGHT?
SO...WHEN ARE YOU GONNA BRING ME TO ONE OF YOUR GROUP NIGHTS?

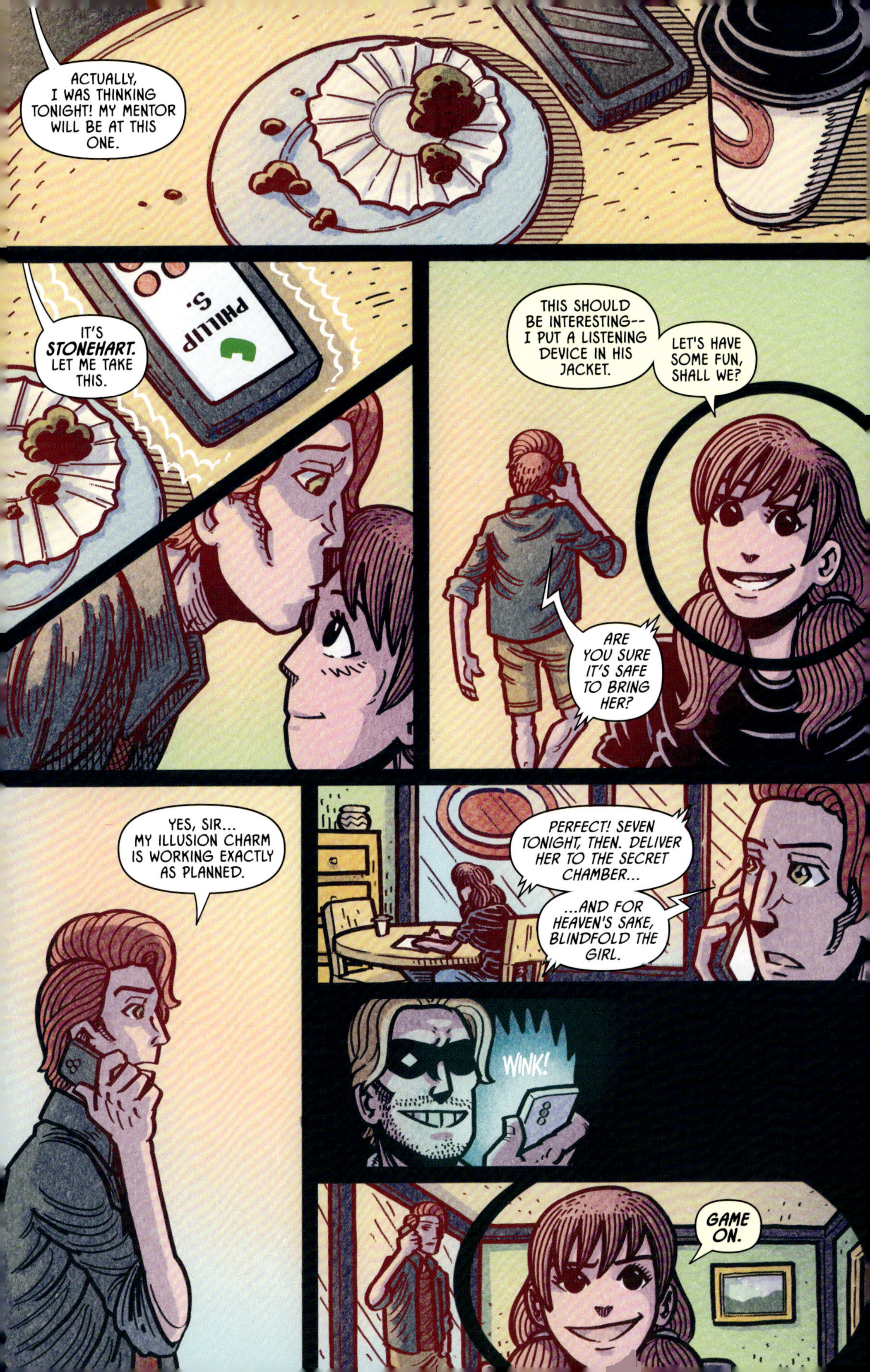
ACTUALLY, I WAS THINKING TONIGHT! MY MENTOR WILL BE AT THIS ONE.
PHILLIP S.
IT'S STONEHART. LET ME TAKE THIS.
THIS SHOULD BE INTERESTING-- I PUT A LISTENING DEVICE IN HIS JACKET.
LET'S HAVE SOME FUN, SHALL WE?
ARE YOU SURE IT'S SAFE TO BRING HER?
YES, SIR... MY ILLUSION CHARM IS WORKING EXACTLY AS PLANNED.
PERFECT! SEVEN TONIGHT, THEN. DELIVER HER TO THE SECRET CHAMBER...
...AND FOR HEAVEN'S SAKE, BLINDFOLD THE GIRL.
WINK!
GAME ON.

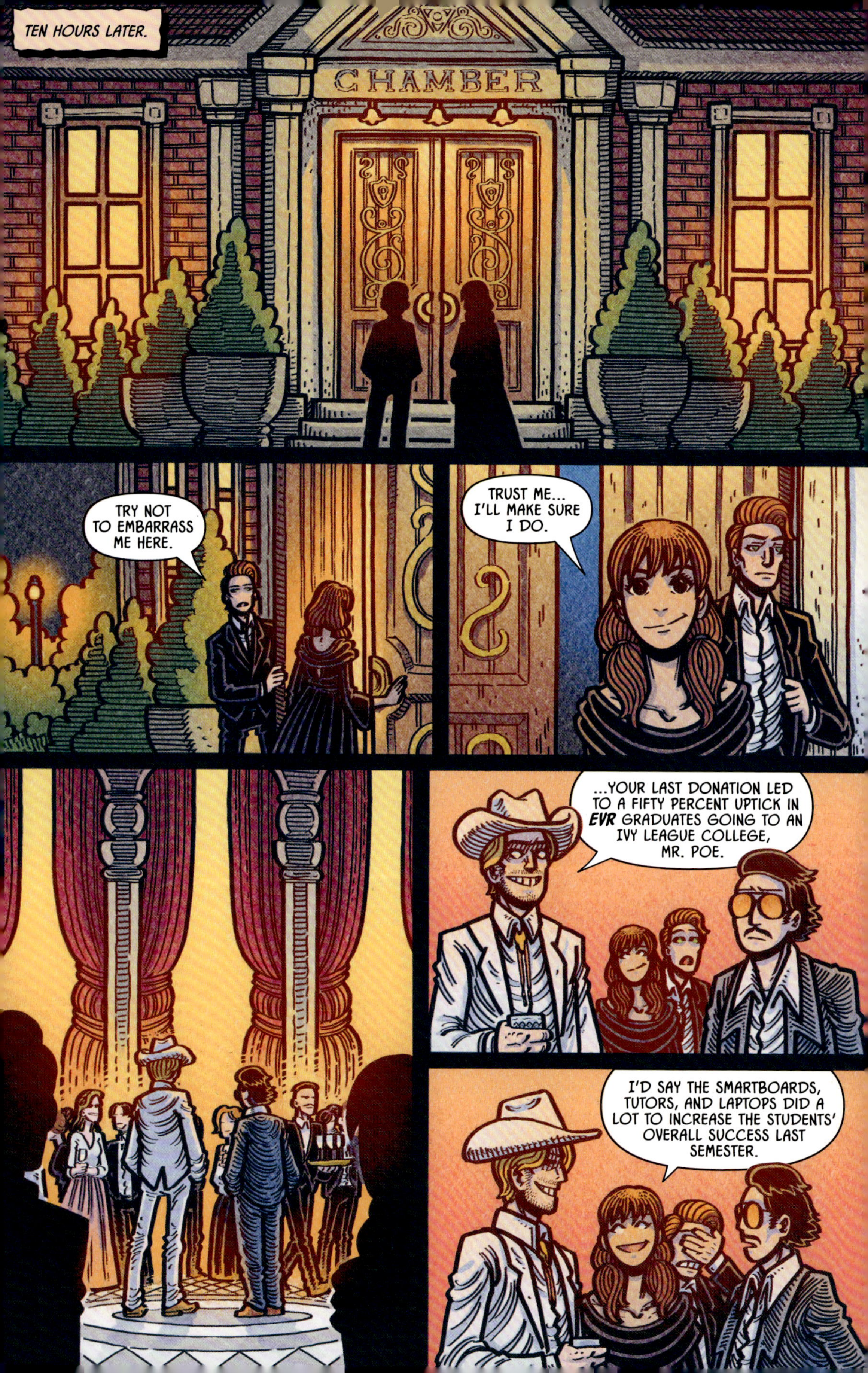
TEN HOURS LATER.
CHAMBER
TRY NOT TO EMBARRASS ME HERE.
TRUST ME... I'LL MAKE SURE I DO.
...YOUR LAST DONATION LED TO A FIFTY PERCENT UPTICK IN **EVR** GRADUATES GOING TO AN IVY LEAGUE COLLEGE, MR. POE.
I'D SAY THE SMARTBOARDS, TUTORS, AND LAPTOPS DID A LOT TO INCREASE THE STUDENTS' OVERALL SUCCESS LAST SEMESTER.

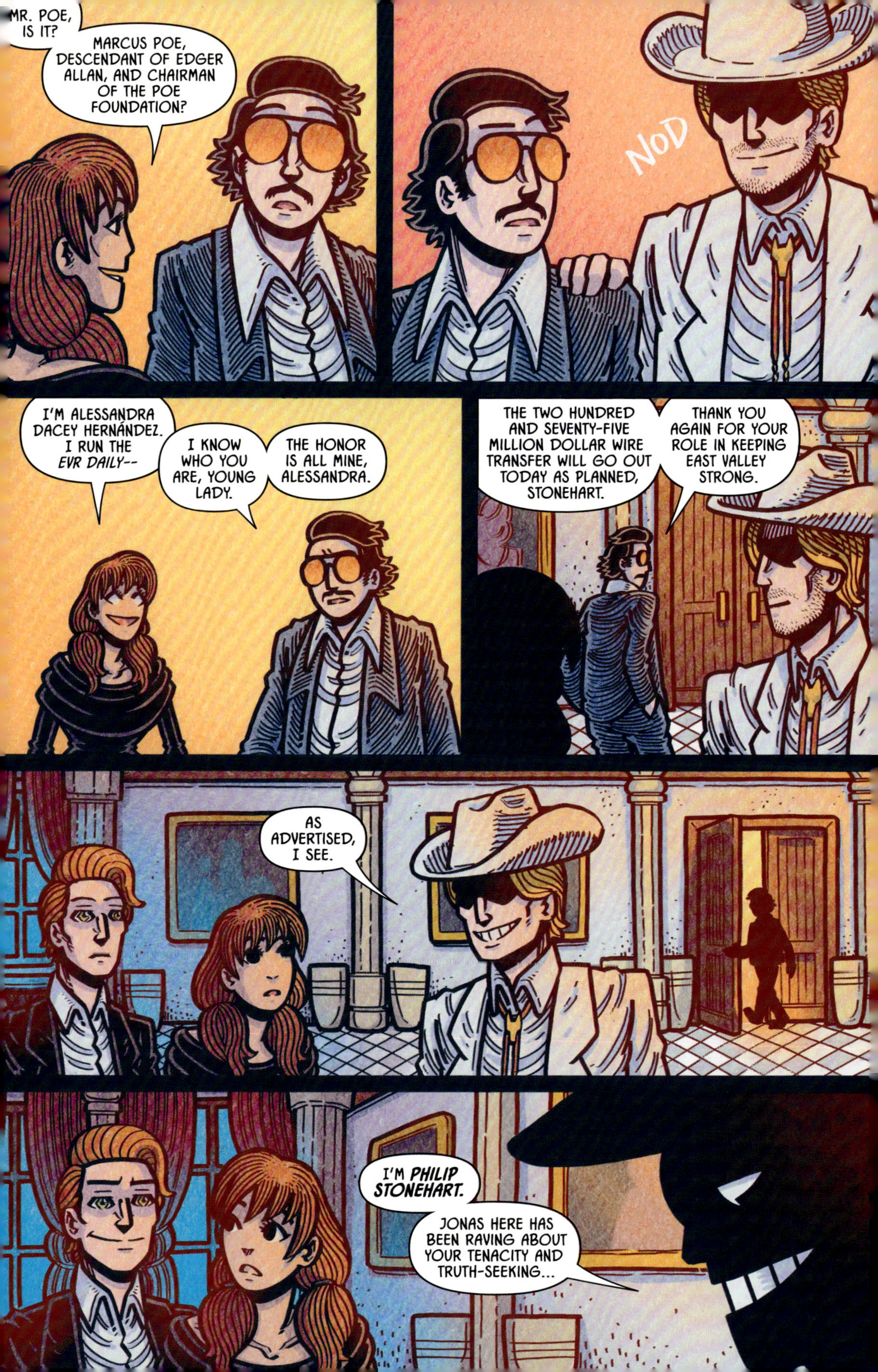
MR. POE, IS IT?
MARCUS POE, DESCENDANT OF EDGER ALLAN, AND CHAIRMAN OF THE POE FOUNDATION?
NOD
I'M ALESSANDRA DACEY HERNÁNDEZ. I RUN THE EVR DAILY--
I KNOW WHO YOU ARE, YOUNG LADY.
THE HONOR IS ALL MINE, ALESSANDRA.
THE TWO HUNDRED AND SEVENTY-FIVE MILLION DOLLAR WIRE TRANSFER WILL GO OUT TODAY AS PLANNED, STONEHART.
THANK YOU AGAIN FOR YOUR ROLE IN KEEPING EAST VALLEY STRONG.
AS ADVERTISED, I SEE.
I'M PHILIP STONEHART.
JONAS HERE HAS BEEN RAVING ABOUT YOUR TENACITY AND TRUTH-SEEKING...

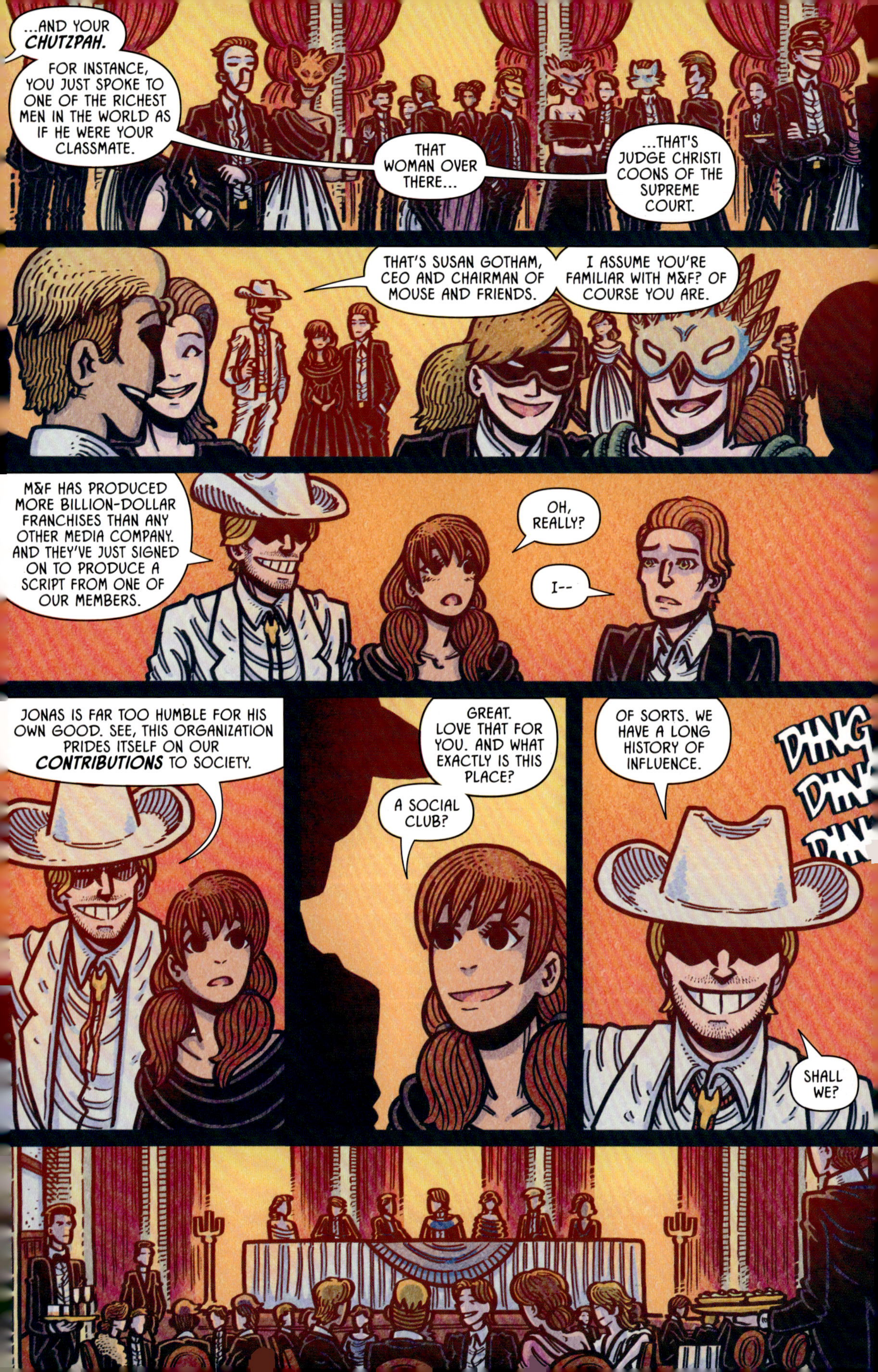
...AND YOUR CHUTZPAH.
FOR INSTANCE, YOU JUST SPOKE TO ONE OF THE RICHEST MEN IN THE WORLD AS IF HE WERE YOUR CLASSMATE.
THAT WOMAN OVER THERE...
...THAT'S JUDGE CHRISTI COONS OF THE SUPREME COURT.
THAT'S SUSAN GOTHAM, CEO AND CHAIRMAN OF MOUSE AND FRIENDS.
I ASSUME YOU'RE FAMILIAR WITH M&F? OF COURSE YOU ARE.
M&F HAS PRODUCED MORE BILLION-DOLLAR FRANCHISES THAN ANY OTHER MEDIA COMPANY. AND THEY'VE JUST SIGNED ON TO PRODUCE A SCRIPT FROM ONE OF OUR MEMBERS.
OH, REALLY?
I--
JONAS IS FAR TOO HUMBLE FOR HIS OWN GOOD. SEE, THIS ORGANIZATION PRIDES ITSELF ON OUR CONTRIBUTIONS TO SOCIETY.
GREAT. LOVE THAT FOR YOU. AND WHAT EXACTLY IS THIS PLACE?
A SOCIAL CLUB?
OF SORTS. WE HAVE A LONG HISTORY OF INFLUENCE.
SHALL WE?

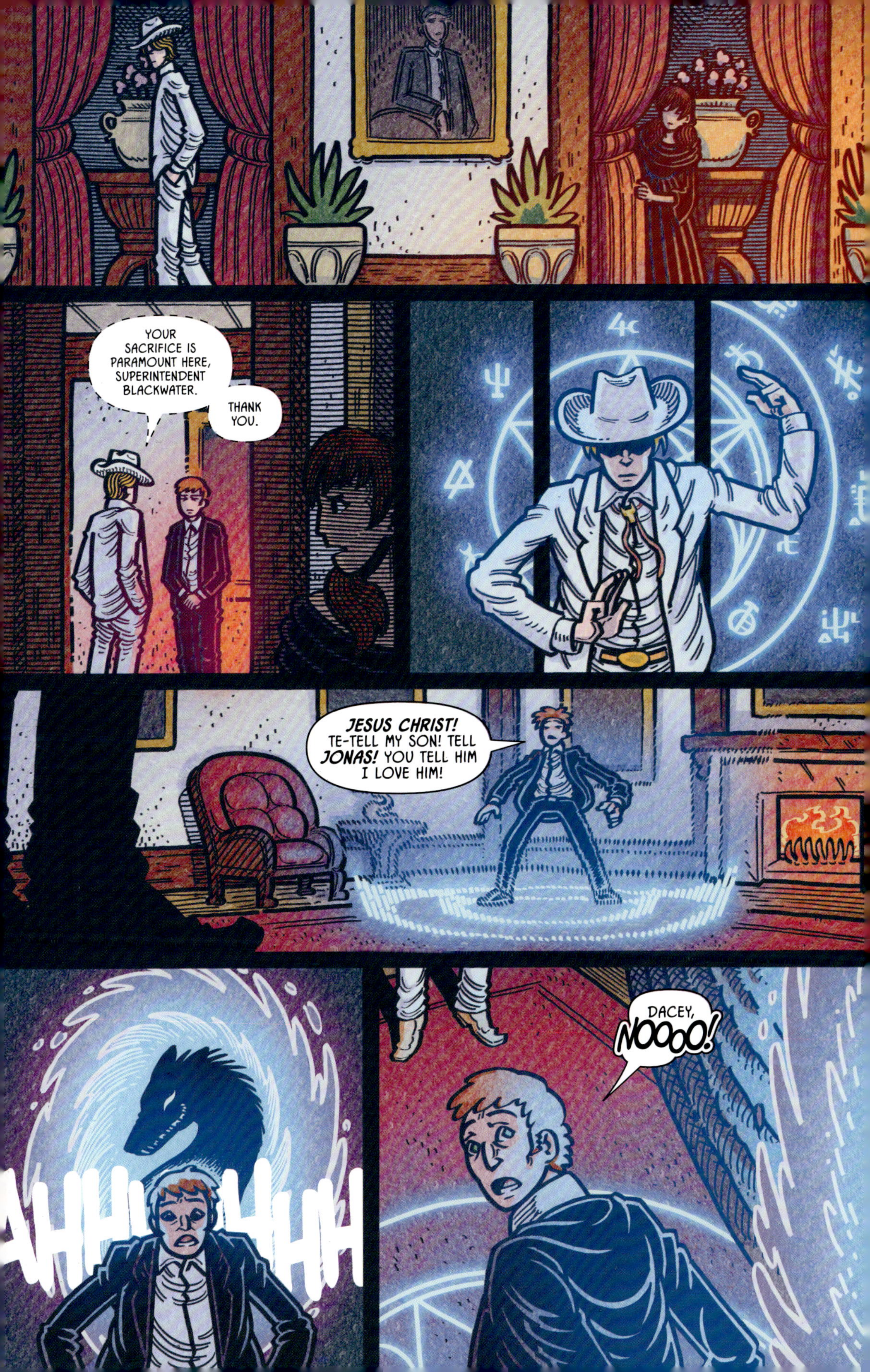
YOUR SACRIFICE IS PARAMOUNT HERE, SUPERINTENDENT BLACKWATER.
THANK YOU.
JESUS CHRIST! TE-TELL MY SON! TELL JONAS! YOU TELL HIM I LOVE HIM!
AHHHHHHH
DACEY, NOOOO!

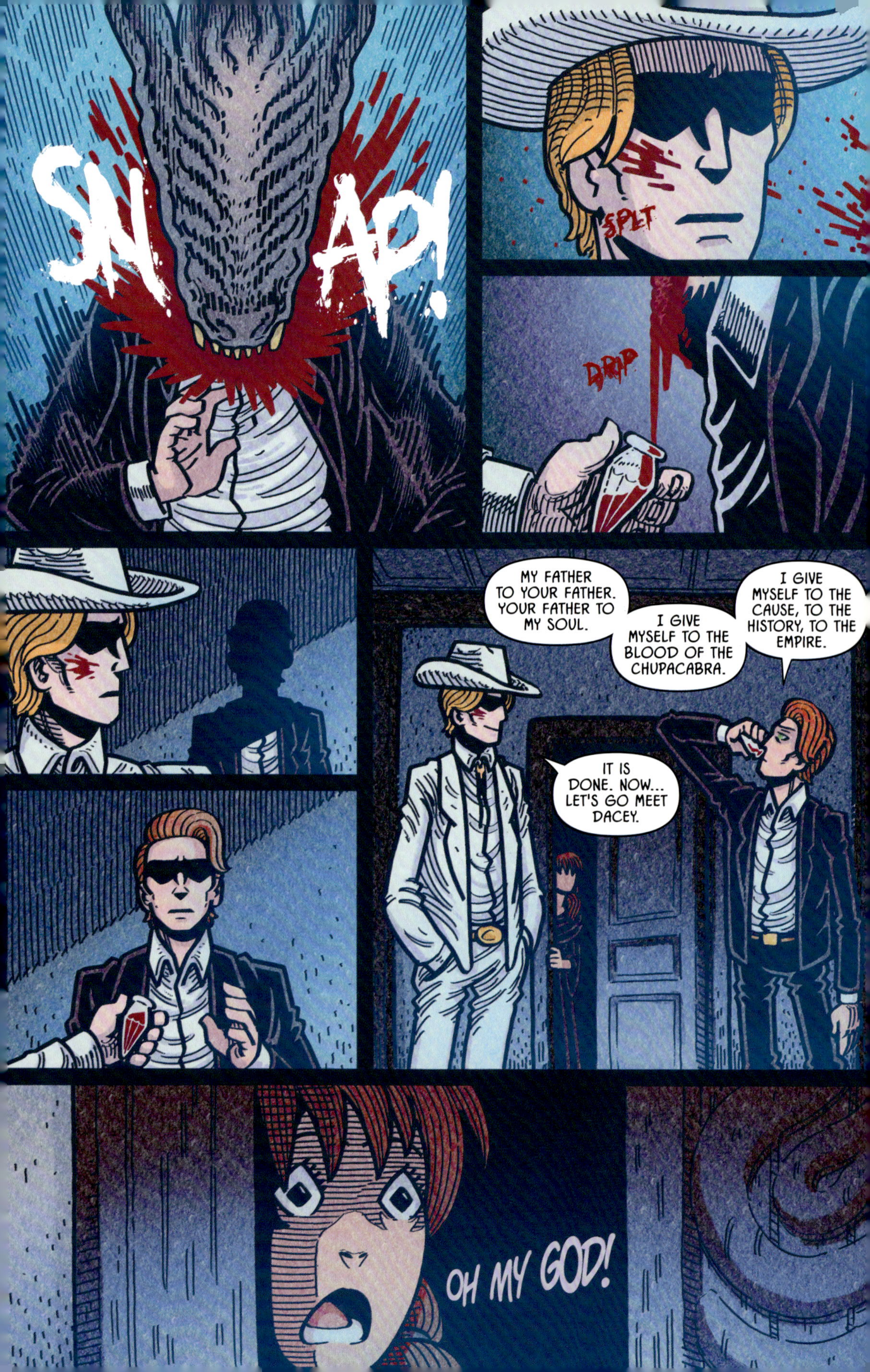
SNAP!
SPLT
DRIP
MY FATHER TO YOUR FATHER. YOUR FATHER TO MY SOUL.
I GIVE MYSELF TO THE BLOOD OF THE CHUPACABRA.
I GIVE MYSELF TO THE CAUSE, TO THE HISTORY, TO THE EMPIRE.
IT IS DONE. NOW... LET'S GO MEET DACEY.
OH MY GOD!

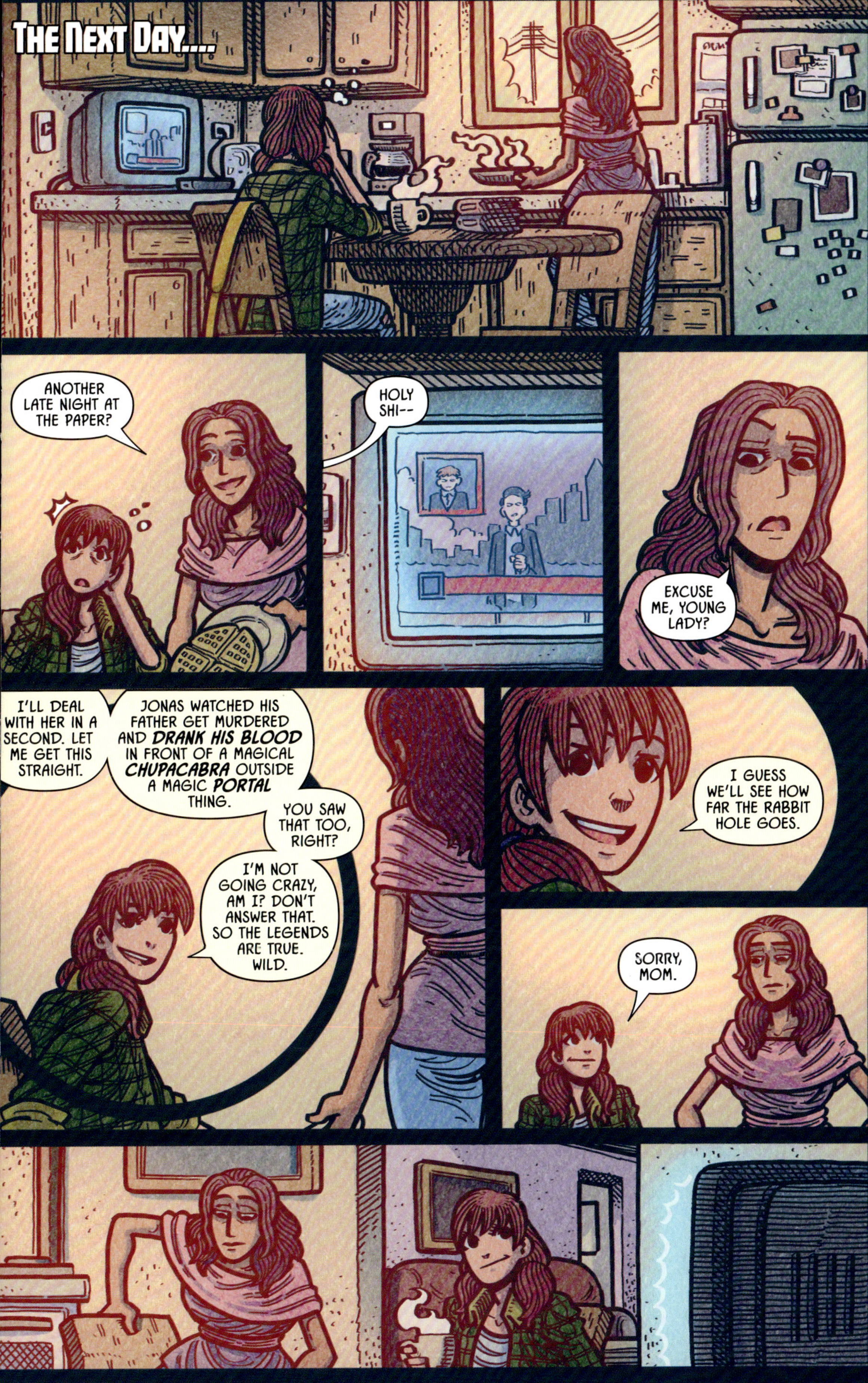
THE NEXT DAY....
ANOTHER LATE NIGHT AT THE PAPER?
HOLY SHI--
EXCUSE ME, YOUNG LADY?
I'LL DEAL WITH HER IN A SECOND. LET ME GET THIS STRAIGHT.
JONAS WATCHED HIS FATHER GET MURDERED AND DRANK HIS BLOOD IN FRONT OF A MAGICAL CHUPACABRA OUTSIDE A MAGIC PORTAL THING.
YOU SAW THAT TOO, RIGHT?
I'M NOT GOING CRAZY, AM I? DON'T ANSWER THAT. SO THE LEGENDS ARE TRUE. WILD.
I GUESS WE'LL SEE HOW FAR THE RABBIT HOLE GOES.
SORRY, MOM.

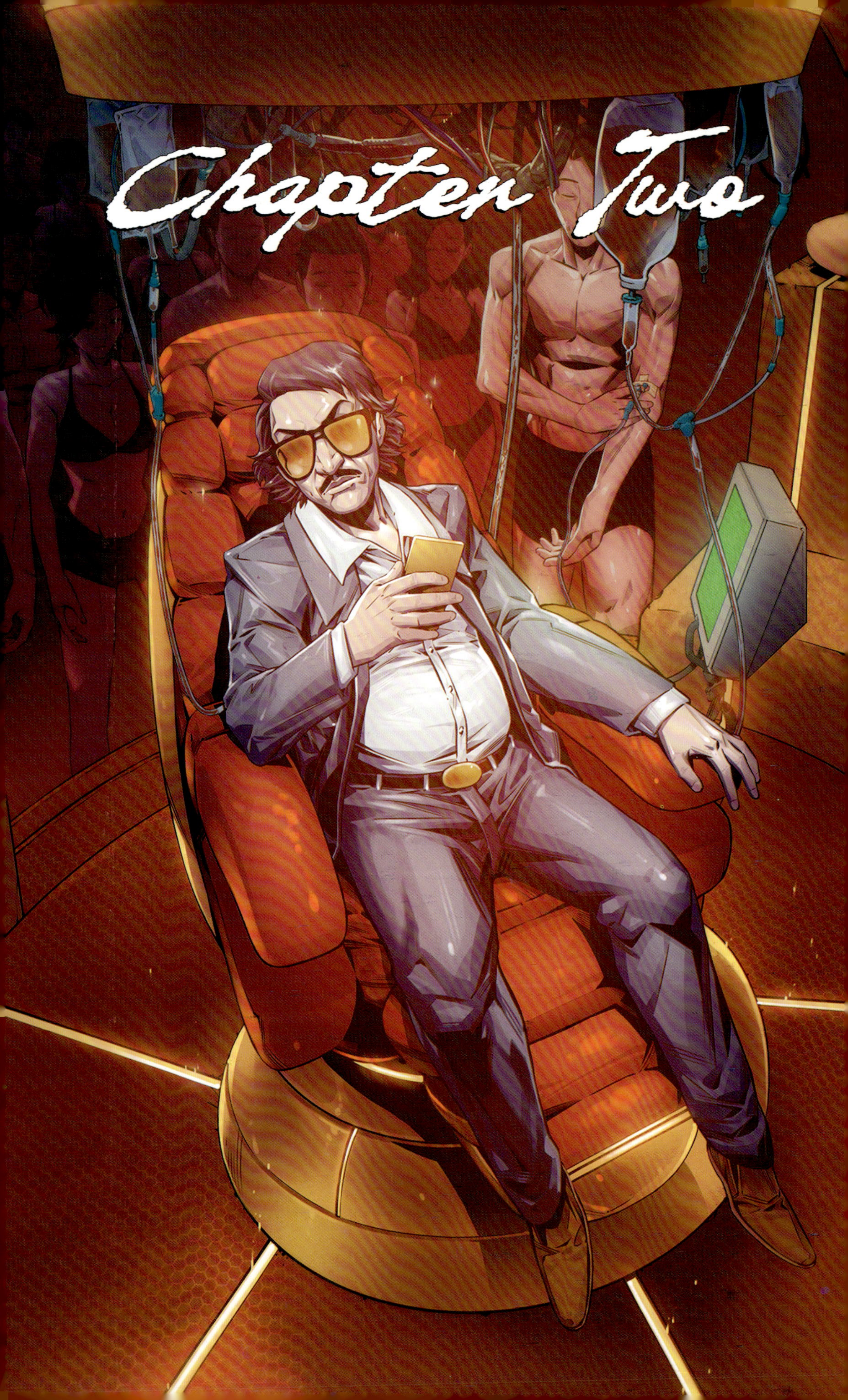
Chapter Two

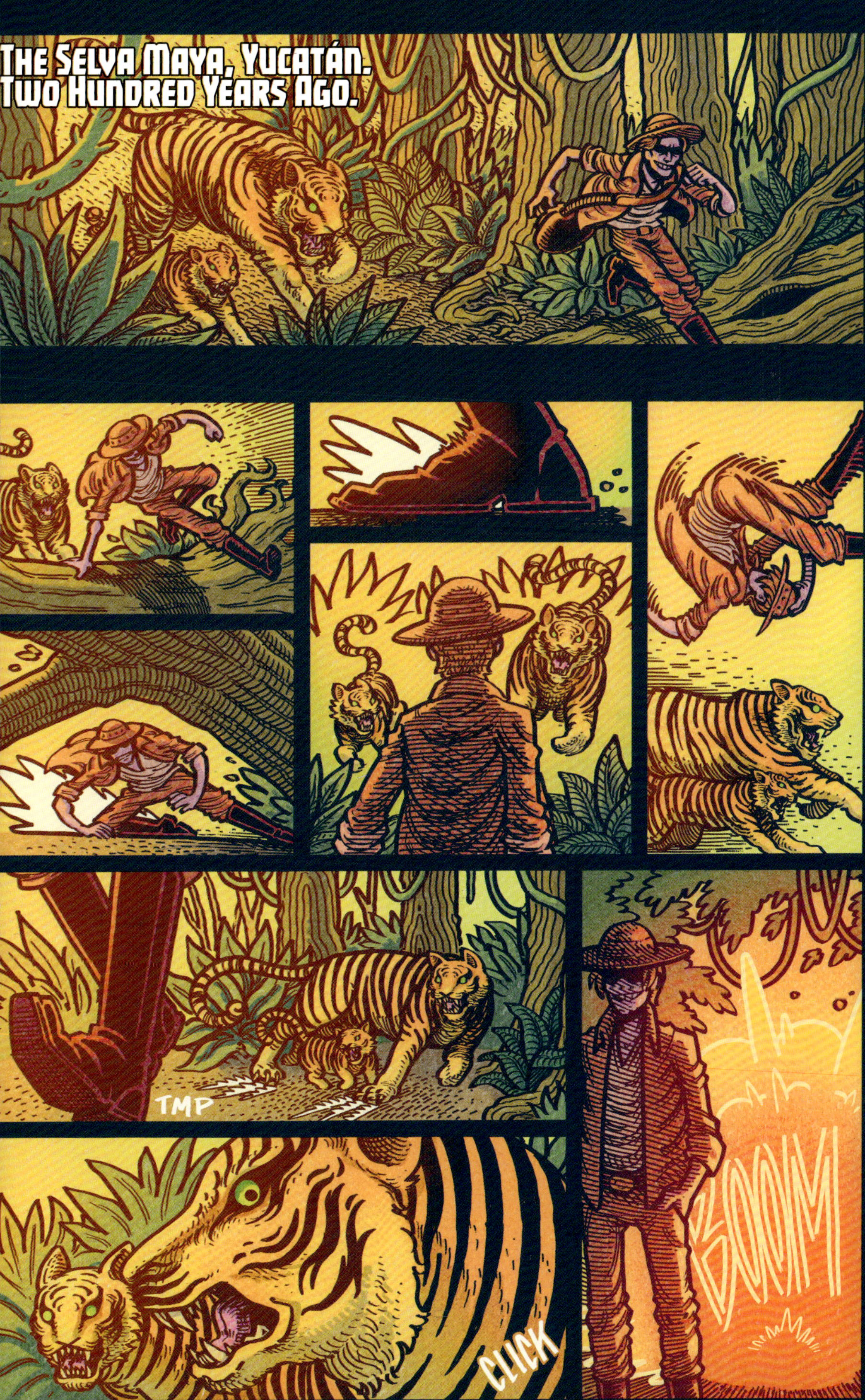
The Selva Maya, Yucatán.
Two Hundred Years Ago.
TMP
CLICK
BOOM

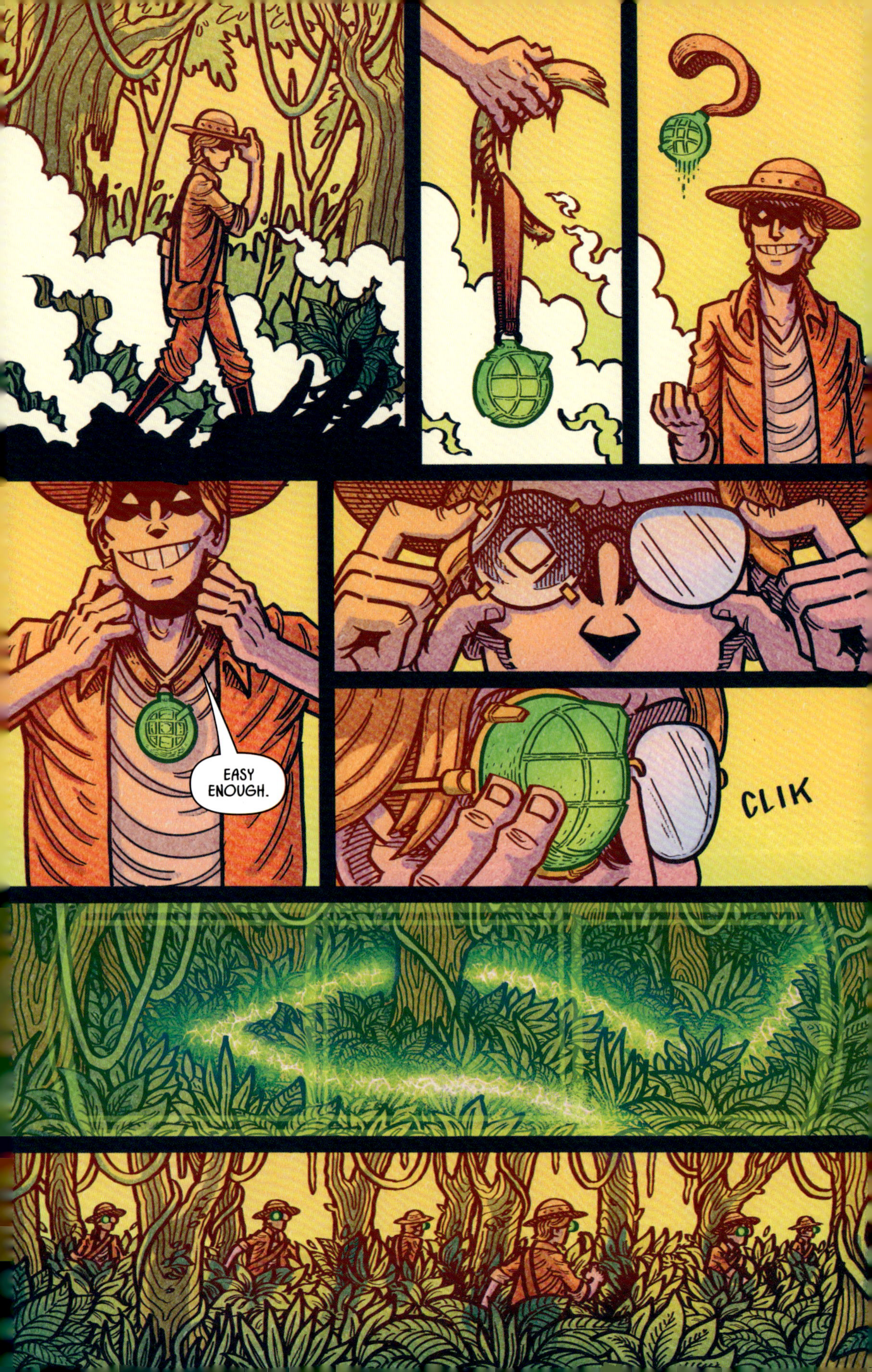
EASY ENOUGH.
CLIK

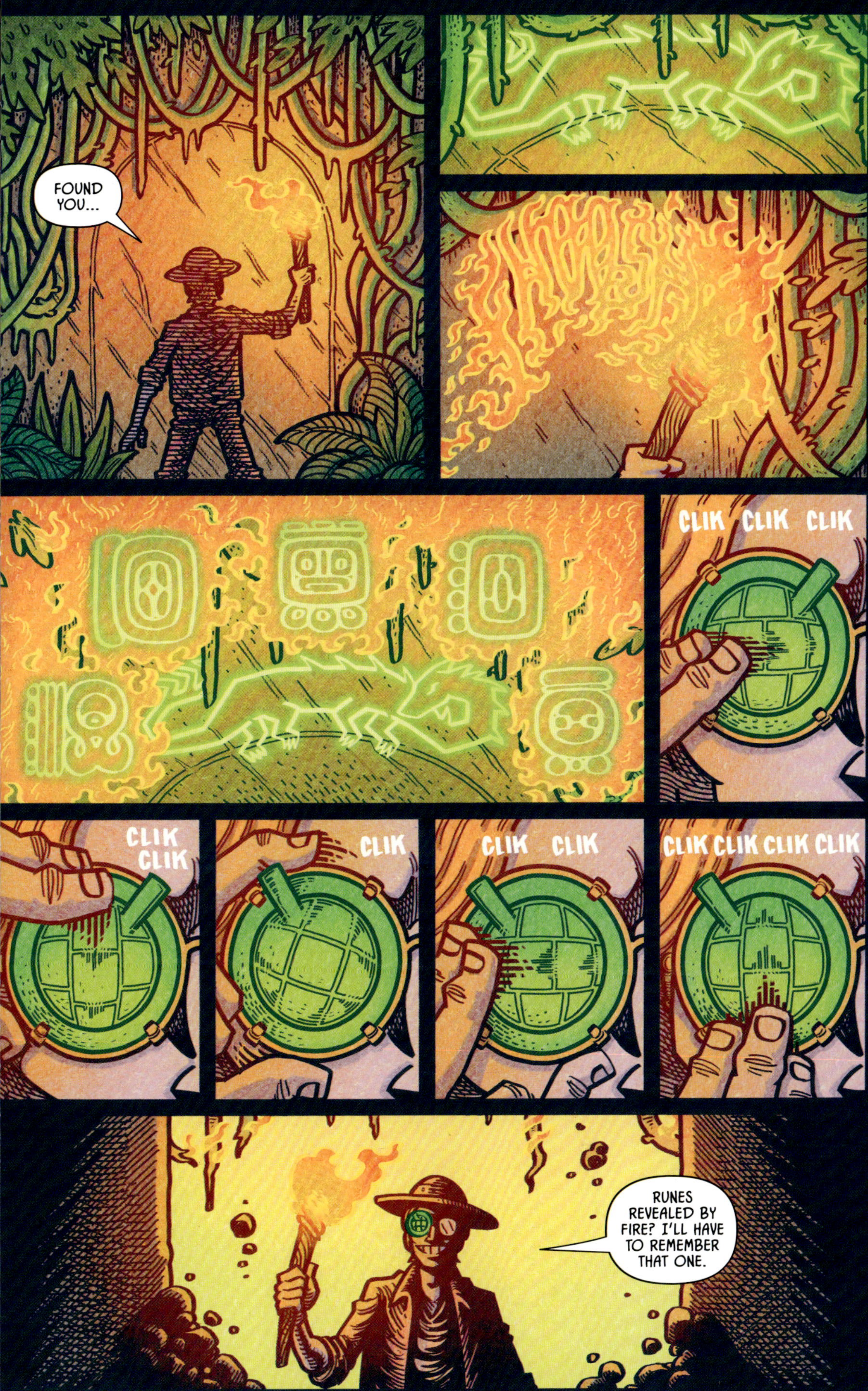
FOUND YOU...
CLIK CLIK CLIK
CLIK CLIK
CLIK
CLIK CLIK
CLIK CLIK CLIK CLIK
RUNES REVEALED BY FIRE? I'LL HAVE TO REMEMBER THAT ONE.

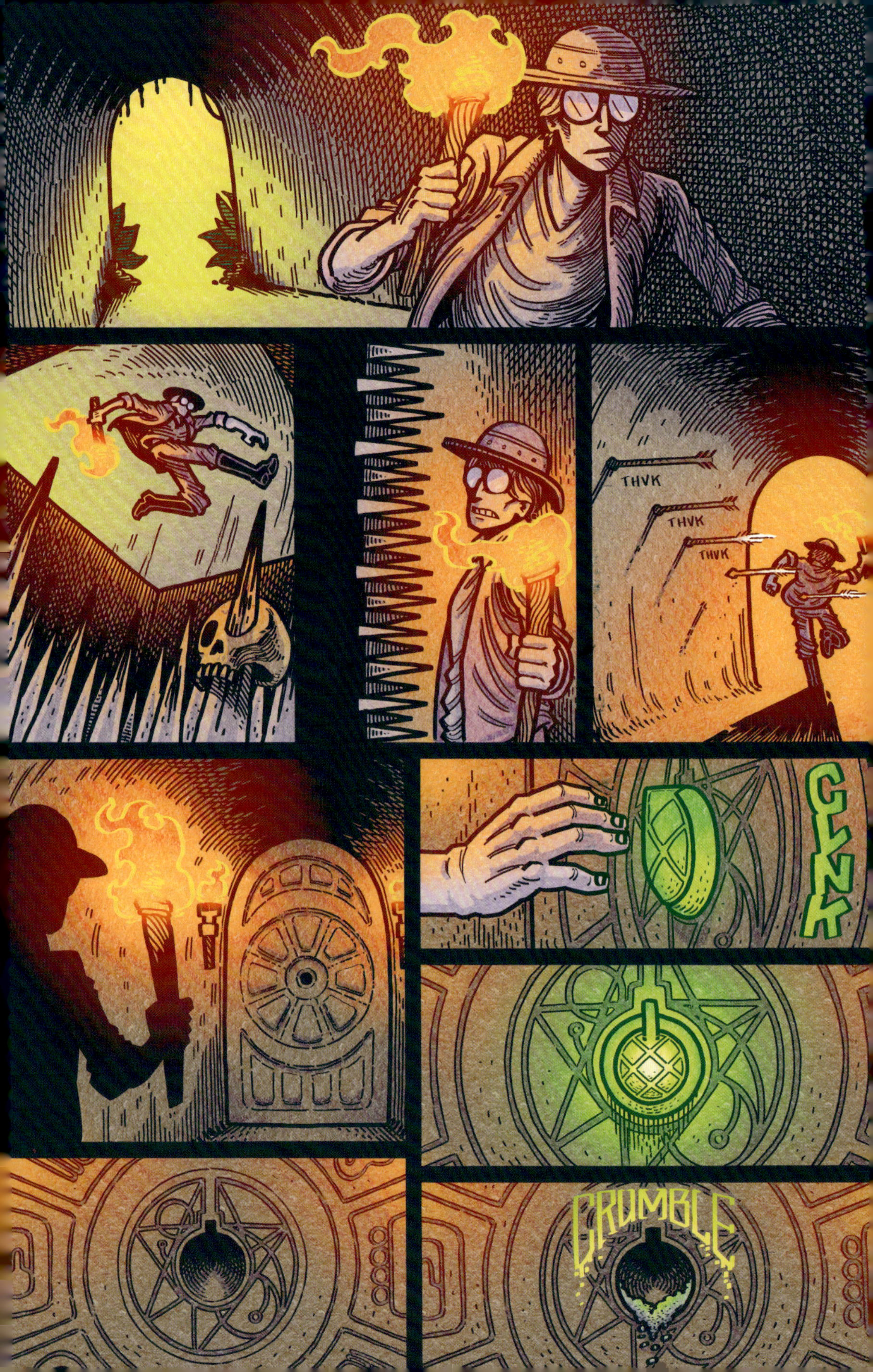
THVK
THVK
THVK
CLNK
CRUMBLE

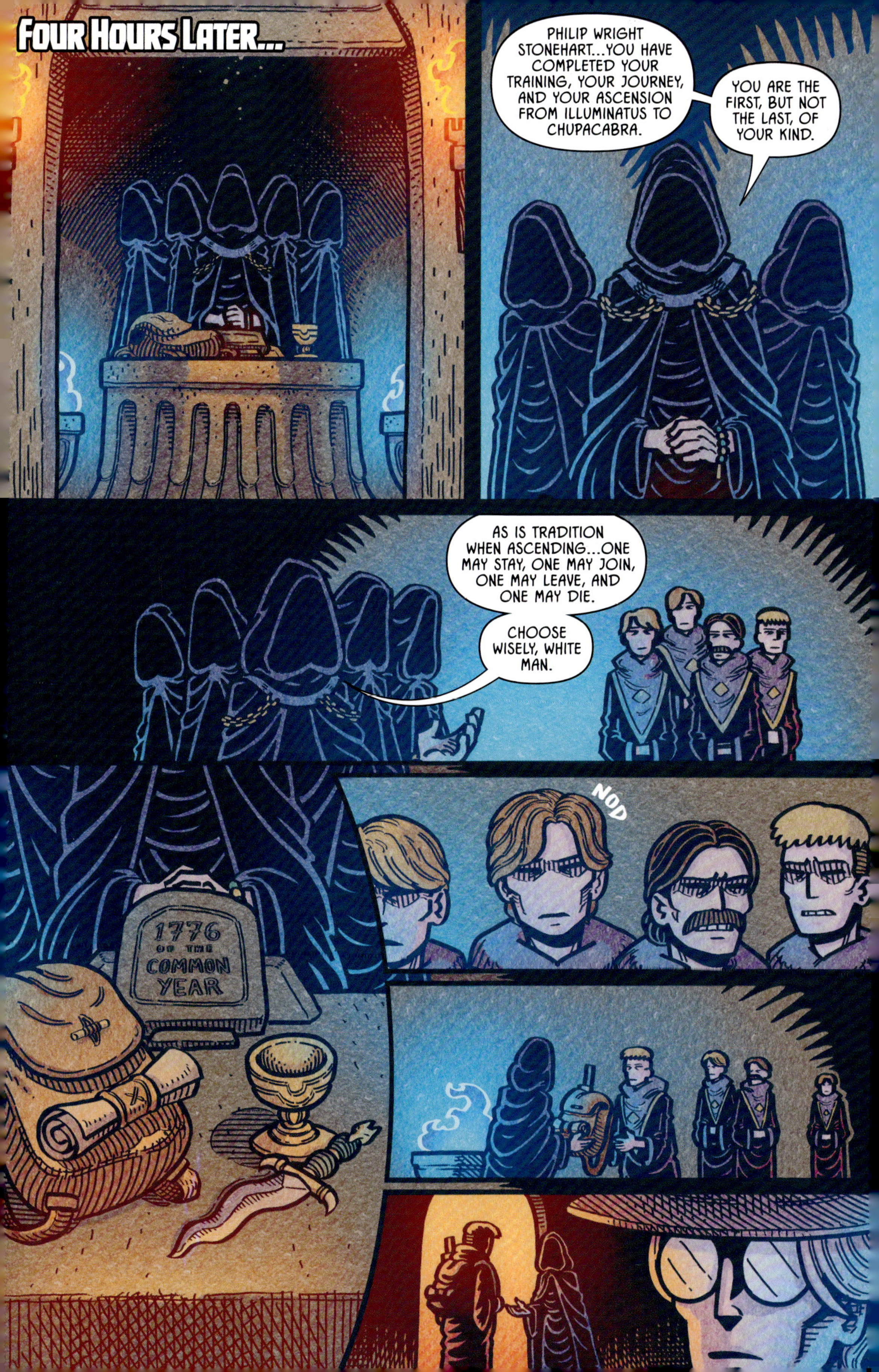
FOUR HOURS LATER...
PHILIP WRIGHT STONEHART...YOU HAVE COMPLETED YOUR TRAINING, YOUR JOURNEY, AND YOUR ASCENSION FROM ILLUMINATUS TO CHUPACABRA.
YOU ARE THE FIRST, BUT NOT THE LAST, OF YOUR KIND.
AS IS TRADITION WHEN ASCENDING...ONE MAY STAY, ONE MAY JOIN, ONE MAY LEAVE, AND ONE MAY DIE.
CHOOSE WISELY, WHITE MAN.
1776 OF THE COMMON YEAR
NOD

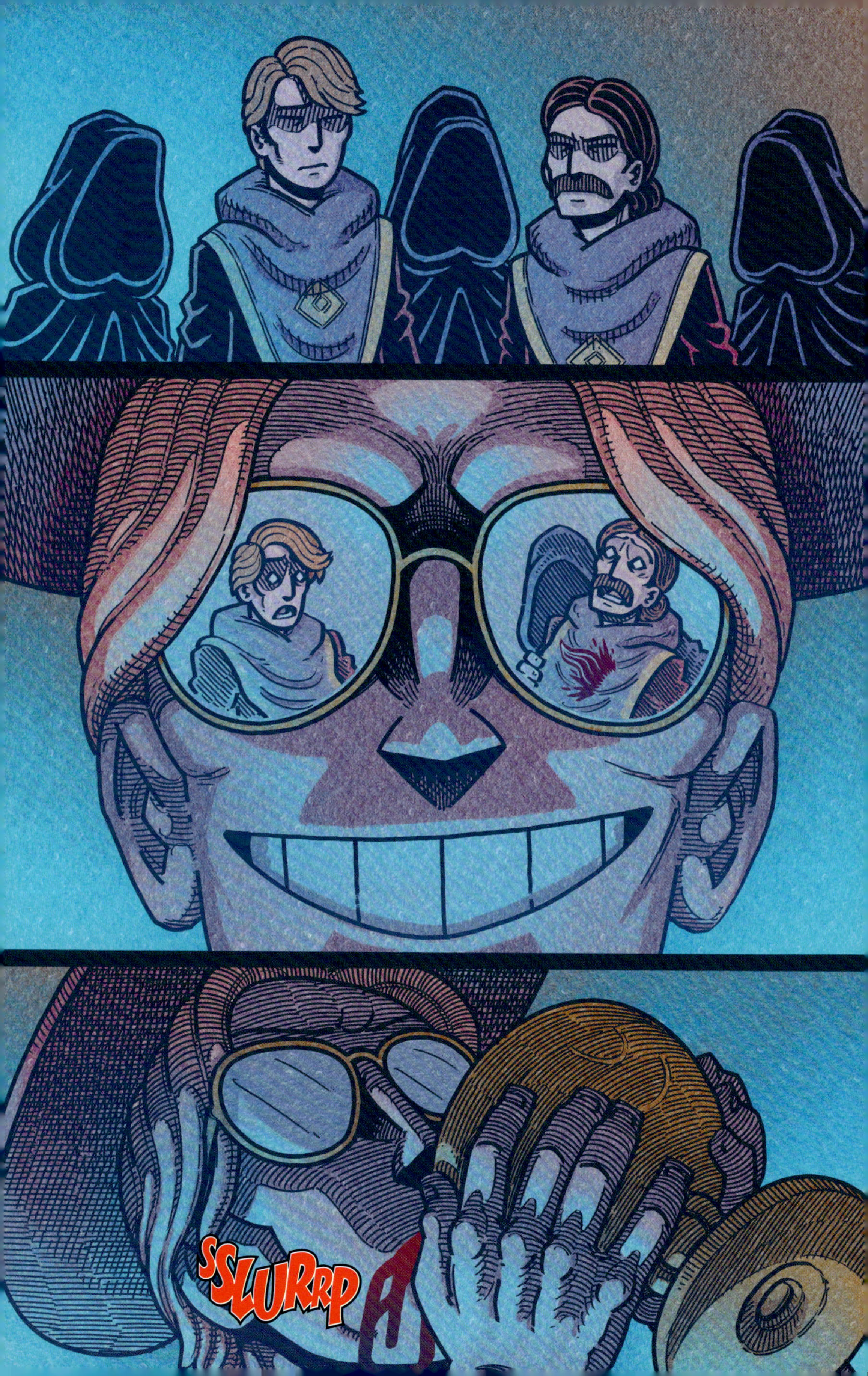
SSLURRP

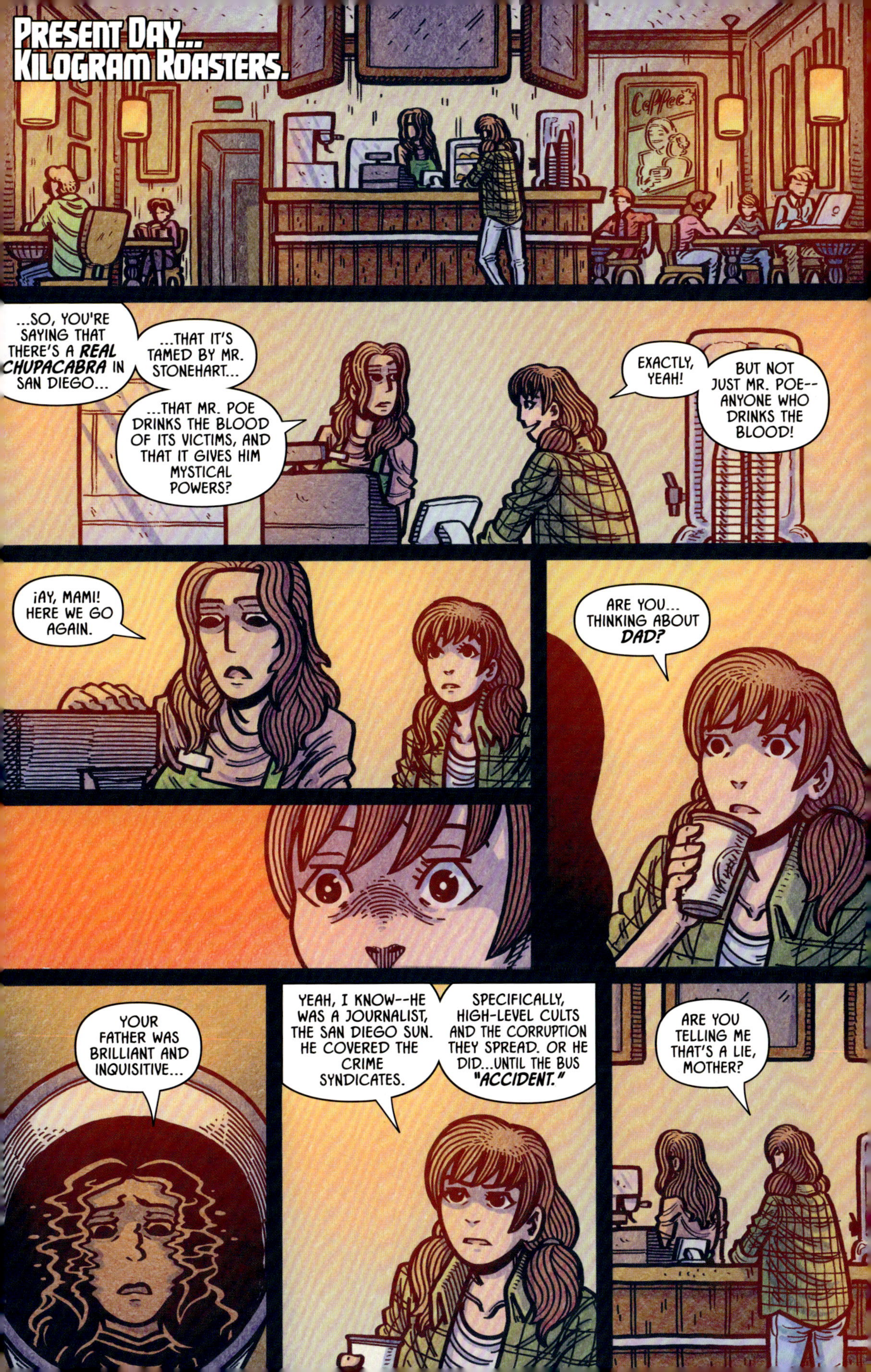
PRESENT DAY... KILOGRAM ROASTERS.
...SO, YOU'RE SAYING THAT THERE'S A REAL CHUPACABRA IN SAN DIEGO...
...THAT IT'S TAMED BY MR. STONEHART...
...THAT MR. POE DRINKS THE BLOOD OF ITS VICTIMS, AND THAT IT GIVES HIM MYSTICAL POWERS?
EXACTLY, YEAH!
BUT NOT JUST MR. POE--ANYONE WHO DRINKS THE BLOOD!
¡AY, MAMI! HERE WE GO AGAIN.
ARE YOU... THINKING ABOUT DAD?
YOUR FATHER WAS BRILLIANT AND INQUISITIVE...
YEAH, I KNOW--HE WAS A JOURNALIST, THE SAN DIEGO SUN. HE COVERED THE CRIME SYNDICATES.
SPECIFICALLY, HIGH-LEVEL CULTS AND THE CORRUPTION THEY SPREAD. OR HE DID...UNTIL THE BUS "ACCIDENT."
ARE YOU TELLING ME THAT'S A LIE, MOTHER?

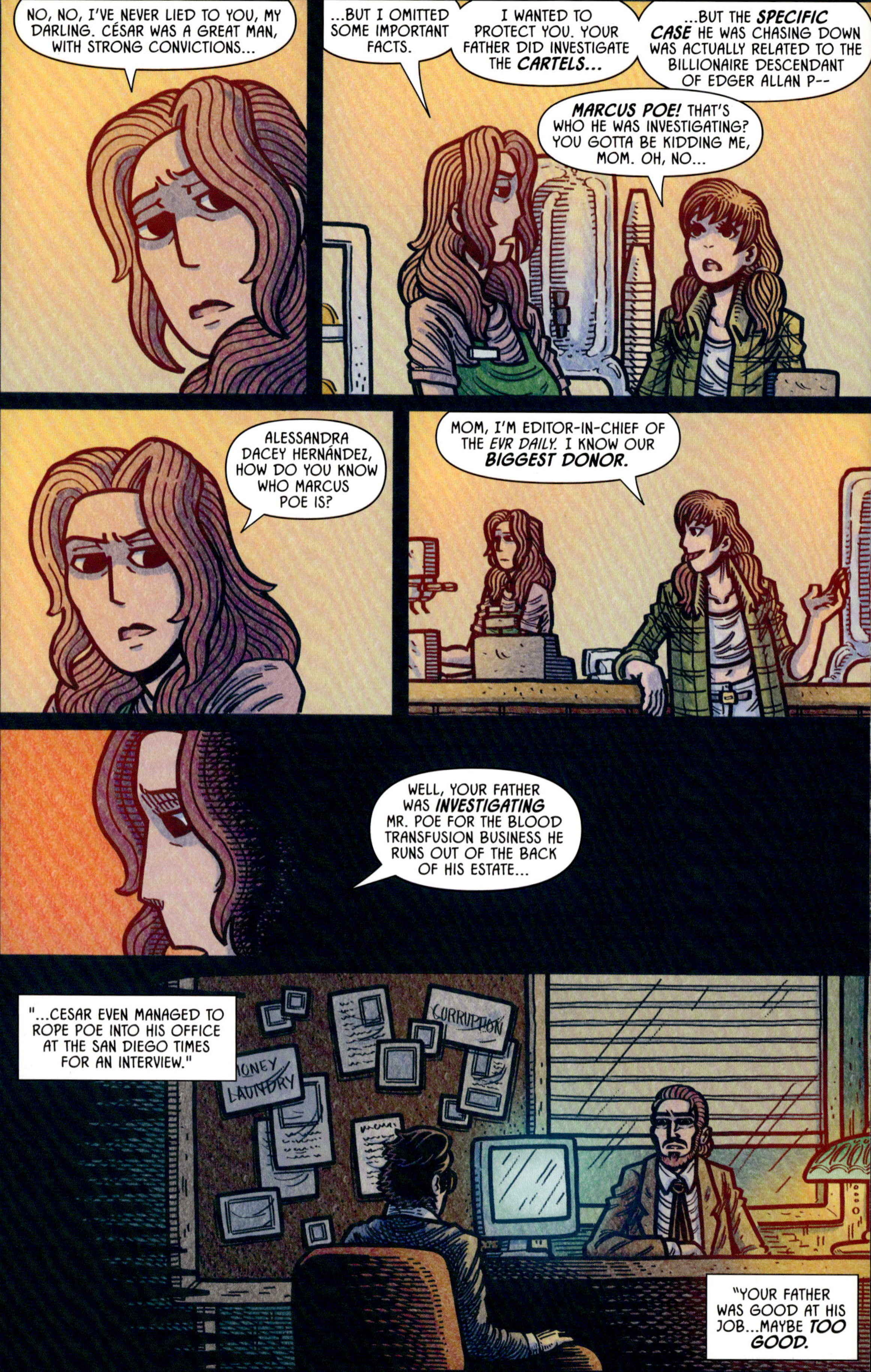
NO, NO, I'VE NEVER LIED TO YOU, MY DARLING. CÉSAR WAS A GREAT MAN, WITH STRONG CONVICTIONS...
...BUT I OMITTED SOME IMPORTANT FACTS.
I WANTED TO PROTECT YOU. YOUR FATHER DID INVESTIGATE THE **CARTELS...**
...BUT THE **SPECIFIC CASE** HE WAS CHASING DOWN WAS ACTUALLY RELATED TO THE BILLIONAIRE DESCENDANT OF EDGER ALLAN P--
MARCUS POE! THAT'S WHO HE WAS INVESTIGATING? YOU GOTTA BE KIDDING ME, MOM. OH, NO...
ALESSANDRA DACEY HERNÁNDEZ, HOW DO YOU KNOW WHO MARCUS POE IS?
MOM, I'M EDITOR-IN-CHIEF OF THE *EVR DAILY.* I KNOW OUR **BIGGEST DONOR.**
WELL, YOUR FATHER WAS **INVESTIGATING** MR. POE FOR THE BLOOD TRANSFUSION BUSINESS HE RUNS OUT OF THE BACK OF HIS ESTATE...
"...CESAR EVEN MANAGED TO ROPE POE INTO HIS OFFICE AT THE SAN DIEGO TIMES FOR AN INTERVIEW."
CORRUPTION
MONEY LAUNDRY
"YOUR FATHER WAS GOOD AT HIS JOB...MAYBE **TOO GOOD.**

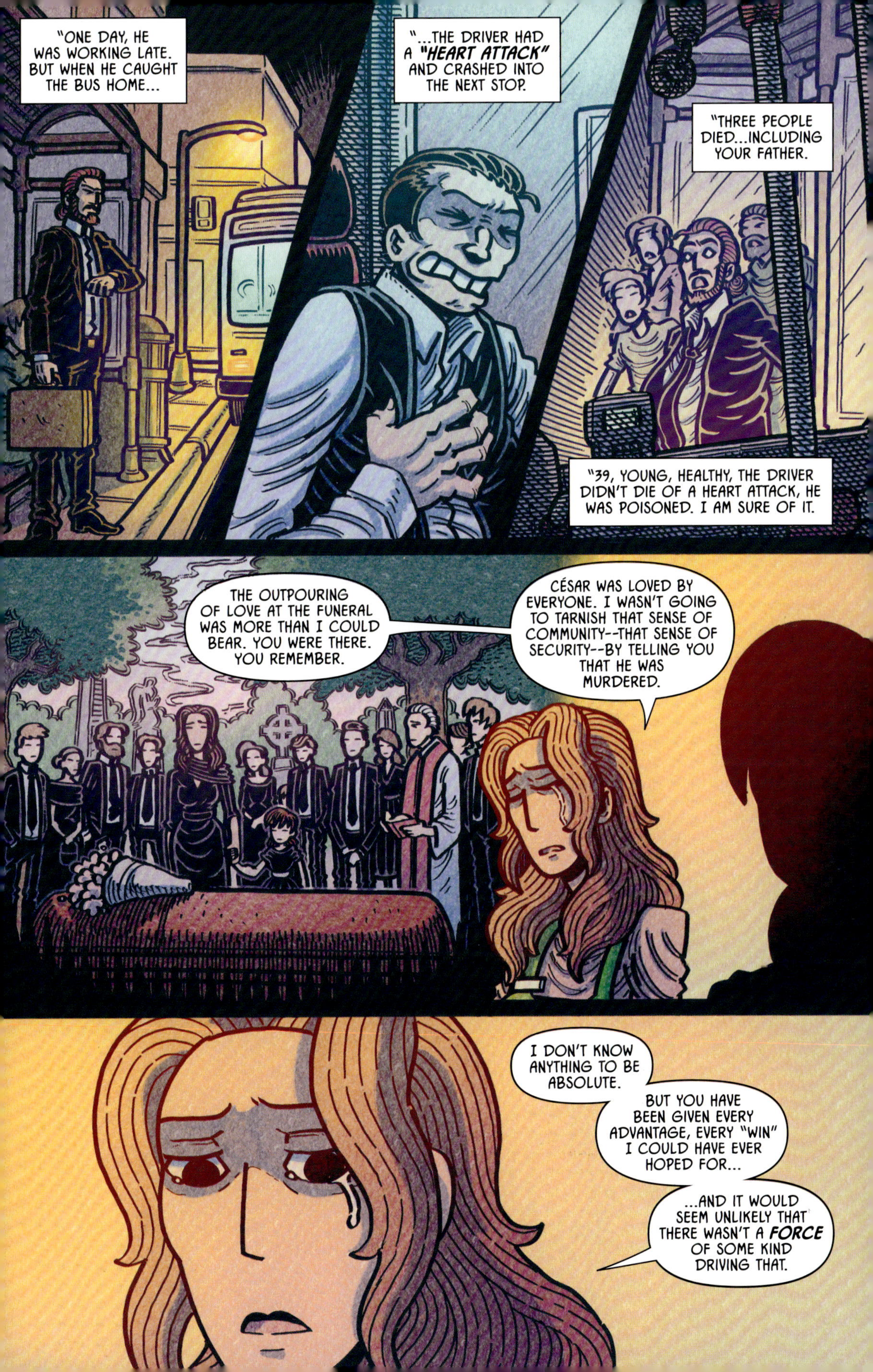
"ONE DAY, HE WAS WORKING LATE. BUT WHEN HE CAUGHT THE BUS HOME...
"...THE DRIVER HAD A "HEART ATTACK" AND CRASHED INTO THE NEXT STOP.
"THREE PEOPLE DIED...INCLUDING YOUR FATHER.
"39, YOUNG, HEALTHY, THE DRIVER DIDN'T DIE OF A HEART ATTACK, HE WAS POISONED. I AM SURE OF IT.
THE OUTPOURING OF LOVE AT THE FUNERAL WAS MORE THAN I COULD BEAR. YOU WERE THERE. YOU REMEMBER.
CÉSAR WAS LOVED BY EVERYONE. I WASN'T GOING TO TARNISH THAT SENSE OF COMMUNITY--THAT SENSE OF SECURITY--BY TELLING YOU THAT HE WAS MURDERED.
I DON'T KNOW ANYTHING TO BE ABSOLUTE.
BUT YOU HAVE BEEN GIVEN EVERY ADVANTAGE, EVERY "WIN" I COULD HAVE EVER HOPED FOR...
...AND IT WOULD SEEM UNLIKELY THAT THERE WASN'T A FORCE OF SOME KIND DRIVING THAT.

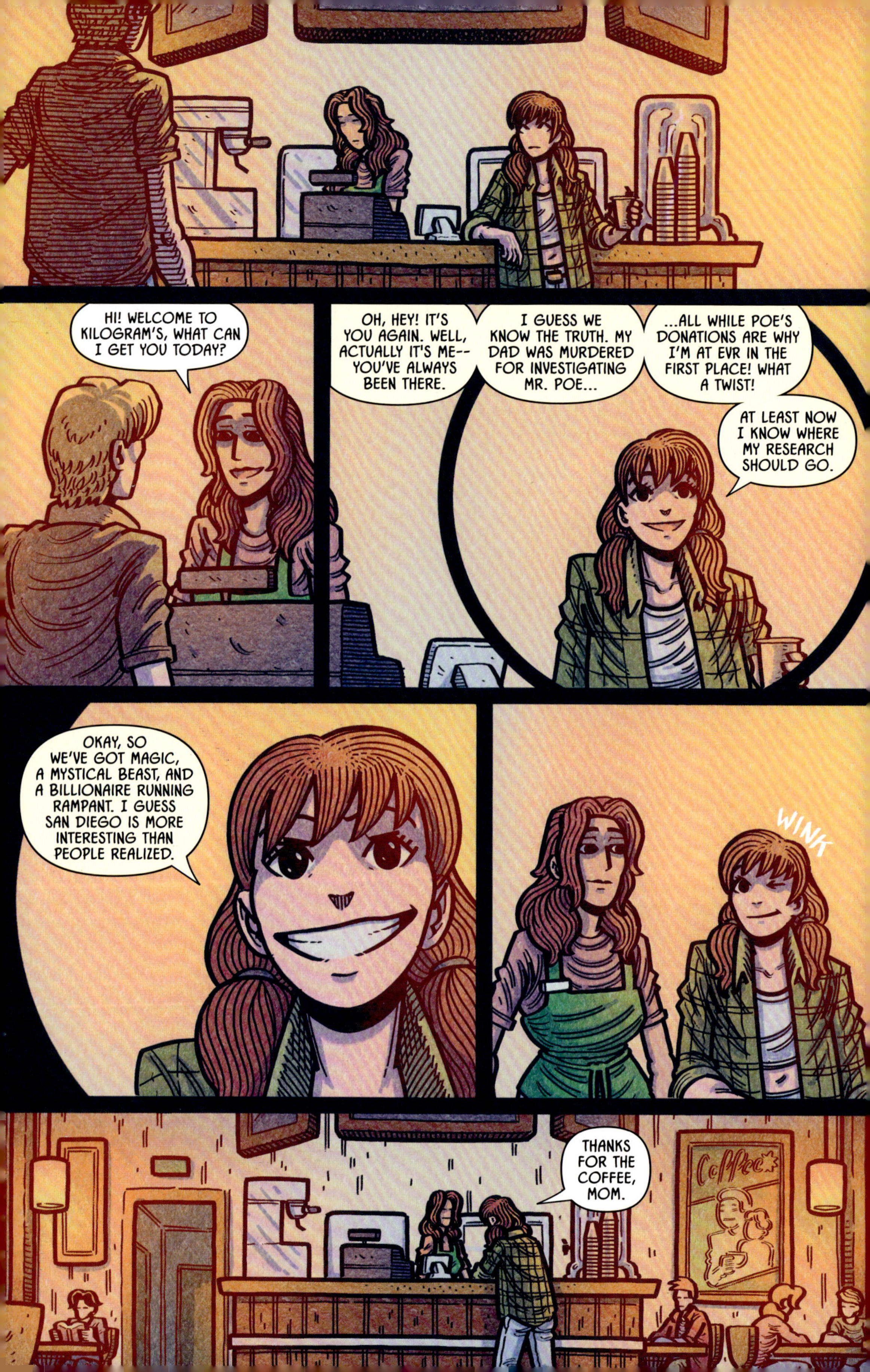
HI! WELCOME TO KILOGRAM'S, WHAT CAN I GET YOU TODAY?
OH, HEY! IT'S YOU AGAIN. WELL, ACTUALLY IT'S ME-- YOU'VE ALWAYS BEEN THERE.
I GUESS WE KNOW THE TRUTH. MY DAD WAS MURDERED FOR INVESTIGATING MR. POE...
...ALL WHILE POE'S DONATIONS ARE WHY I'M AT EVR IN THE FIRST PLACE! WHAT A TWIST!
AT LEAST NOW I KNOW WHERE MY RESEARCH SHOULD GO.
OKAY, SO WE'VE GOT MAGIC, A MYSTICAL BEAST, AND A BILLIONAIRE RUNNING RAMPANT. I GUESS SAN DIEGO IS MORE INTERESTING THAN PEOPLE REALIZED.
WINK
THANKS FOR THE COFFEE, MOM.
Coffee

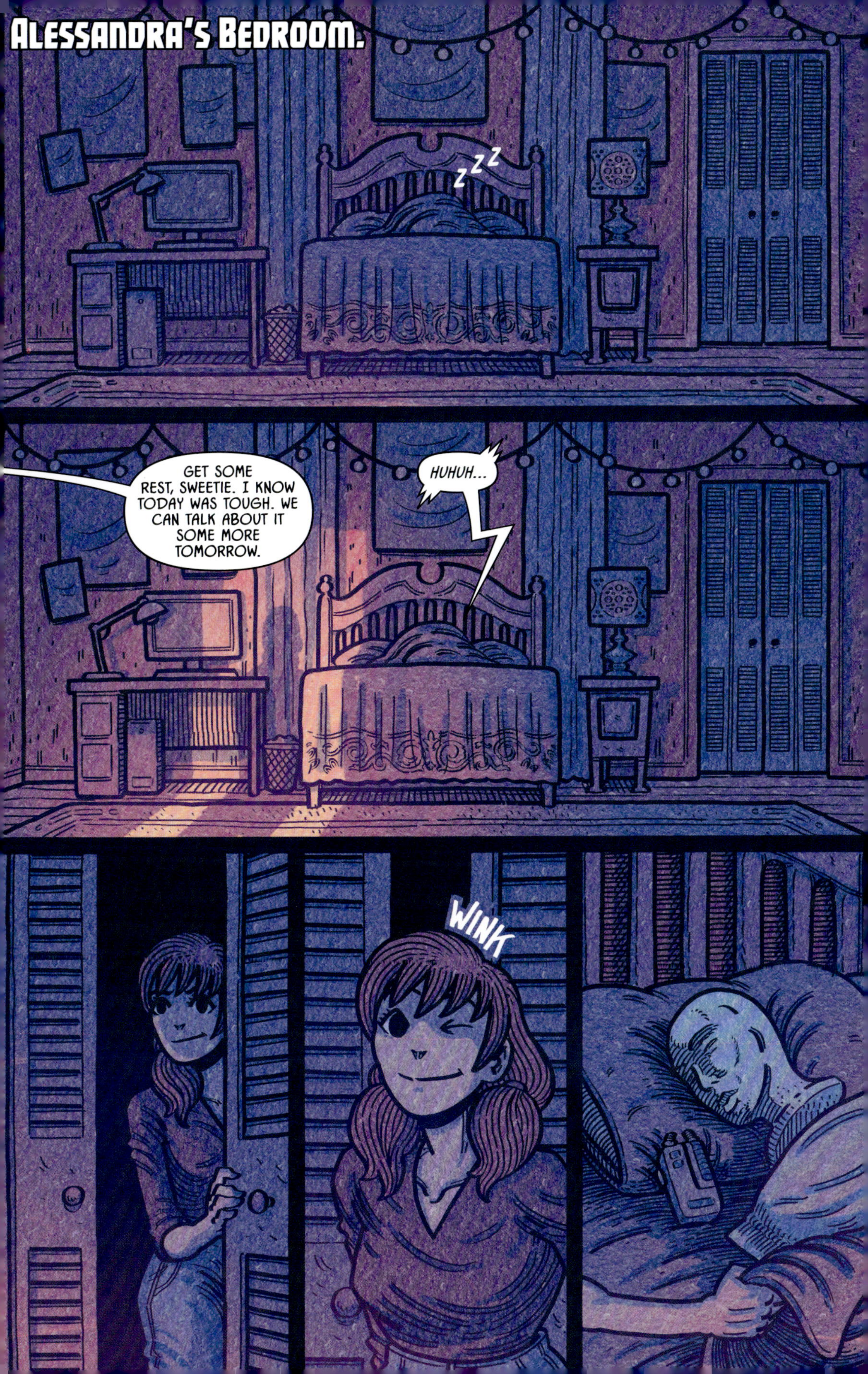
Alessandra's Bedroom.
Z Z Z
GET SOME REST, SWEETIE. I KNOW TODAY WAS TOUGH. WE CAN TALK ABOUT IT SOME MORE TOMORROW.
HUHUH...
WINK

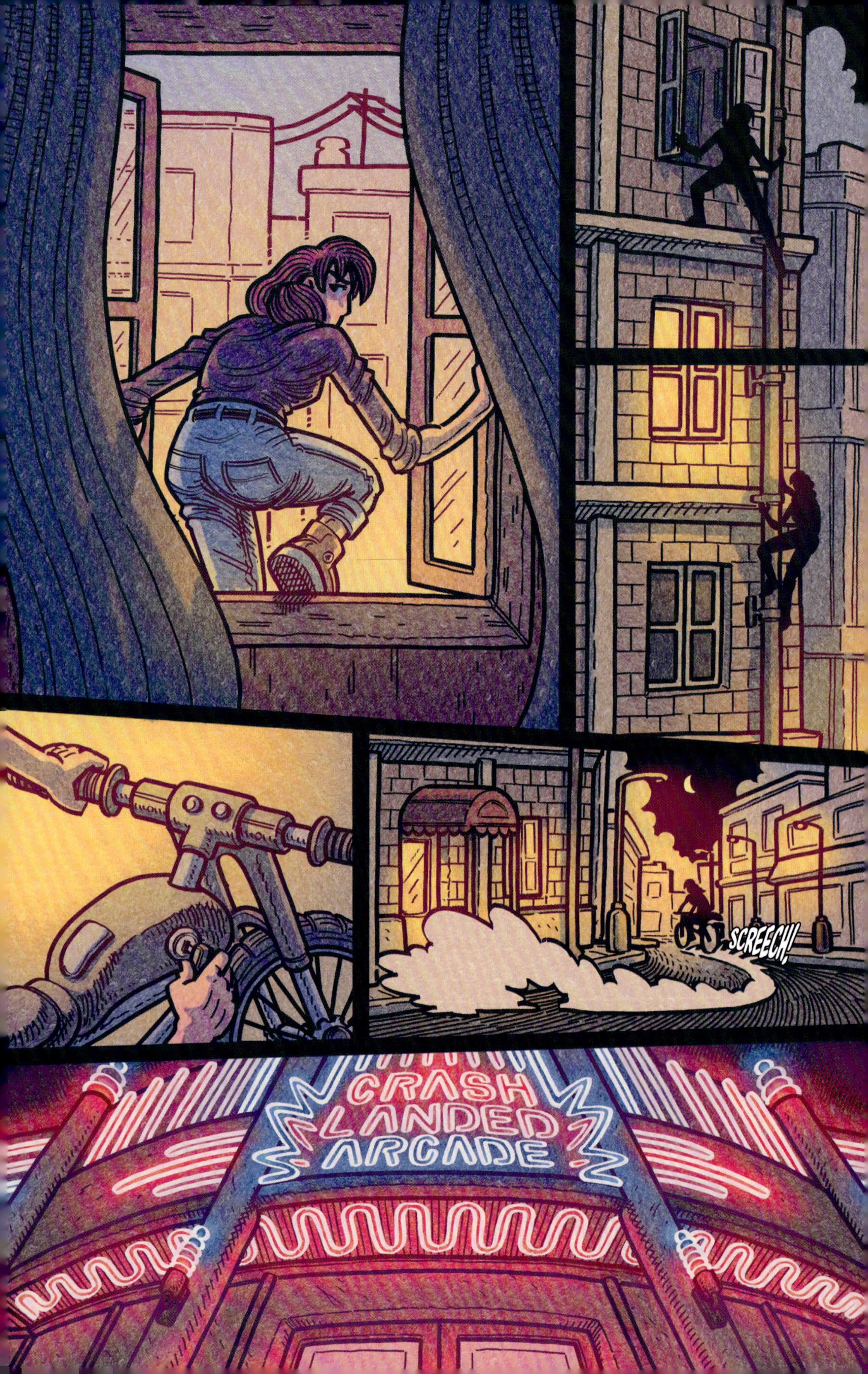
SCREECH!
CRASH LANDED ARCADE

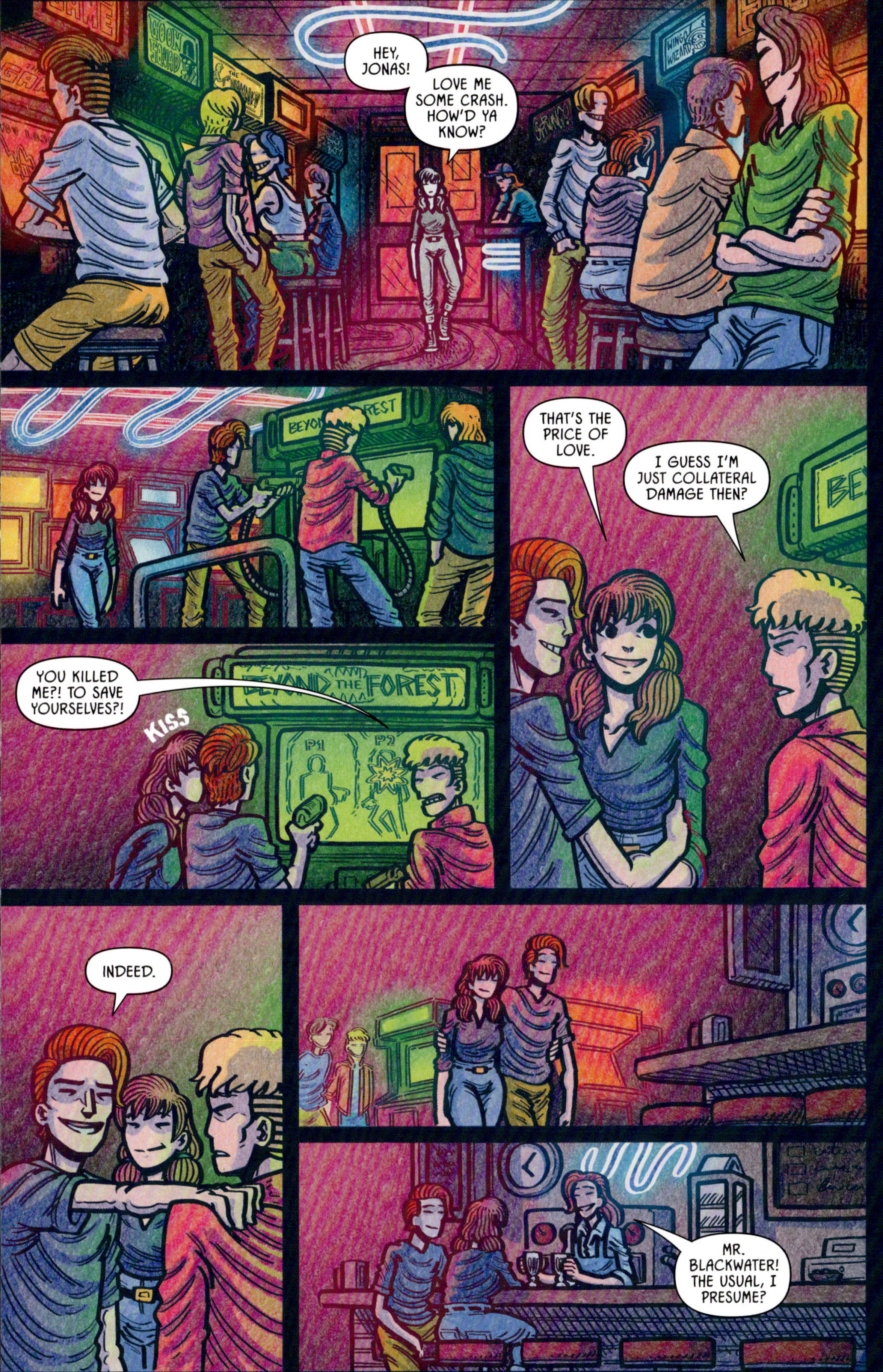
HEY, JONAS!
LOVE ME SOME CRASH. HOW'D YA KNOW?
THAT'S THE PRICE OF LOVE.
I GUESS I'M JUST COLLATERAL DAMAGE THEN?
YOU KILLED ME?! TO SAVE YOURSELVES?!
KISS
BEYOND THE FOREST
INDEED.
MR. BLACKWATER! THE USUAL, I PRESUME?

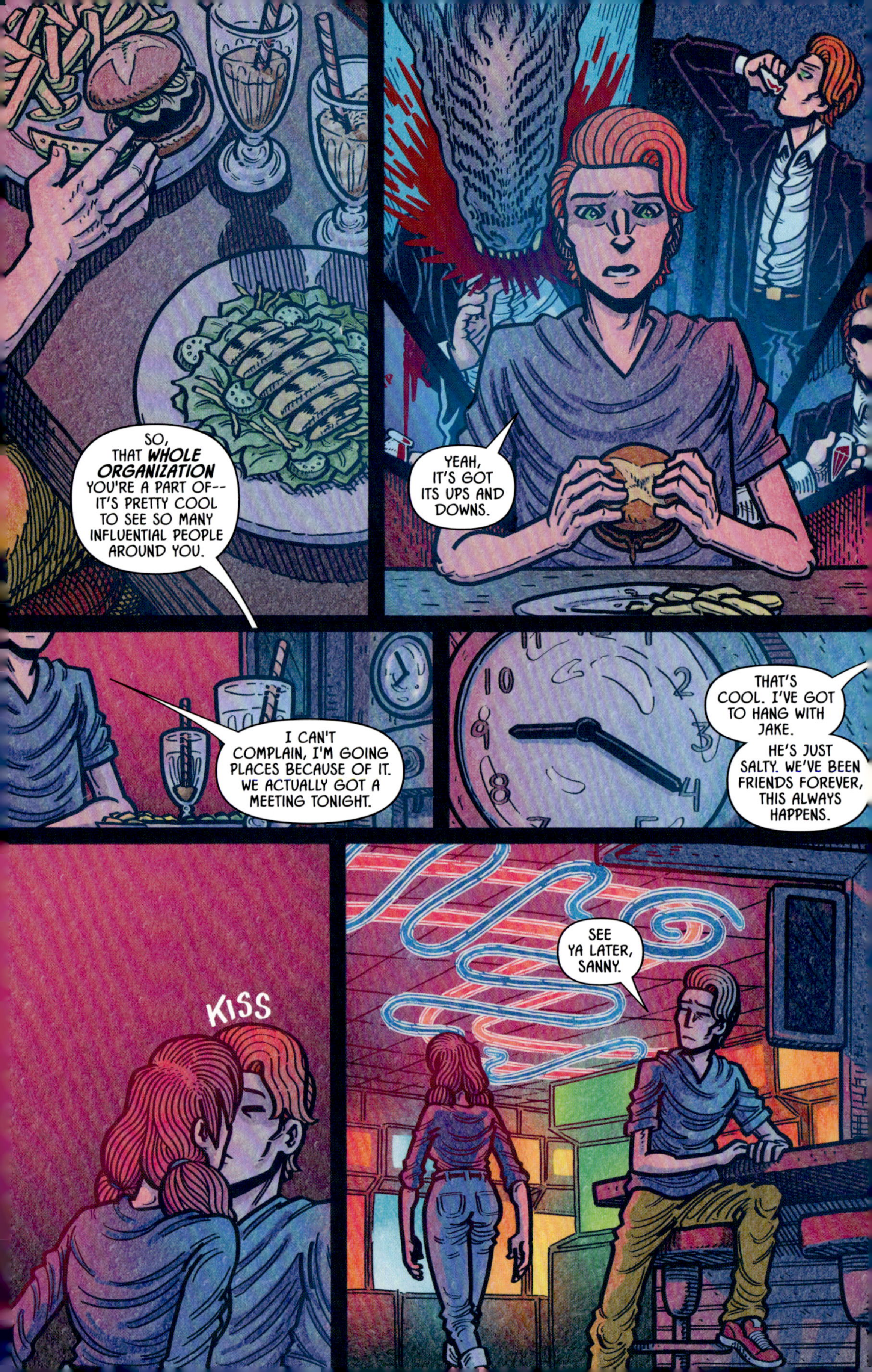
SO, THAT **WHOLE ORGANIZATION** YOU'RE A PART OF-- IT'S PRETTY COOL TO SEE SO MANY INFLUENTIAL PEOPLE AROUND YOU.
YEAH, IT'S GOT ITS UPS AND DOWNS.
I CAN'T COMPLAIN, I'M GOING PLACES BECAUSE OF IT. WE ACTUALLY GOT A MEETING TONIGHT.
THAT'S COOL. I'VE GOT TO HANG WITH JAKE.
HE'S JUST SALTY. WE'VE BEEN FRIENDS FOREVER, THIS ALWAYS HAPPENS.
KISS
SEE YA LATER, SANNY.

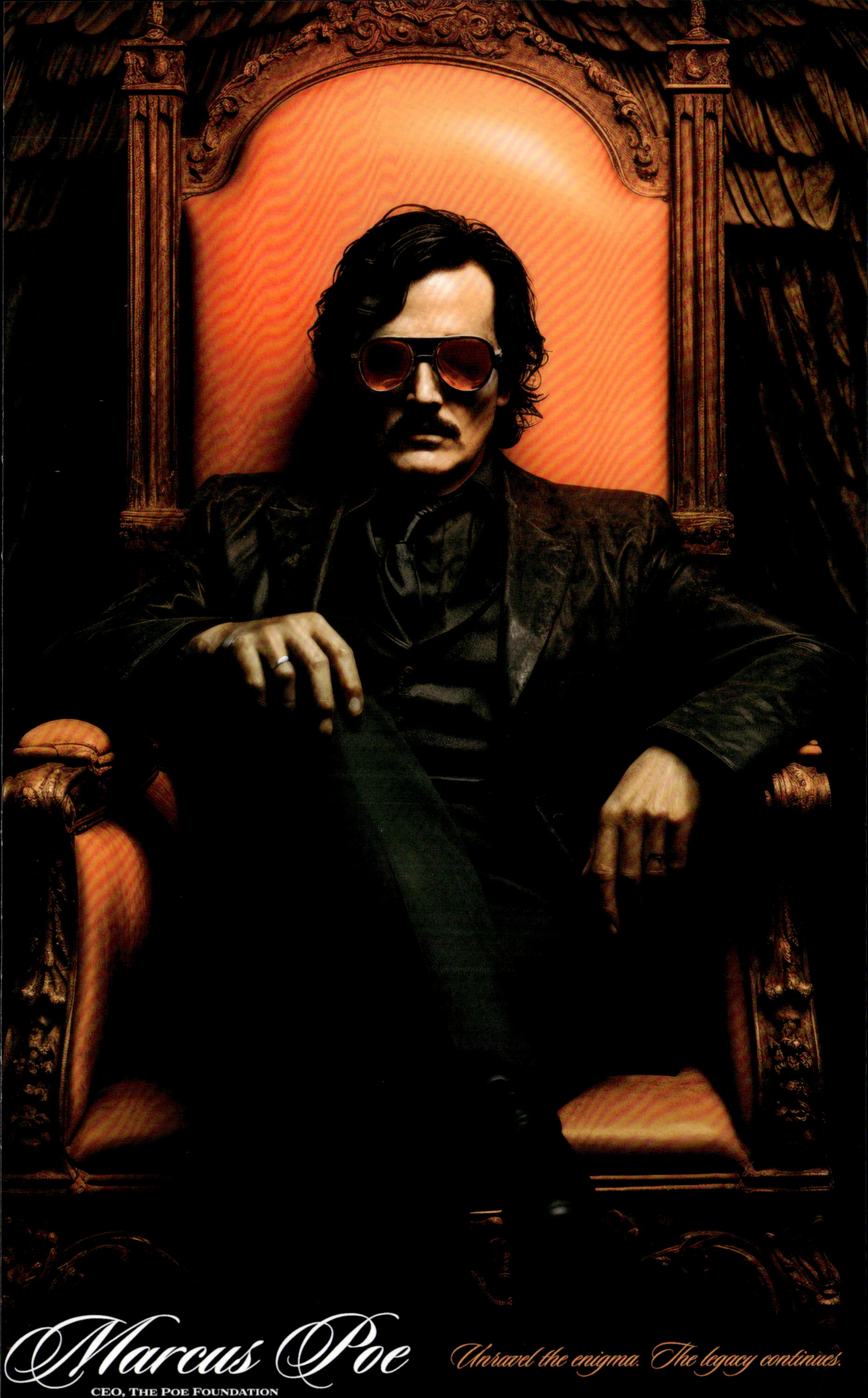
Marcus Poe
CEO, The Poe Foundation
Unravel the enigma. The legacy continues.

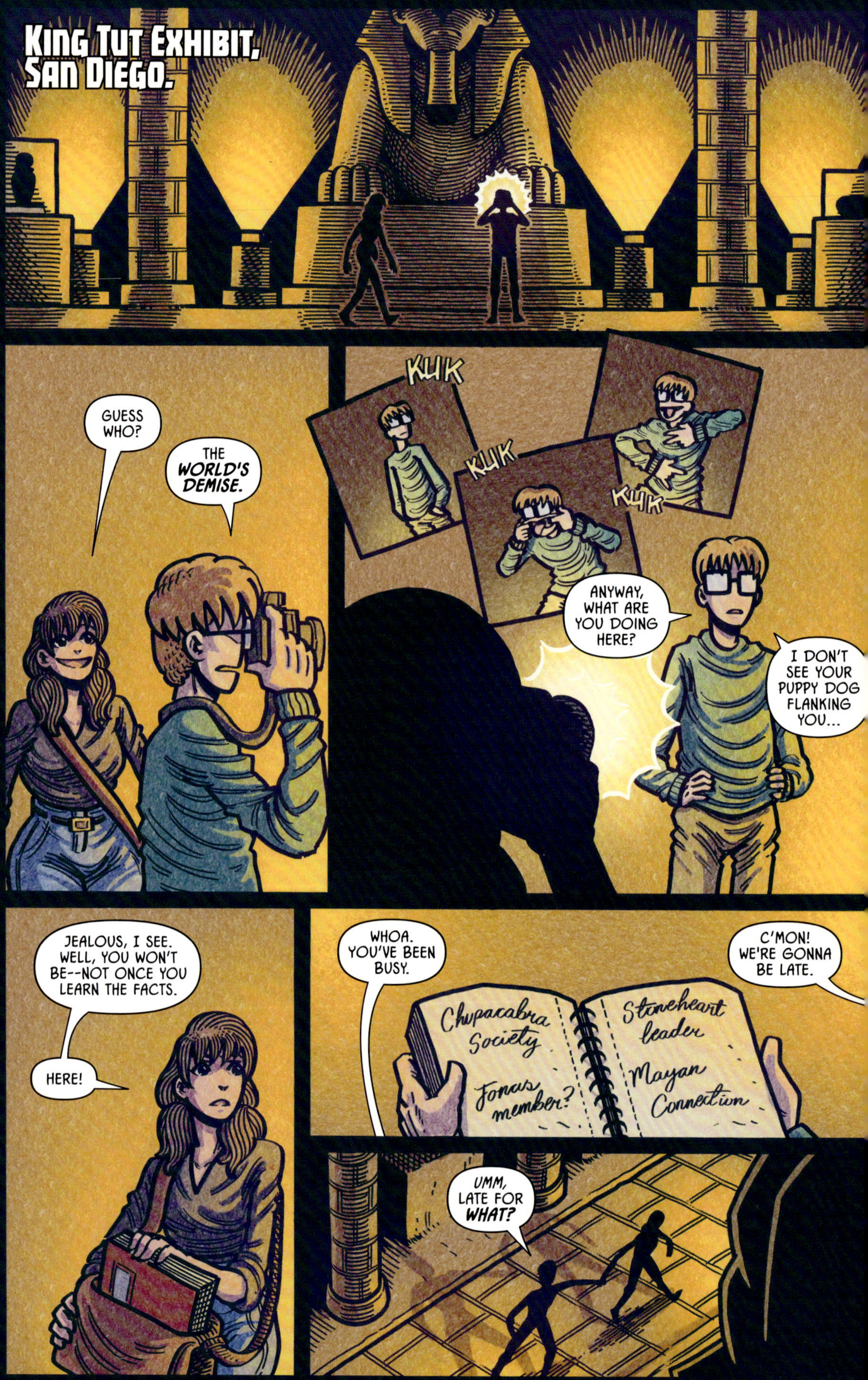
KING TUT EXHIBIT, SAN DIEGO.
GUESS WHO?
THE WORLD'S DEMISE.
KLIK
KLIK
KLIK
ANYWAY, WHAT ARE YOU DOING HERE?
I DON'T SEE YOUR PUPPY DOG FLANKING YOU...
JEALOUS, I SEE. WELL, YOU WON'T BE--NOT ONCE YOU LEARN THE FACTS.
HERE!
WHOA. YOU'VE BEEN BUSY.
Chupacabra Society
Jonas member?
Stoneheart leader
Mayan Connection
C'MON! WE'RE GONNA BE LATE.
UMM, LATE FOR WHAT?

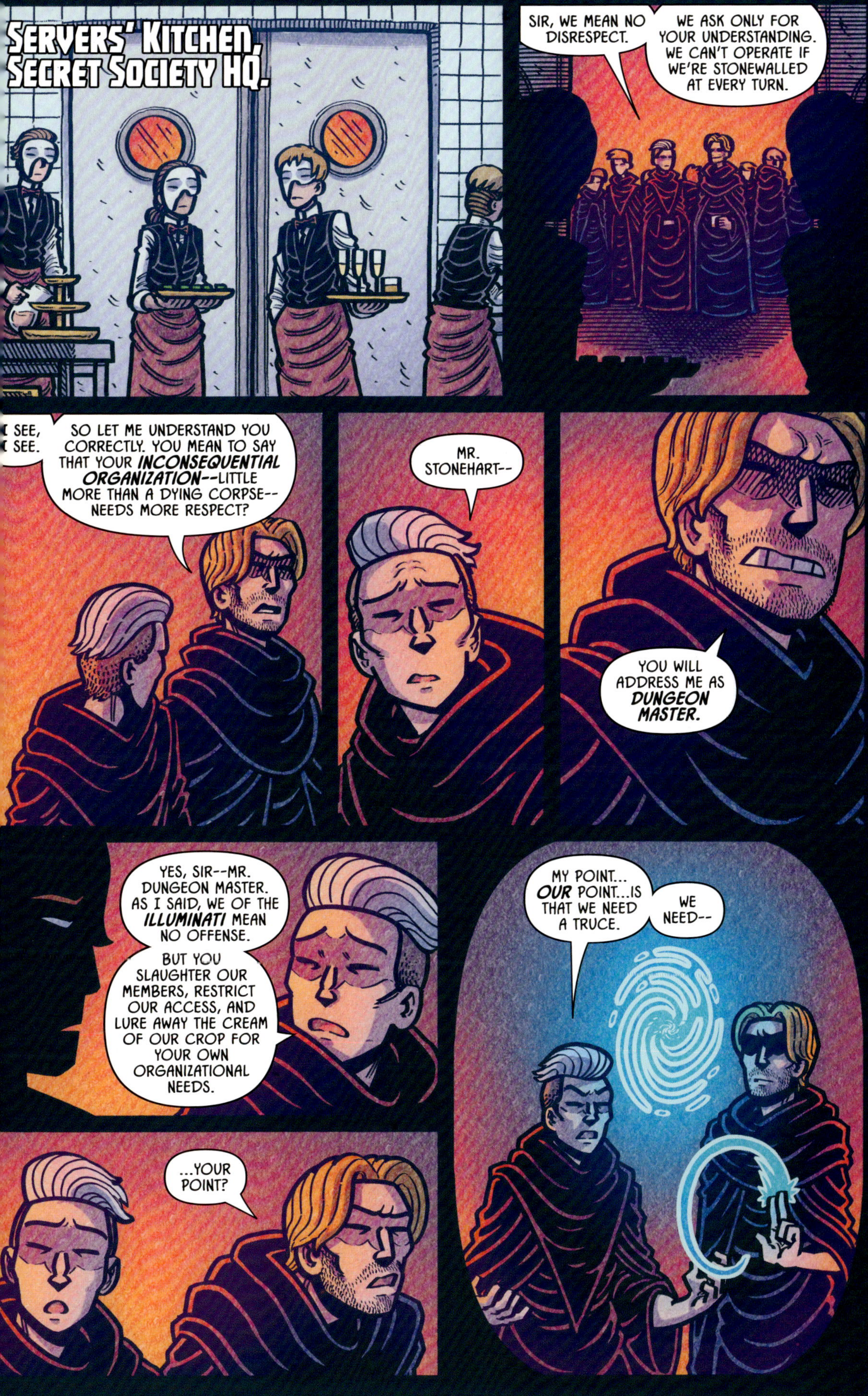
SERVERS' KITCHEN, SECRET SOCIETY HQ.
SIR, WE MEAN NO DISRESPECT.
WE ASK ONLY FOR YOUR UNDERSTANDING. WE CAN'T OPERATE IF WE'RE STONEWALLED AT EVERY TURN.
I SEE, I SEE.
SO LET ME UNDERSTAND YOU CORRECTLY. YOU MEAN TO SAY THAT YOUR INCONSEQUENTIAL ORGANIZATION--LITTLE MORE THAN A DYING CORPSE--NEEDS MORE RESPECT?
MR. STONEHART--
YOU WILL ADDRESS ME AS DUNGEON MASTER.
YES, SIR--MR. DUNGEON MASTER. AS I SAID, WE OF THE ILLUMINATI MEAN NO OFFENSE.
BUT YOU SLAUGHTER OUR MEMBERS, RESTRICT OUR ACCESS, AND LURE AWAY THE CREAM OF OUR CROP FOR YOUR OWN ORGANIZATIONAL NEEDS.
...YOUR POINT?
MY POINT... OUR POINT...IS THAT WE NEED A TRUCE.
WE NEED--

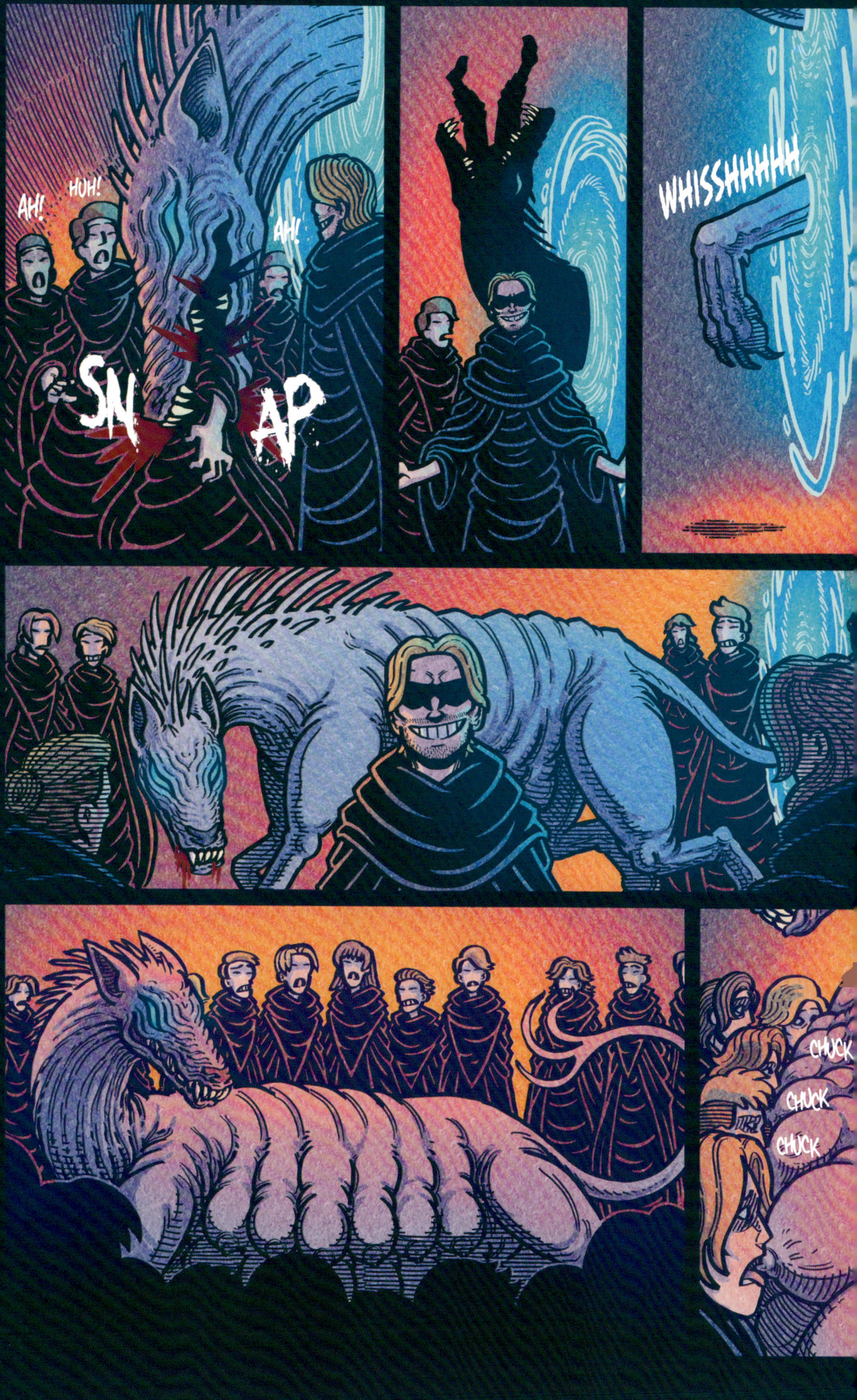

AH!
HUH!
AH!
SNAP
WHISSHHHHH
CHUCK
CHUCK
CHUCK

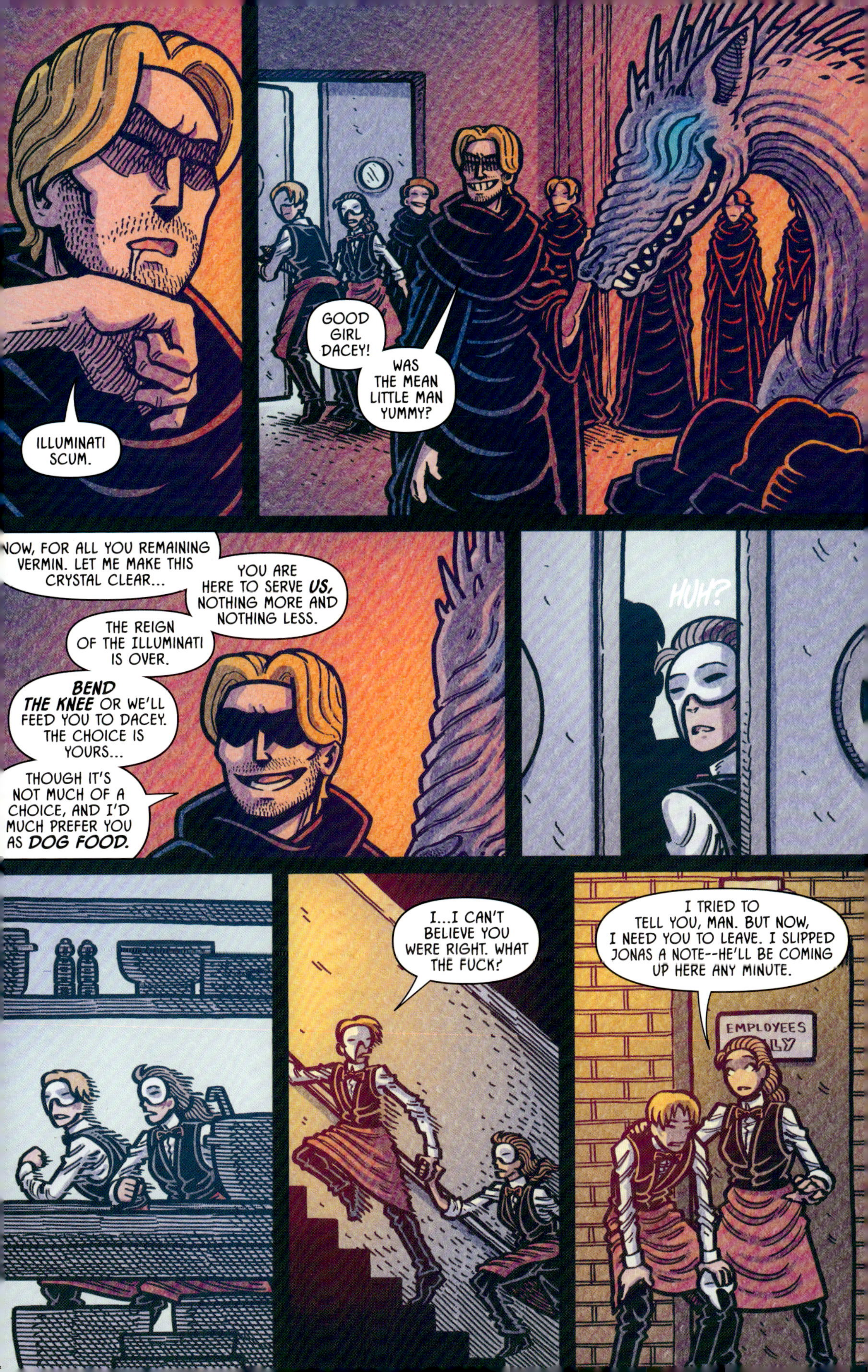
ILLUMINATI SCUM.
GOOD GIRL DACEY!
WAS THE MEAN LITTLE MAN YUMMY?
NOW, FOR ALL YOU REMAINING VERMIN. LET ME MAKE THIS CRYSTAL CLEAR...
YOU ARE HERE TO SERVE US, NOTHING MORE AND NOTHING LESS.
THE REIGN OF THE ILLUMINATI IS OVER.
BEND THE KNEE OR WE'LL FEED YOU TO DACEY. THE CHOICE IS YOURS...
THOUGH IT'S NOT MUCH OF A CHOICE, AND I'D MUCH PREFER YOU AS DOG FOOD.
HUH?
I...I CAN'T BELIEVE YOU WERE RIGHT. WHAT THE FUCK?
I TRIED TO TELL YOU, MAN. BUT NOW, I NEED YOU TO LEAVE. I SLIPPED JONAS A NOTE--HE'LL BE COMING UP HERE ANY MINUTE.
EMPLOYEES

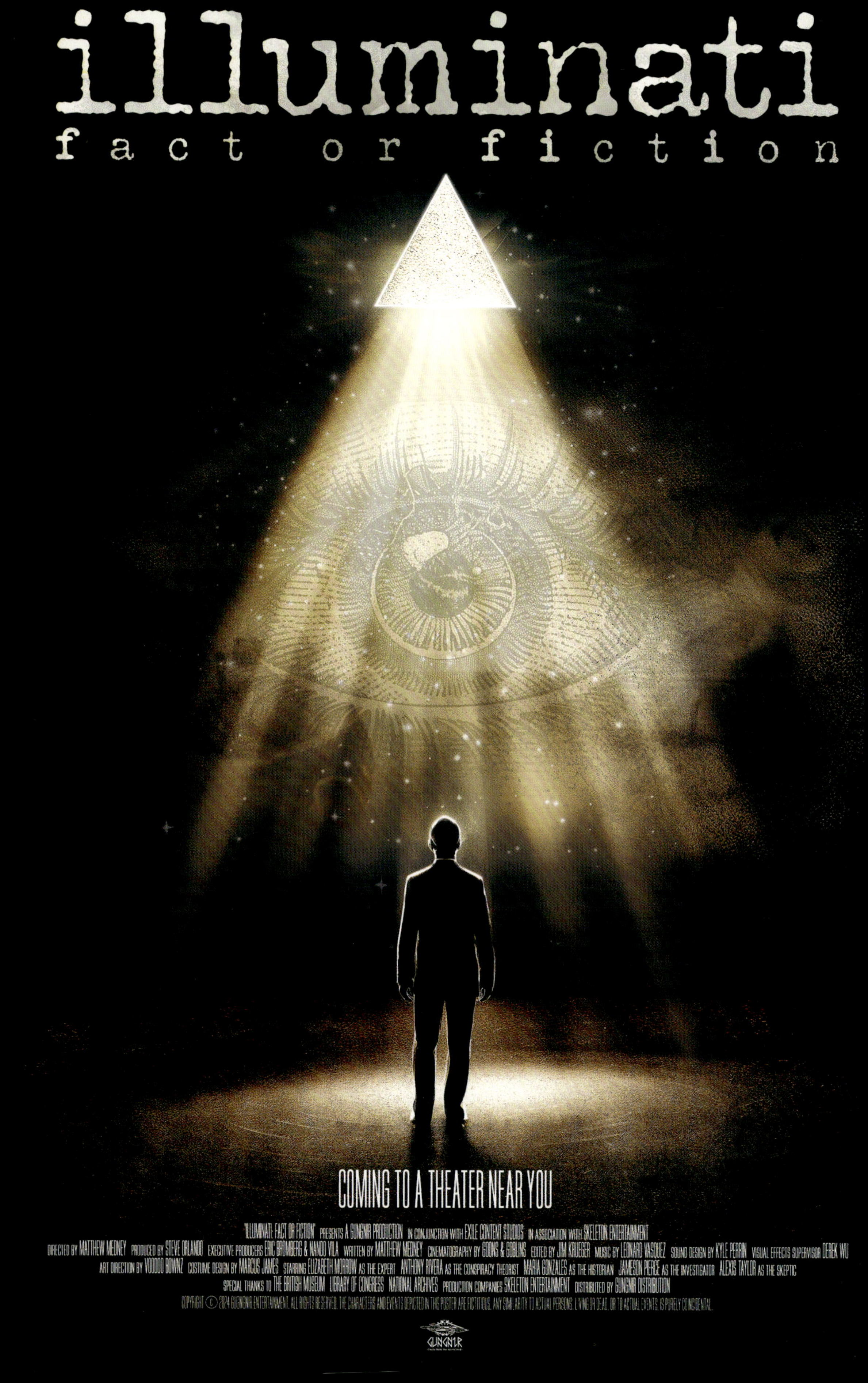
illuminati
fact or fiction
COMING TO A THEATER NEAR YOU
"ILLUMINATI: FACT OR FICTION" PRESENTS A GUNGNIR PRODUCTION IN CONJUNCTION WITH EXILE CONTENT STUDIOS IN ASSOCIATION WITH SKELETON ENTERTAINMENT
DIRECTED BY MATTHEW MEDNEY PRODUCED BY STEVE ORLANDO EXECUTIVE PRODUCERS ERIC BROMBERG & NANDO VILA WRITTEN BY MATTHEW MEDNEY CINEMATOGRAPHY BY GOONS & GOBLINS EDITED BY JIM KRUEGER MUSIC BY LEONARD VASQUEZ SOUND DESIGN BY KYLE PERRIN VISUAL EFFECTS SUPERVISOR DEREK WU
ART DIRECTION BY VOODOO BOWNZ COSTUME DESIGN BY MARCUS JAMES STARRING ELIZABETH MORROW AS THE EXPERT ANTHONY RIVERA AS THE CONSPIRACY THEORIST MARIA GONZALES AS THE HISTORIAN JAMESON PIERCE AS THE INVESTIGATOR ALEXIS TAYLOR AS THE SKEPTIC
SPECIAL THANKS TO THE BRITISH MUSEUM LIBRARY OF CONGRESS NATIONAL ARCHIVES PRODUCTION COMPANIES SKELETON ENTERTAINMENT DISTRIBUTED BY GUNGNIR DISTRIBUTION
COPYRIGHT © 2024 GUGNGNIR ENTERTAINMENT. ALL RIGHTS RESERVED. THE CHARACTERS AND EVENTS DEPICTED IN THIS POSTER ARE FICTITIOUS. ANY SIMILARITY TO ACTUAL PERSONS, LIVING OR DEAD, OR TO ACTUAL EVENTS, IS PURELY CONCIDENTAL.
GUNGNIR

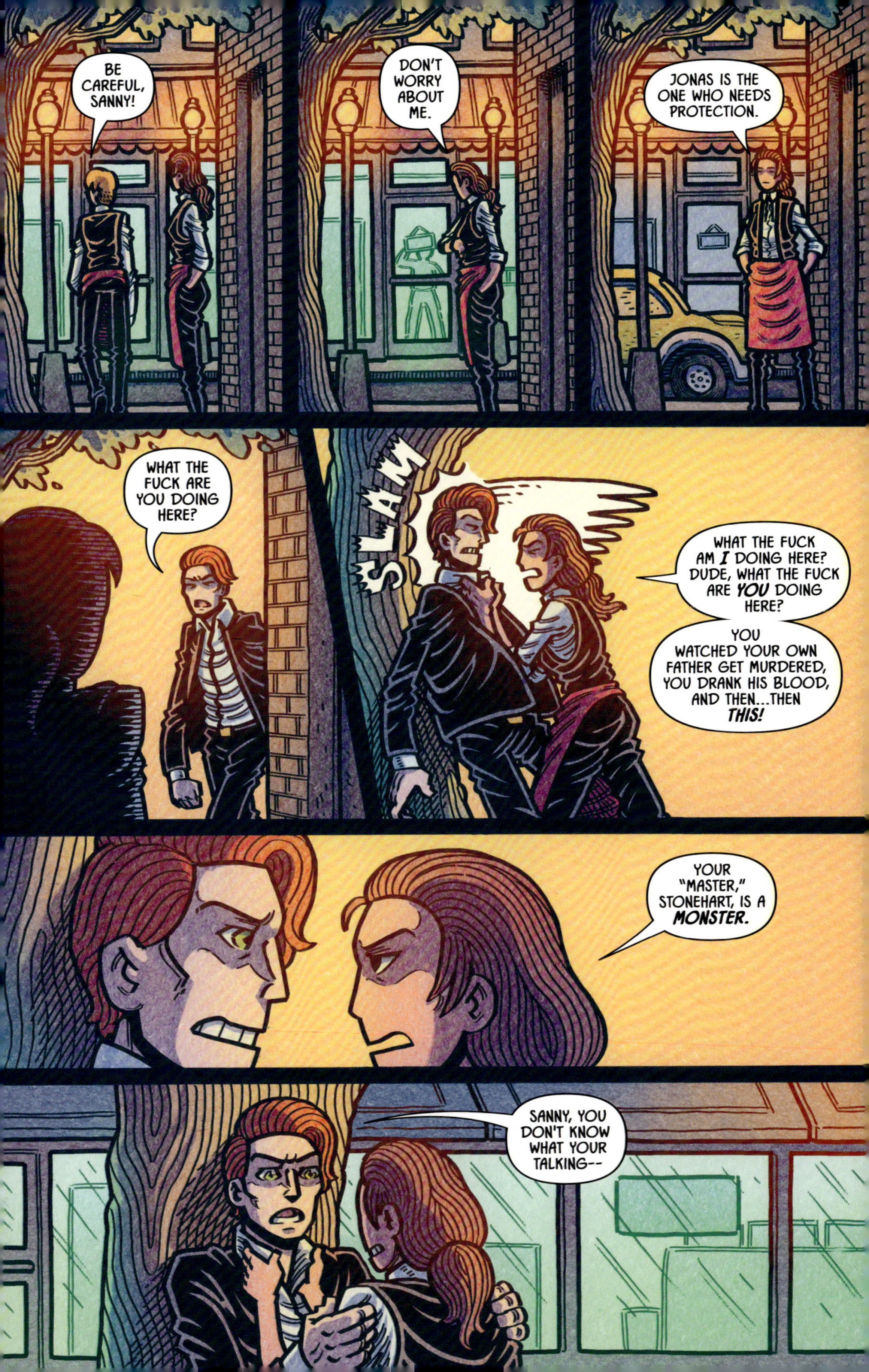
BE CAREFUL, SANNY!
DON'T WORRY ABOUT ME.
JONAS IS THE ONE WHO NEEDS PROTECTION.
WHAT THE FUCK ARE YOU DOING HERE?
SLAM
WHAT THE FUCK AM *I* DOING HERE? DUDE, WHAT THE FUCK ARE *YOU* DOING HERE?
YOU WATCHED YOUR OWN FATHER GET MURDERED, YOU DRANK HIS BLOOD, AND THEN...THEN *THIS!*
YOUR "MASTER," STONEHART, IS A *MONSTER.*
SANNY, YOU DON'T KNOW WHAT YOUR TALKING--

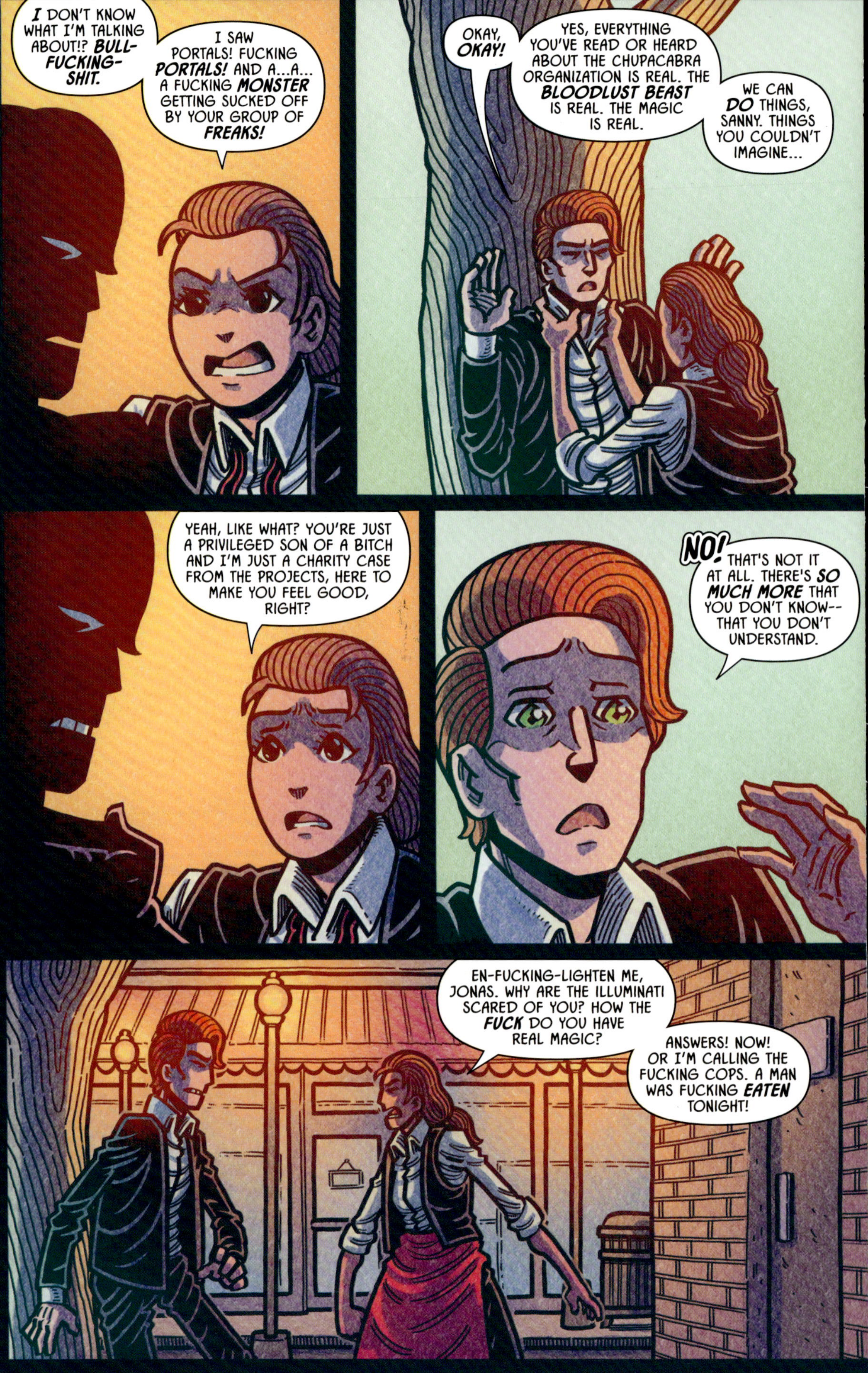
I DON'T KNOW WHAT I'M TALKING ABOUT!? BULL-FUCKING-SHIT.
I SAW PORTALS! FUCKING PORTALS! AND A...A... A FUCKING MONSTER GETTING SUCKED OFF BY YOUR GROUP OF FREAKS!
OKAY, OKAY!
YES, EVERYTHING YOU'VE READ OR HEARD ABOUT THE CHUPACABRA ORGANIZATION IS REAL. THE BLOODLUST BEAST IS REAL. THE MAGIC IS REAL.
WE CAN DO THINGS, SANNY. THINGS YOU COULDN'T IMAGINE...
YEAH, LIKE WHAT? YOU'RE JUST A PRIVILEGED SON OF A BITCH AND I'M JUST A CHARITY CASE FROM THE PROJECTS, HERE TO MAKE YOU FEEL GOOD, RIGHT?
NO! THAT'S NOT IT AT ALL. THERE'S SO MUCH MORE THAT YOU DON'T KNOW-- THAT YOU DON'T UNDERSTAND.
EN-FUCKING-LIGHTEN ME, JONAS. WHY ARE THE ILLUMINATI SCARED OF YOU? HOW THE FUCK DO YOU HAVE REAL MAGIC?
ANSWERS! NOW! OR I'M CALLING THE FUCKING COPS. A MAN WAS FUCKING EATEN TONIGHT!

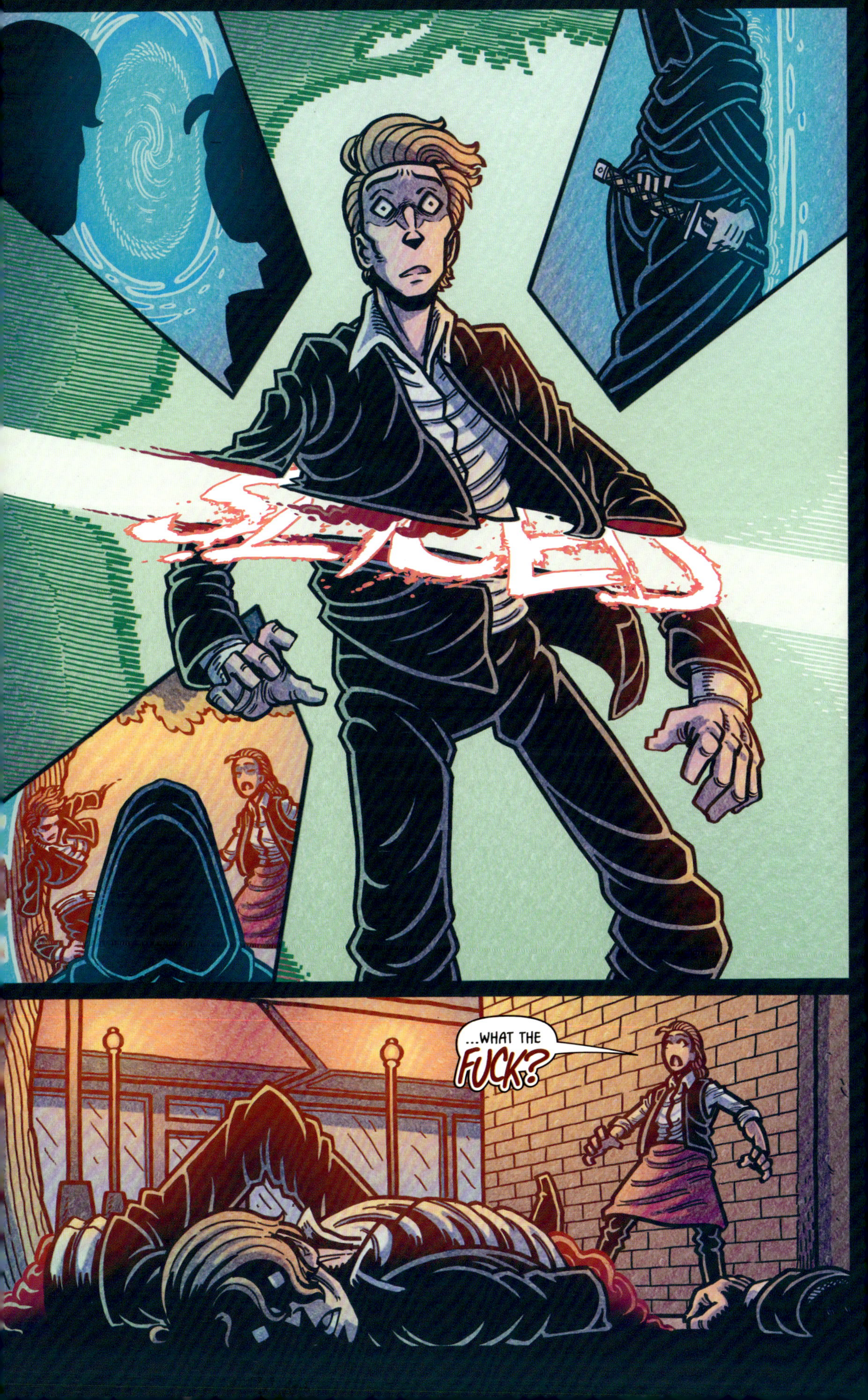
SLICED
...WHAT THE FUCK?

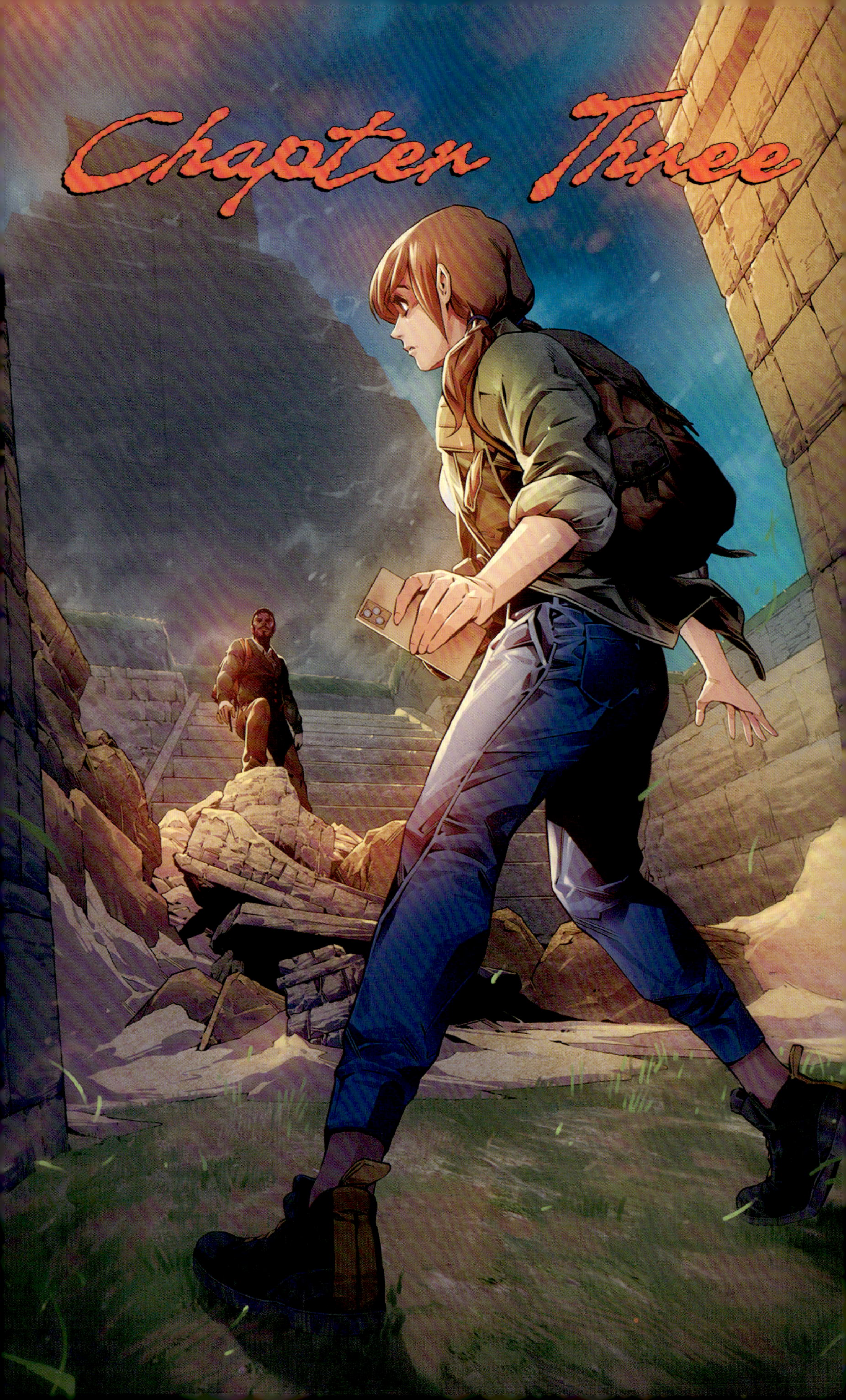
Chapter Three

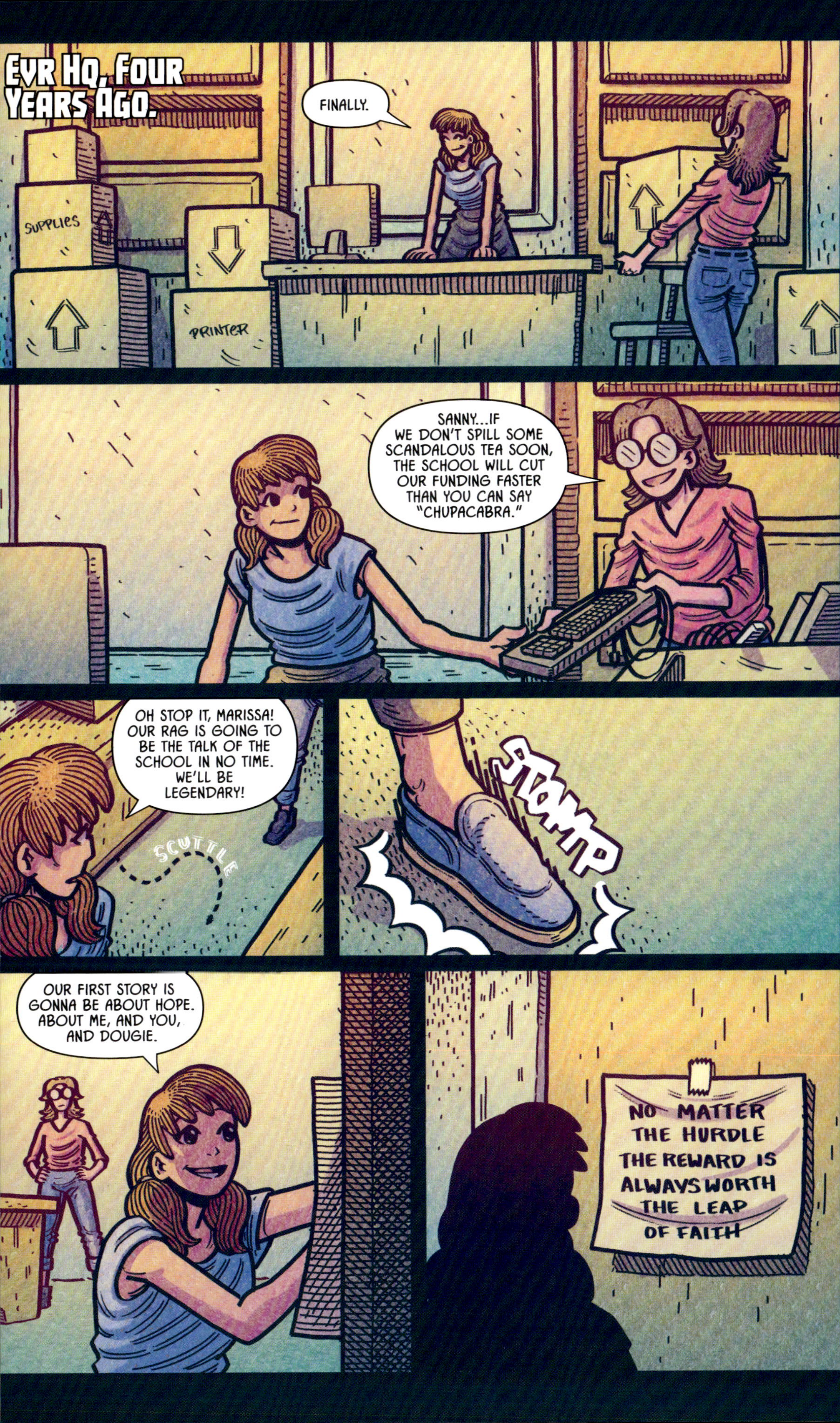
EVR HQ, FOUR YEARS AGO.
FINALLY.
SUPPLIES
PRINTER
SANNY...IF WE DON'T SPILL SOME SCANDALOUS TEA SOON, THE SCHOOL WILL CUT OUR FUNDING FASTER THAN YOU CAN SAY "CHUPACABRA."
OH STOP IT, MARISSA! OUR RAG IS GOING TO BE THE TALK OF THE SCHOOL IN NO TIME. WE'LL BE LEGENDARY!
SCUTTLE
STOMP
OUR FIRST STORY IS GONNA BE ABOUT HOPE. ABOUT ME, AND YOU, AND DOUGIE.
NO MATTER THE HURDLE THE REWARD IS ALWAYS WORTH THE LEAP OF FAITH

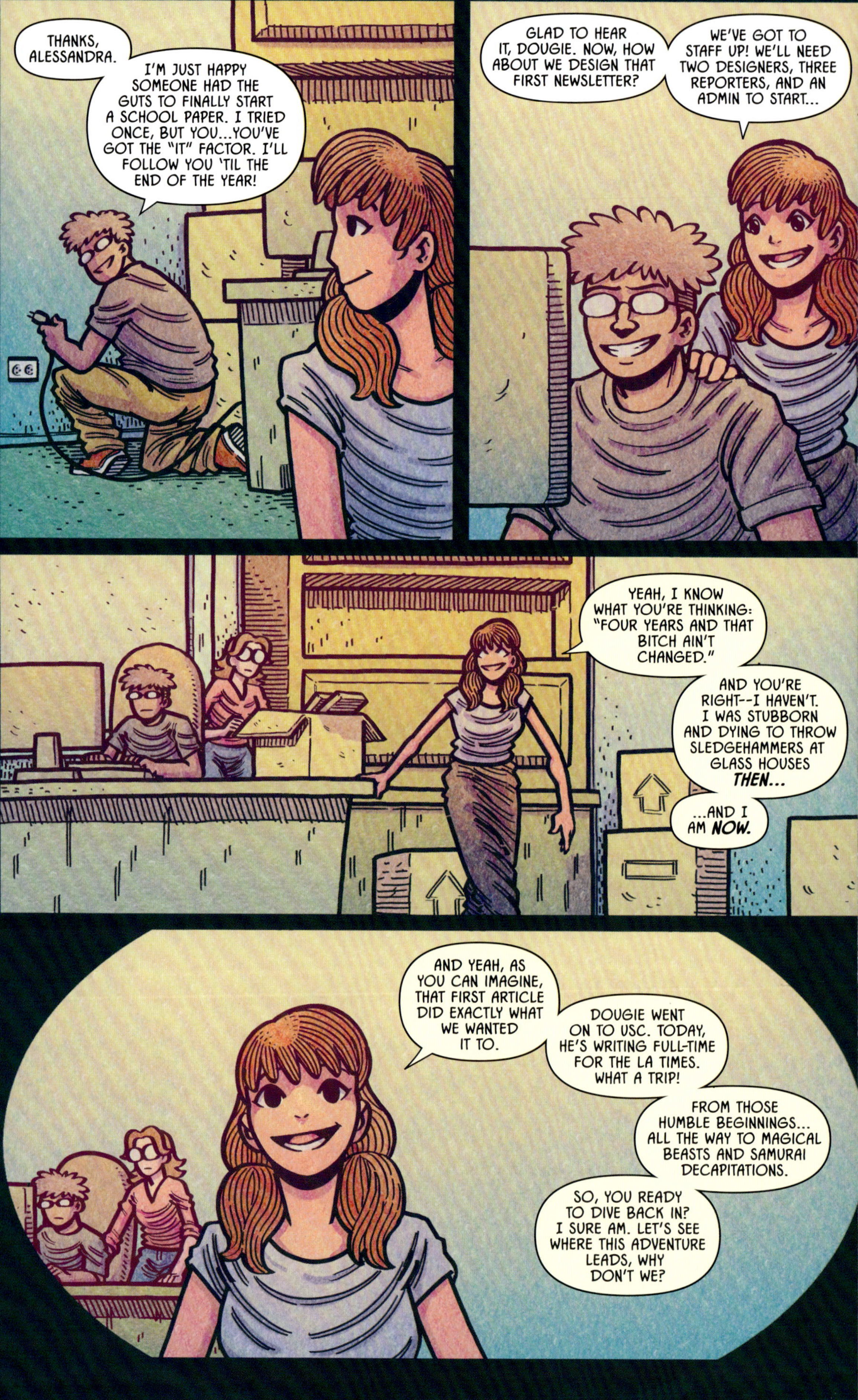
THANKS, ALESSANDRA.
I'M JUST HAPPY SOMEONE HAD THE GUTS TO FINALLY START A SCHOOL PAPER. I TRIED ONCE, BUT YOU...YOU'VE GOT THE "IT" FACTOR. I'LL FOLLOW YOU 'TIL THE END OF THE YEAR!
GLAD TO HEAR IT, DOUGIE. NOW, HOW ABOUT WE DESIGN THAT FIRST NEWSLETTER?
WE'VE GOT TO STAFF UP! WE'LL NEED TWO DESIGNERS, THREE REPORTERS, AND AN ADMIN TO START...
YEAH, I KNOW WHAT YOU'RE THINKING: "FOUR YEARS AND THAT BITCH AIN'T CHANGED."
AND YOU'RE RIGHT--I HAVEN'T. I WAS STUBBORN AND DYING TO THROW SLEDGEHAMMERS AT GLASS HOUSES ***THEN...***
...AND I AM ***NOW.***
AND YEAH, AS YOU CAN IMAGINE, THAT FIRST ARTICLE DID EXACTLY WHAT WE WANTED IT TO.
DOUGIE WENT ON TO USC. TODAY, HE'S WRITING FULL-TIME FOR THE LA TIMES. WHAT A TRIP!
FROM THOSE HUMBLE BEGINNINGS... ALL THE WAY TO MAGICAL BEASTS AND SAMURAI DECAPITATIONS.
SO, YOU READY TO DIVE BACK IN? I SURE AM. LET'S SEE WHERE THIS ADVENTURE LEADS, WHY DON'T WE?

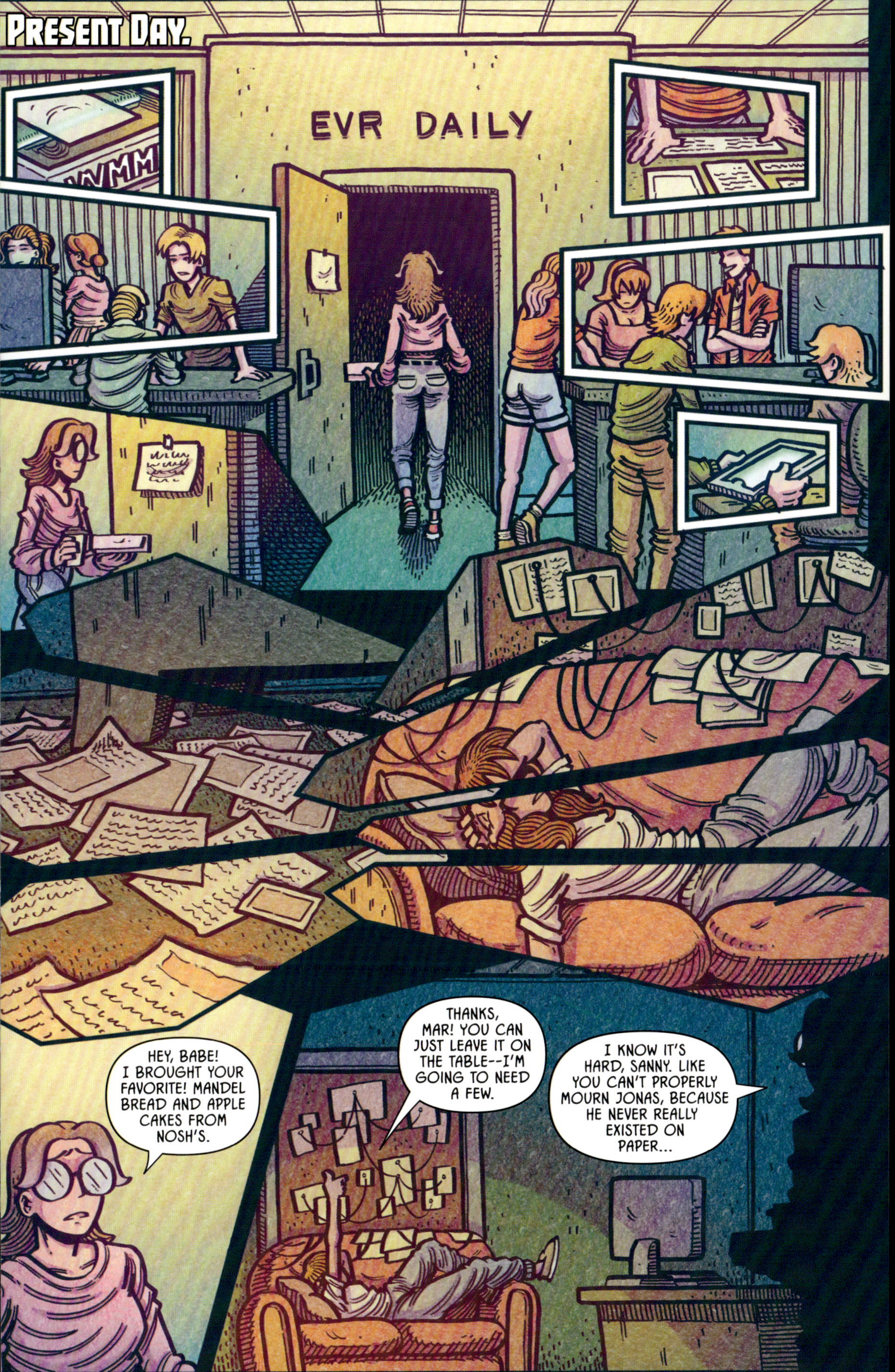
PRESENT DAY.
EVR DAILY
HEY, BABE! I BROUGHT YOUR FAVORITE! MANDEL BREAD AND APPLE CAKES FROM NOSH'S.
THANKS, MAR! YOU CAN JUST LEAVE IT ON THE TABLE--I'M GOING TO NEED A FEW.
I KNOW IT'S HARD, SANNY. LIKE YOU CAN'T PROPERLY MOURN JONAS, BECAUSE HE NEVER REALLY EXISTED ON PAPER...

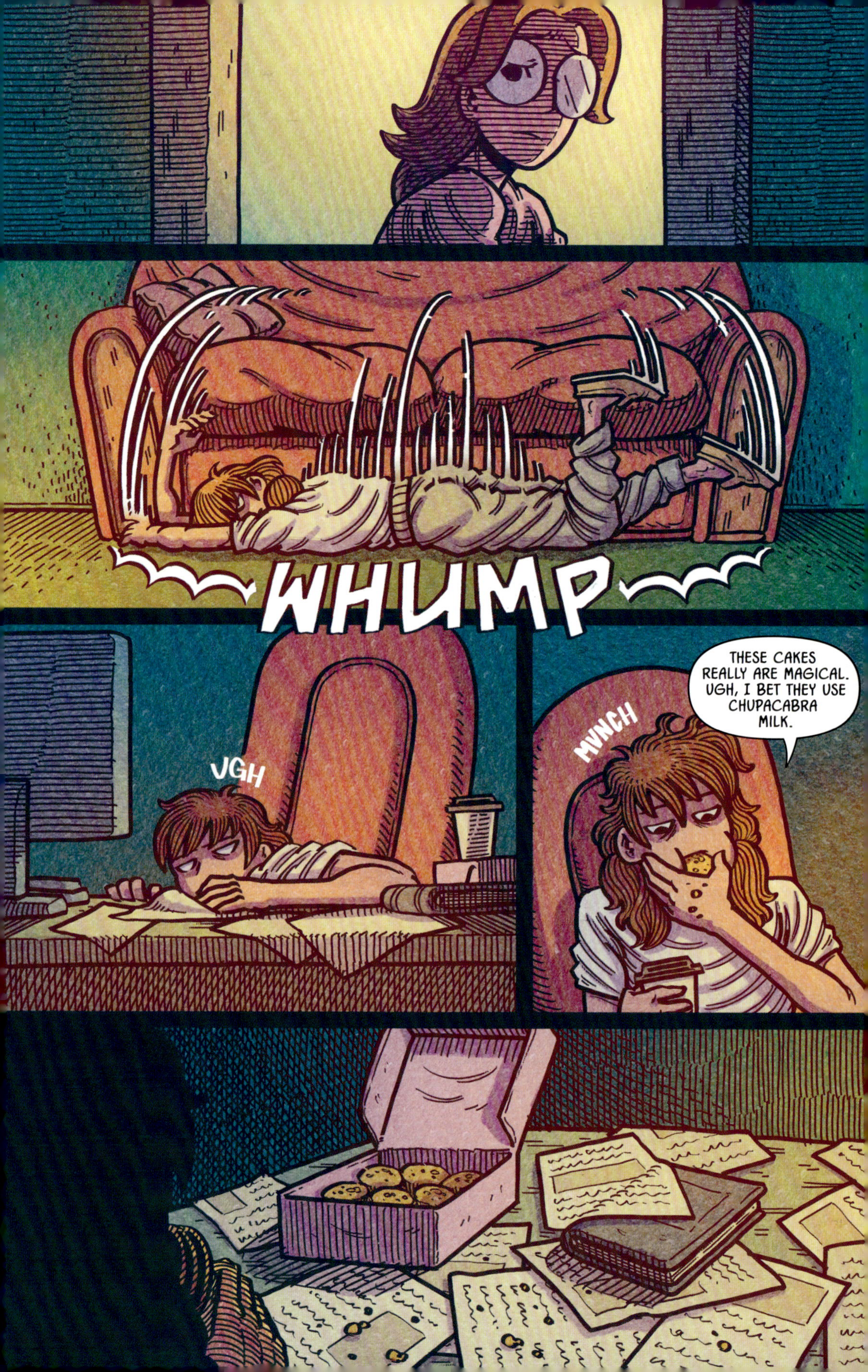
WHUMP
VGH
MVNCH
THESE CAKES REALLY ARE MAGICAL. UGH, I BET THEY USE CHUPACABRA MILK.

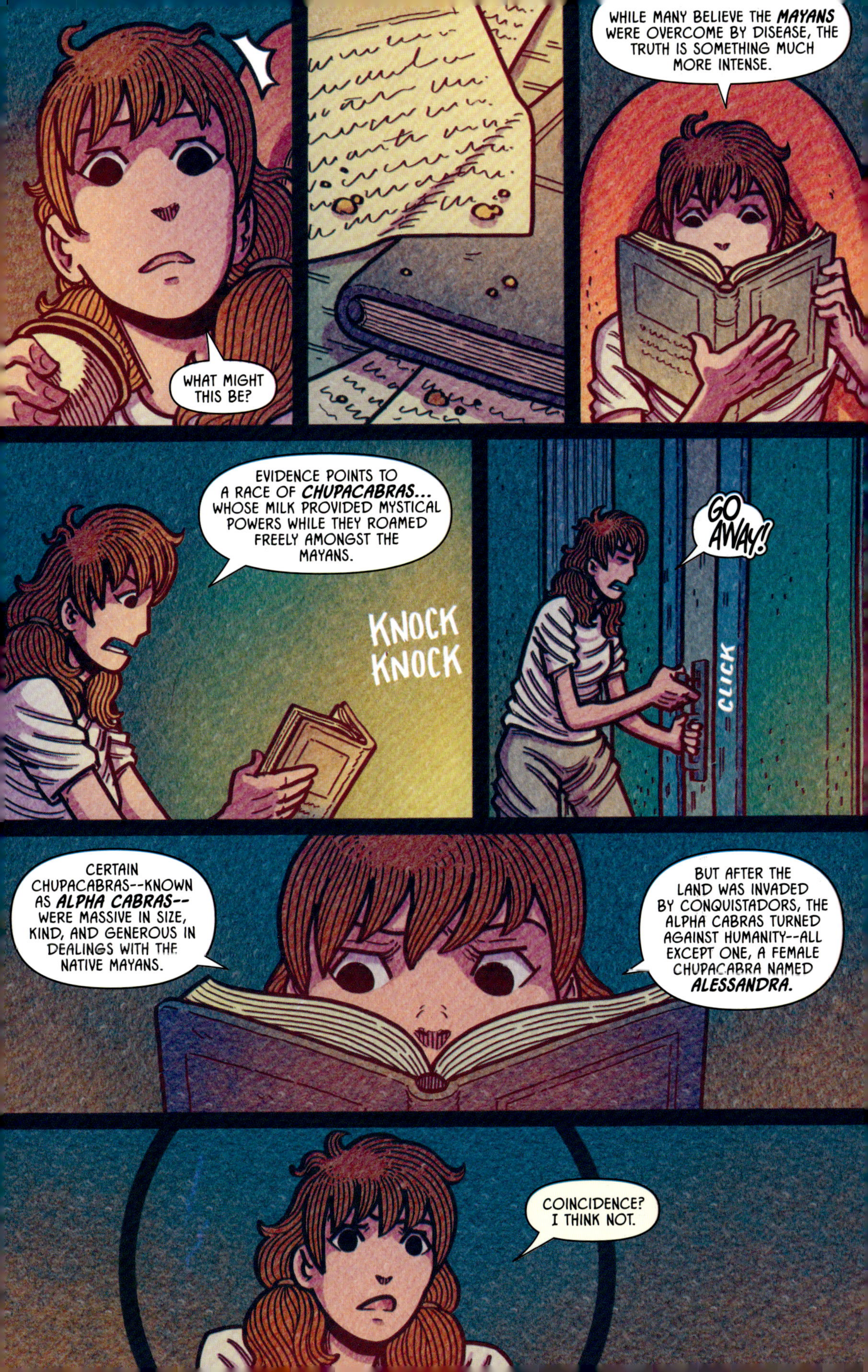
WHAT MIGHT THIS BE?
WHILE MANY BELIEVE THE MAYANS WERE OVERCOME BY DISEASE, THE TRUTH IS SOMETHING MUCH MORE INTENSE.
EVIDENCE POINTS TO A RACE OF CHUPACABRAS... WHOSE MILK PROVIDED MYSTICAL POWERS WHILE THEY ROAMED FREELY AMONGST THE MAYANS.
KNOCK KNOCK
GO AWAY!
CLICK
CERTAIN CHUPACABRAS--KNOWN AS ALPHA CABRAS--WERE MASSIVE IN SIZE, KIND, AND GENEROUS IN DEALINGS WITH THE NATIVE MAYANS.
BUT AFTER THE LAND WAS INVADED BY CONQUISTADORS, THE ALPHA CABRAS TURNED AGAINST HUMANITY--ALL EXCEPT ONE, A FEMALE CHUPACABRA NAMED ALESSANDRA.
COINCIDENCE? I THINK NOT.

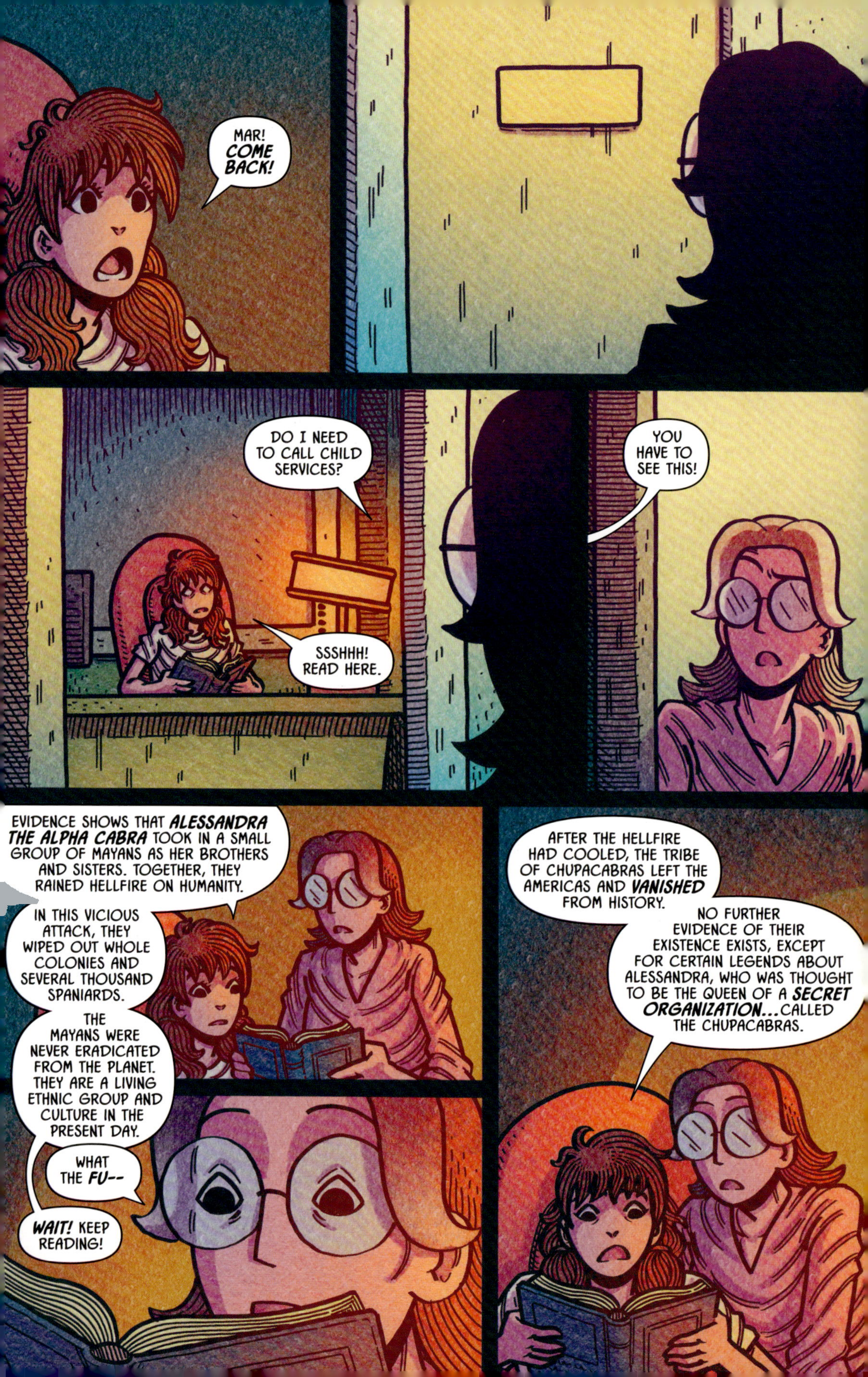
MAR! COME BACK!
DO I NEED TO CALL CHILD SERVICES?
SSSHHH! READ HERE.
YOU HAVE TO SEE THIS!
EVIDENCE SHOWS THAT ALESSANDRA THE ALPHA CABRA TOOK IN A SMALL GROUP OF MAYANS AS HER BROTHERS AND SISTERS. TOGETHER, THEY RAINED HELLFIRE ON HUMANITY.
IN THIS VICIOUS ATTACK, THEY WIPED OUT WHOLE COLONIES AND SEVERAL THOUSAND SPANIARDS.
THE MAYANS WERE NEVER ERADICATED FROM THE PLANET. THEY ARE A LIVING ETHNIC GROUP AND CULTURE IN THE PRESENT DAY.
WHAT THE FU--
WAIT! KEEP READING!
AFTER THE HELLFIRE HAD COOLED, THE TRIBE OF CHUPACABRAS LEFT THE AMERICAS AND VANISHED FROM HISTORY.
NO FURTHER EVIDENCE OF THEIR EXISTENCE EXISTS, EXCEPT FOR CERTAIN LEGENDS ABOUT ALESSANDRA, WHO WAS THOUGHT TO BE THE QUEEN OF A SECRET ORGANIZATION...CALLED THE CHUPACABRAS.

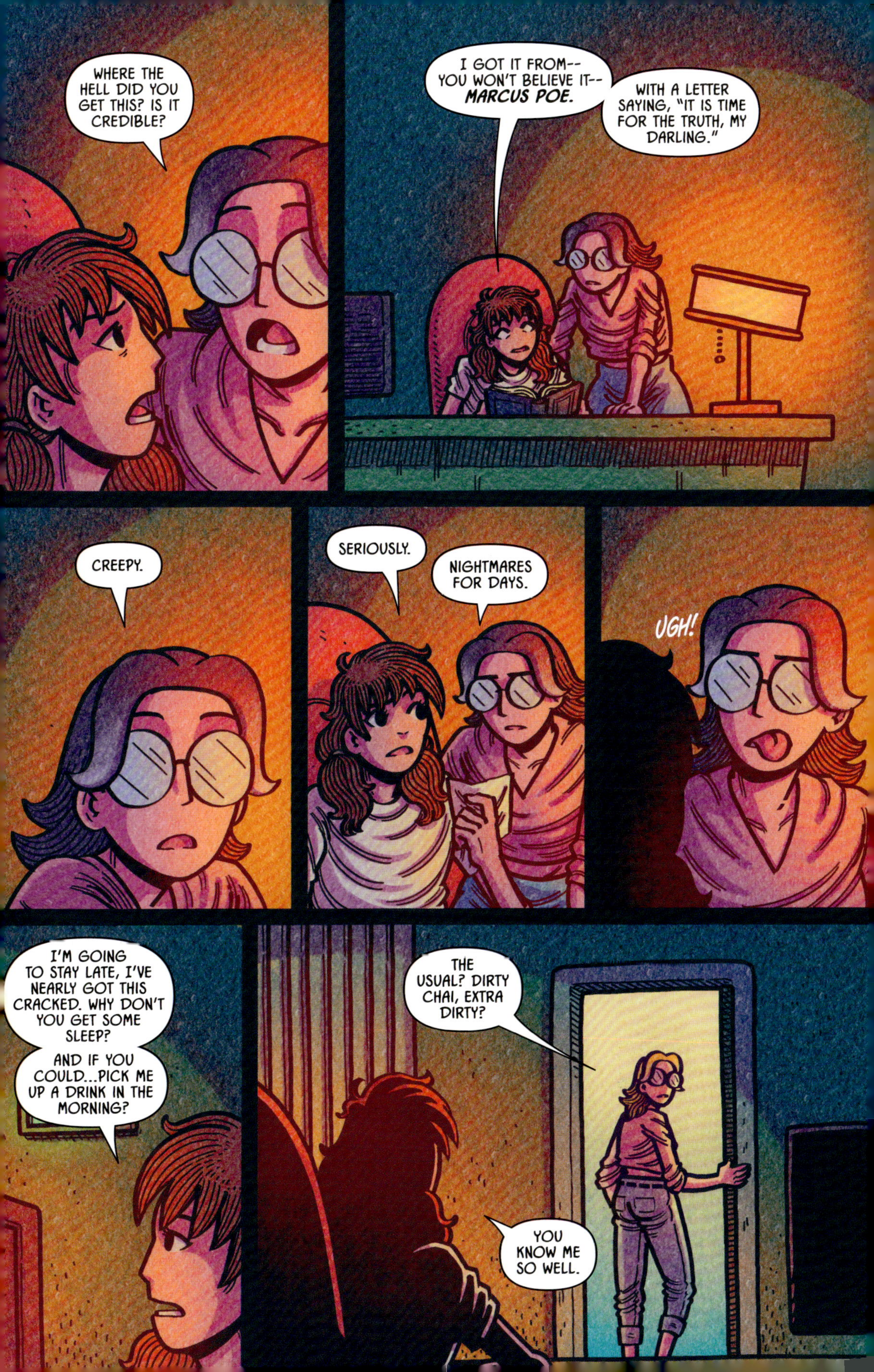
WHERE THE HELL DID YOU GET THIS? IS IT CREDIBLE?
I GOT IT FROM-- YOU WON'T BELIEVE IT-- MARCUS POE.
WITH A LETTER SAYING, "IT IS TIME FOR THE TRUTH, MY DARLING."
CREEPY.
SERIOUSLY.
NIGHTMARES FOR DAYS.
UGH!
I'M GOING TO STAY LATE, I'VE NEARLY GOT THIS CRACKED. WHY DON'T YOU GET SOME SLEEP?
AND IF YOU COULD...PICK ME UP A DRINK IN THE MORNING?
THE USUAL? DIRTY CHAI, EXTRA DIRTY?
YOU KNOW ME SO WELL.

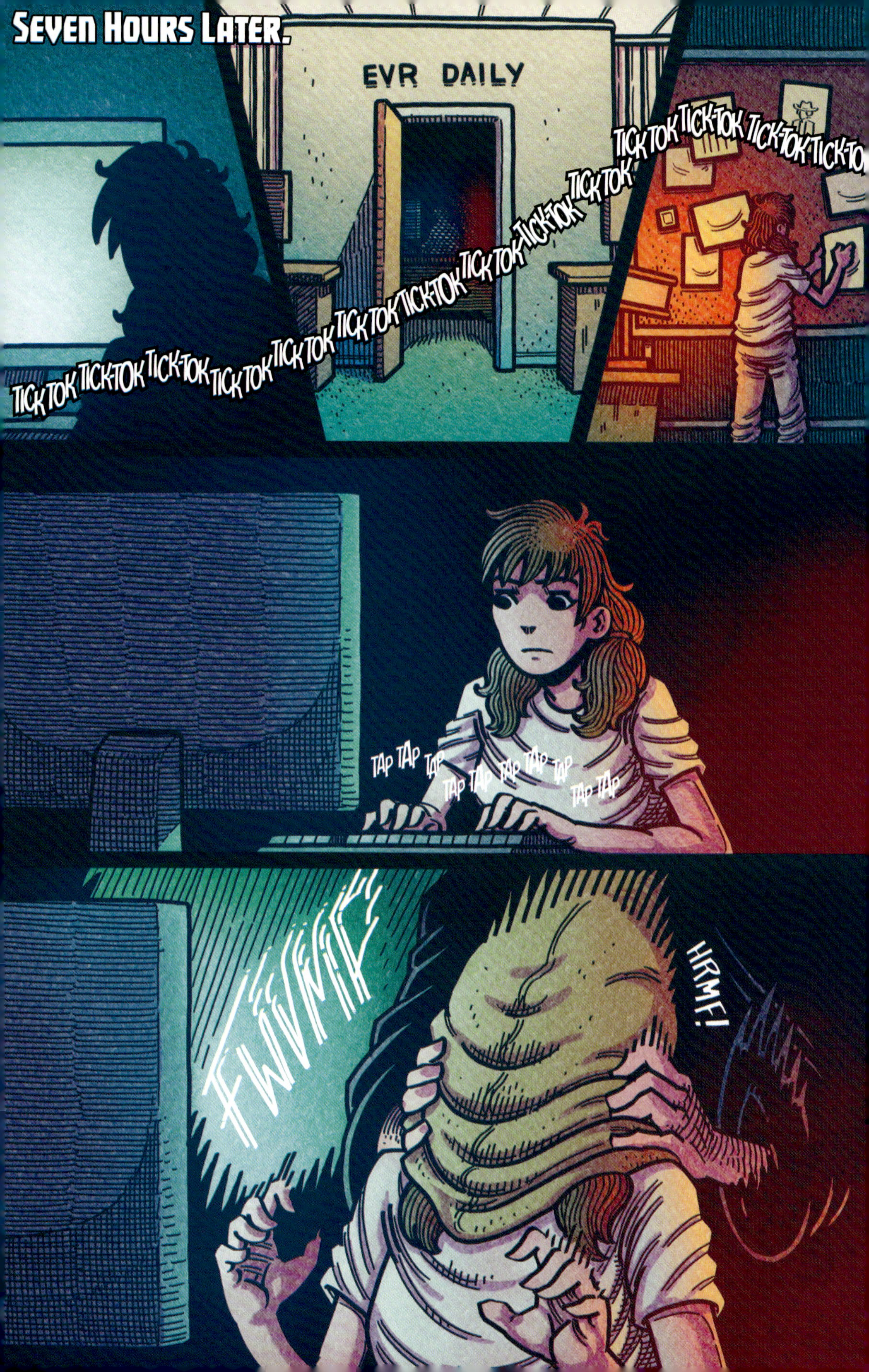

Seven Hours Later.
EVR DAILY
TICK TOK TICK-TOK TICK-TOK TICK TOK TICK TOK TICK TOK TICK-TOK TICK TOK TICK-TOK TICK TOK TICK TOK TICK-TOK TICK-TOK TICK-TO
TAP TAP TAP TAP TAP TAP TAP TAP TAP TAP
FWWMP
HRMF!

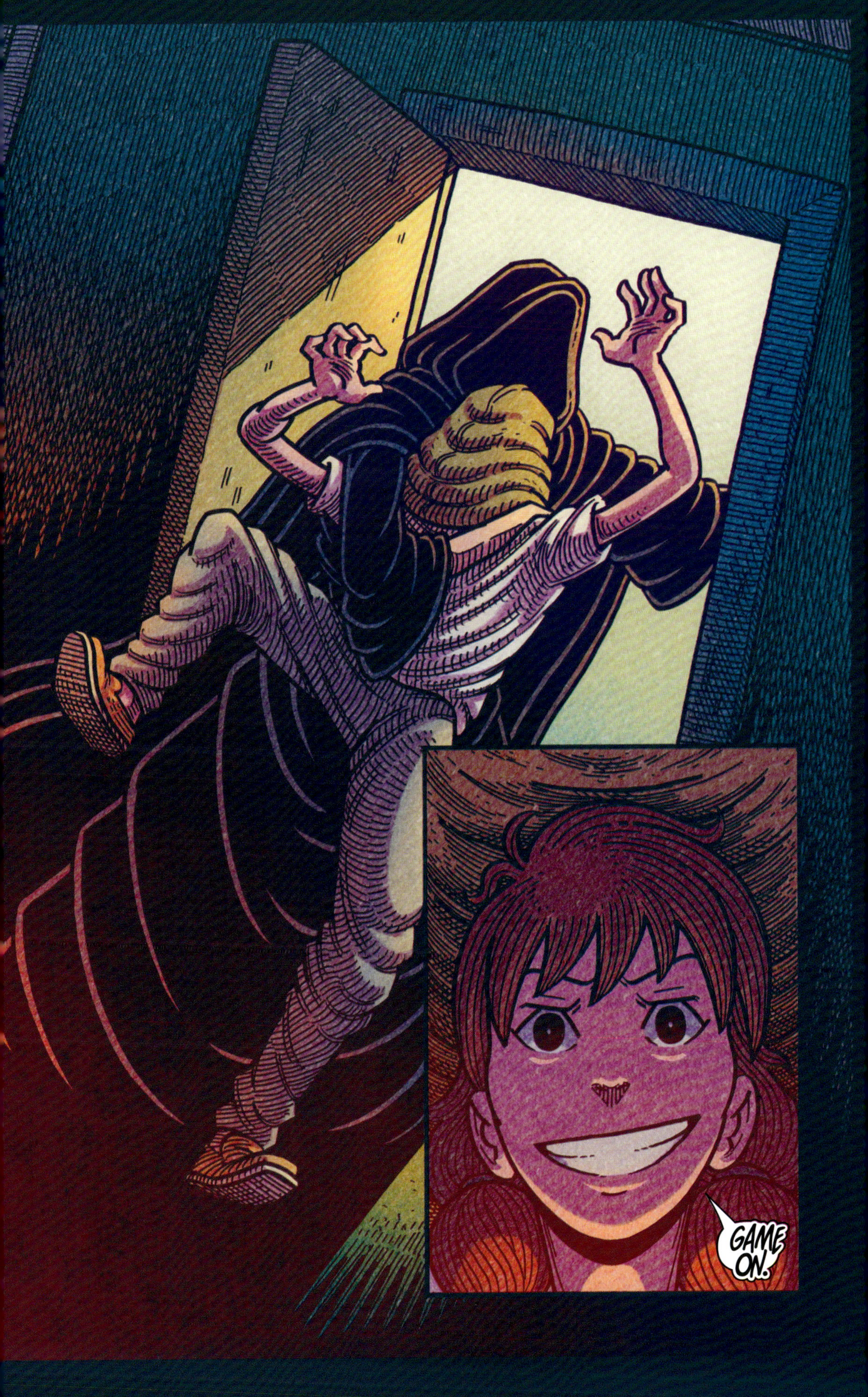
GAME ON.

EVR Daily Times

VOL. I...No. 1 CONTACT@EVRDAILYTIMES.COM NEWS FOR TODAY EVRDAILYTIMES.COM PRICE $ .99

BREAKING NEWS

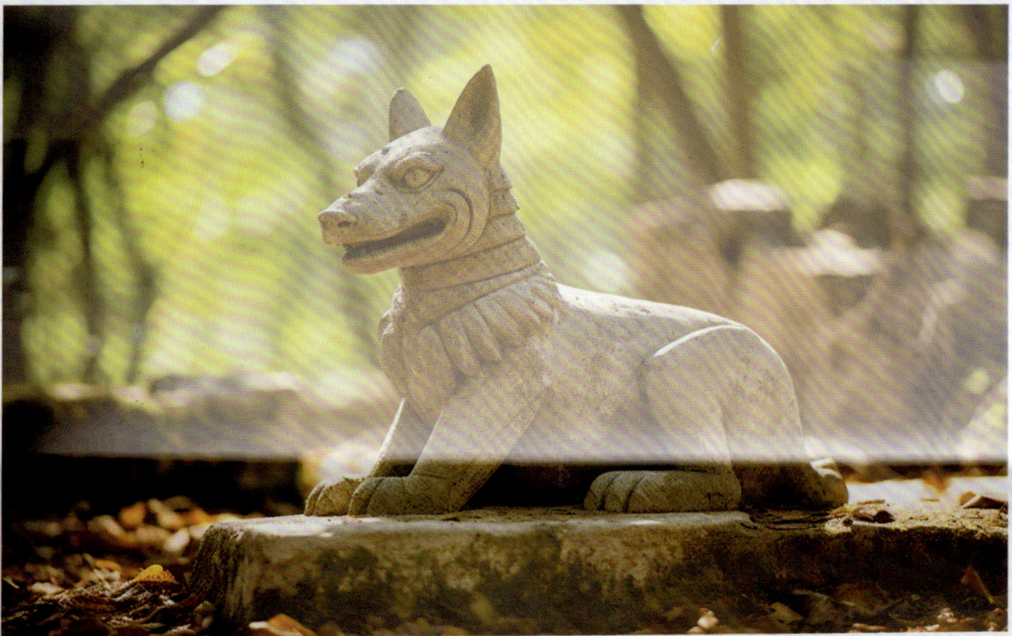

Unearthed Secrets: An Expedition to the Yucatan

Story by
Alessandra Dacey Hernández, Editor-in-Chief, EVR Daily

Fifteen years ago, my life was irrevocably changed when my father, a relentless reporter, met an untimely and suspicious end. His last assignment was anything but ordinary—a pursuit of the mythical Chupacabra, an elusive creature that has captured human imagination for decades.

Last week, the enigmatic beast resurfaced, not in folklore, but in a very real, very tangible excavation site in the Yucatan. I knew I had to go there. With a determined team of student journalists from EVR Daily and accompanied by a school chaperone well-versed in archaeology, we set out to uncover the truth.

As our plane touched down in the Yucatan, the air was thick with a mix of humidity and anticipation. We were met by local experts who guided us to the dig sites, where teams were already busy sifting through layers of earth and history. The excavation was a hive of activity, each digger engrossed in their own small universe of dirt and discovery. Contrary to popular belief, these digs are not rare. "We think we've found a Chupacabra once every 18 months," our teacher informed us, "but we've never actually found one."

As I stood there, staring at the multiple dig sites, something clicked. Call it intuition or a reporter's gut feeling; I felt we were on the brink of a monumental discovery. I couldn't help but remember my father's steadfast belief in the existence of the Chupacabra. Could this be the moment he had lost his life pursuing?

Our trip to the Yucatan was not just an academic field trip; it was a journey to validate a narrative that had long been manipulated by others. We may not have found definitive proof of the Chupacabra, but we unearthed something equally valuable—our own voice in a world quick to silence inconvenient truths.

As I flip through the pages of my own newspaper, preparing for our next adventure, I know one thing is for sure: The story is far from over, and EVR Daily will be there to tell it.

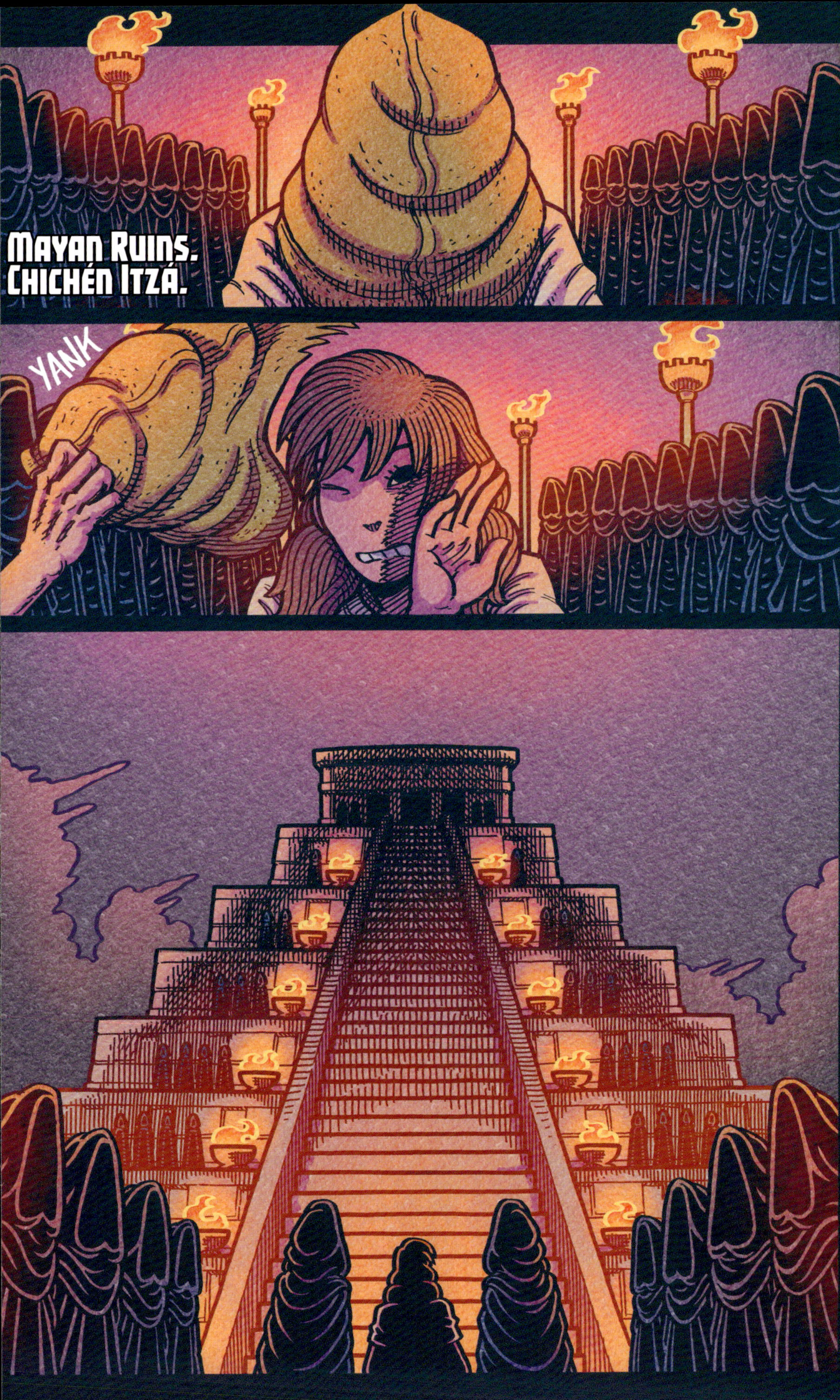
Mayan Ruins.
Chichén Itzá.
YANK

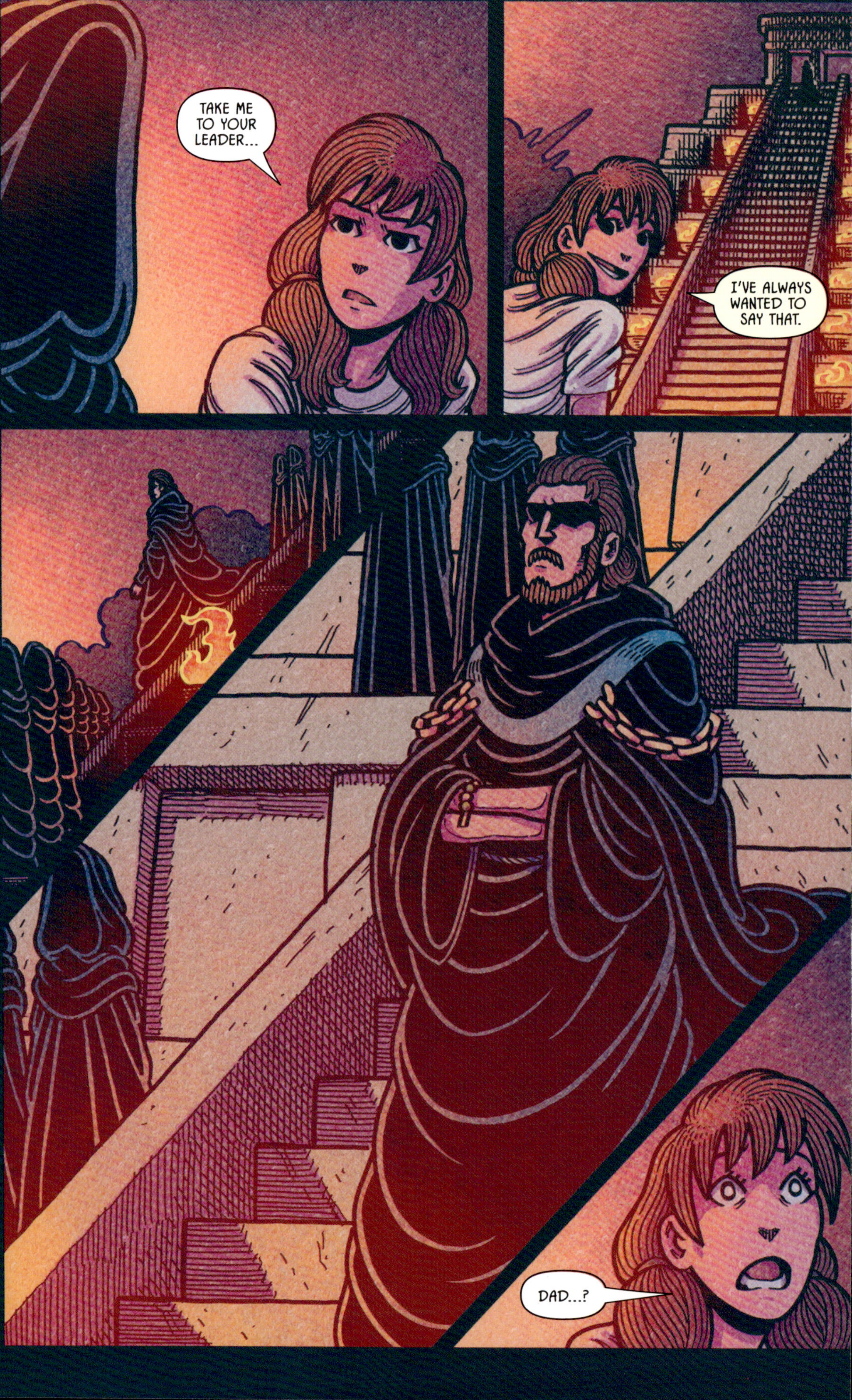
TAKE ME TO YOUR LEADER...
I'VE ALWAYS WANTED TO SAY THAT.
DAD...?

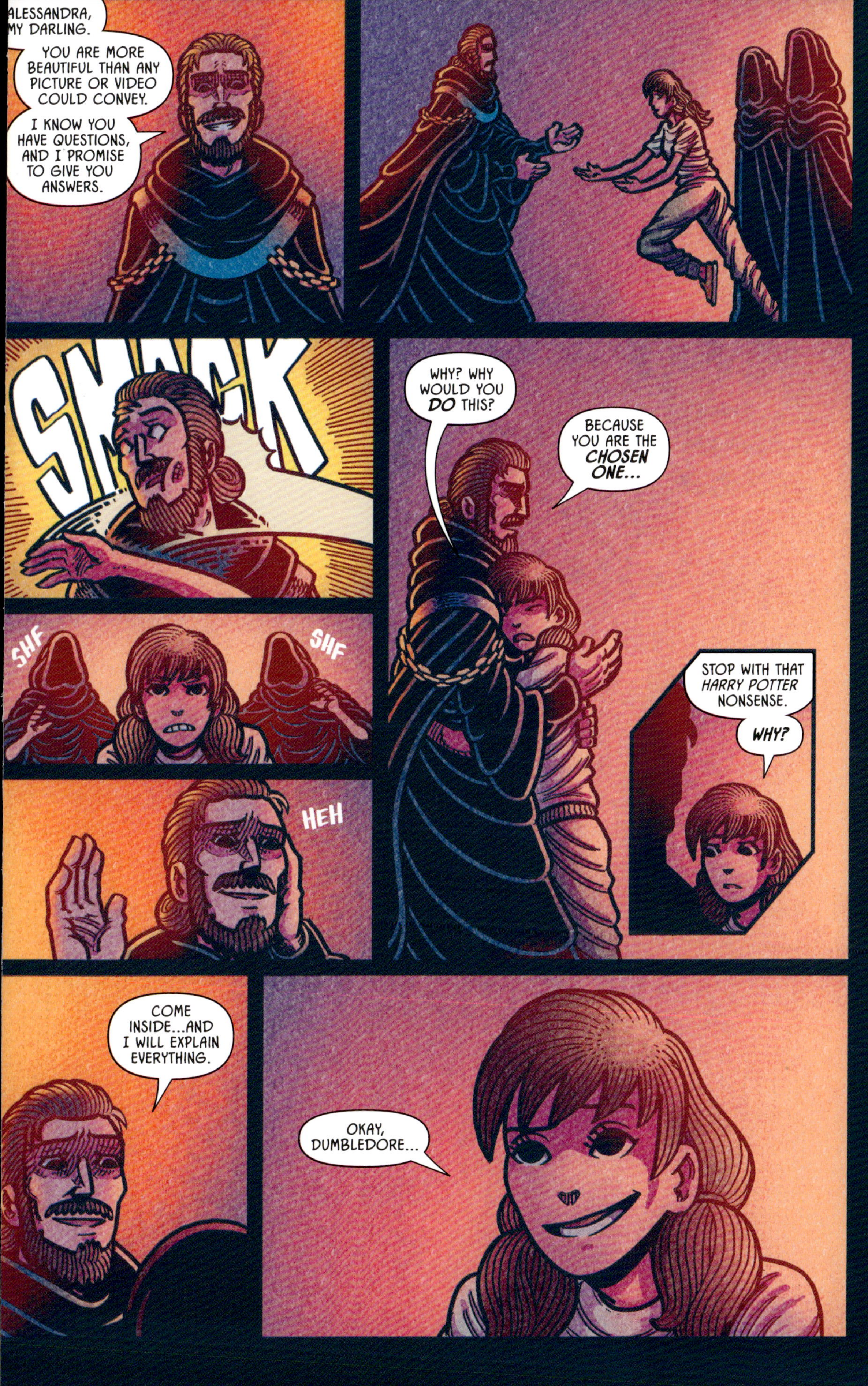

ALESSANDRA, MY DARLING.
YOU ARE MORE BEAUTIFUL THAN ANY PICTURE OR VIDEO COULD CONVEY.
I KNOW YOU HAVE QUESTIONS, AND I PROMISE TO GIVE YOU ANSWERS.
SMACK
SHF
SHF
HEH
WHY? WHY WOULD YOU *DO* THIS?
BECAUSE YOU ARE THE *CHOSEN ONE...*
STOP WITH THAT *HARRY POTTER* NONSENSE.
WHY?
COME INSIDE...AND I WILL EXPLAIN EVERYTHING.
OKAY, DUMBLEDORE...

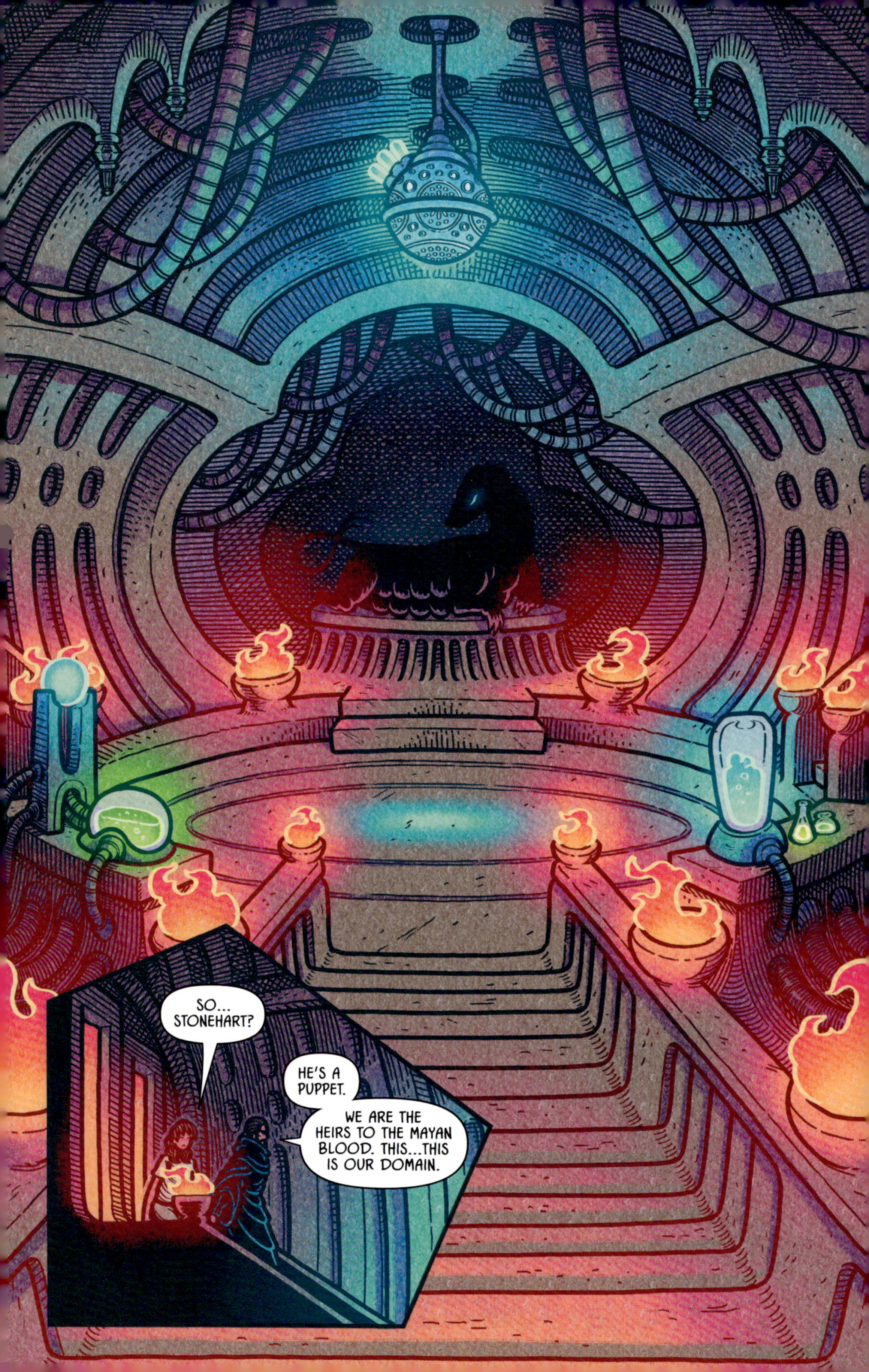
SO... STONEHART?
HE'S A PUPPET.
WE ARE THE HEIRS TO THE MAYAN BLOOD. THIS...THIS IS OUR DOMAIN.

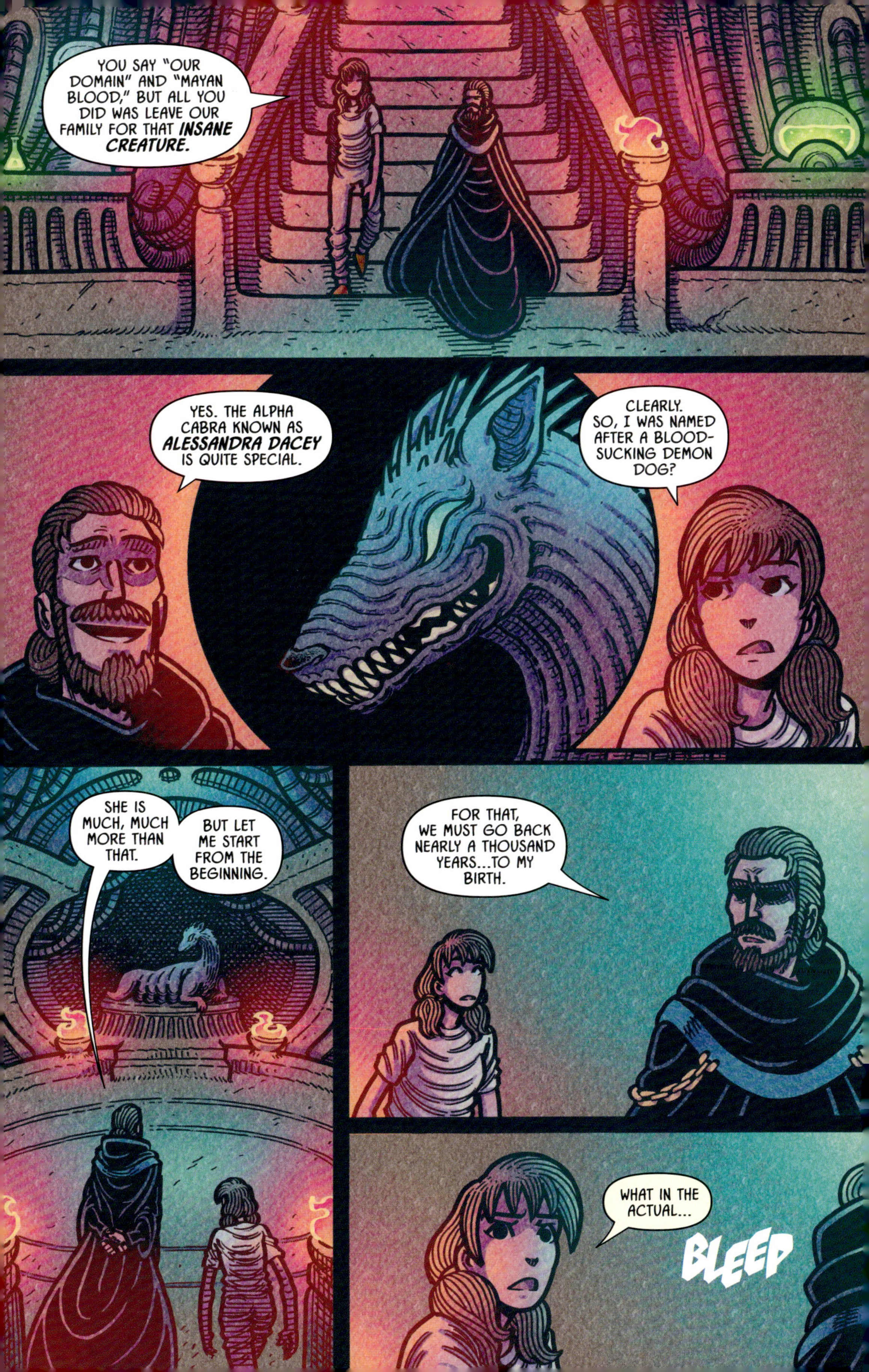
YOU SAY "OUR DOMAIN" AND "MAYAN BLOOD," BUT ALL YOU DID WAS LEAVE OUR FAMILY FOR THAT *INSANE CREATURE.*
YES. THE ALPHA CABRA KNOWN AS *ALESSANDRA DACEY* IS QUITE SPECIAL.
CLEARLY. SO, I WAS NAMED AFTER A BLOOD-SUCKING DEMON DOG?
SHE IS MUCH, MUCH MORE THAN THAT.
BUT LET ME START FROM THE BEGINNING.
FOR THAT, WE MUST GO BACK NEARLY A THOUSAND YEARS...TO MY BIRTH.
WHAT IN THE ACTUAL...
BLEEP

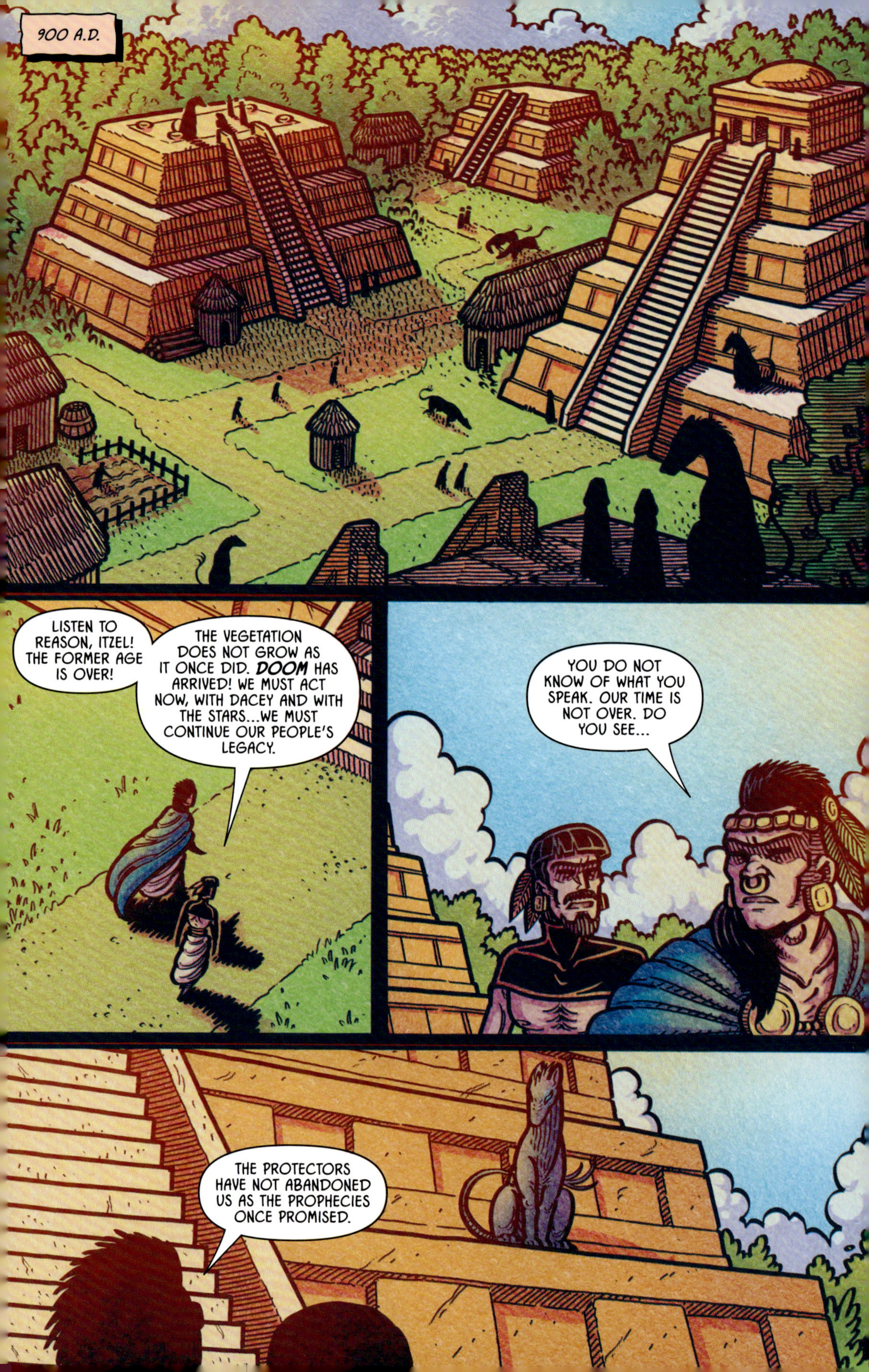
900 A.D.
LISTEN TO REASON, ITZEL! THE FORMER AGE IS OVER!
THE VEGETATION DOES NOT GROW AS IT ONCE DID. DOOM HAS ARRIVED! WE MUST ACT NOW, WITH DACEY AND WITH THE STARS...WE MUST CONTINUE OUR PEOPLE'S LEGACY.
YOU DO NOT KNOW OF WHAT YOU SPEAK. OUR TIME IS NOT OVER. DO YOU SEE...
THE PROTECTORS HAVE NOT ABANDONED US AS THE PROPHECIES ONCE PROMISED.

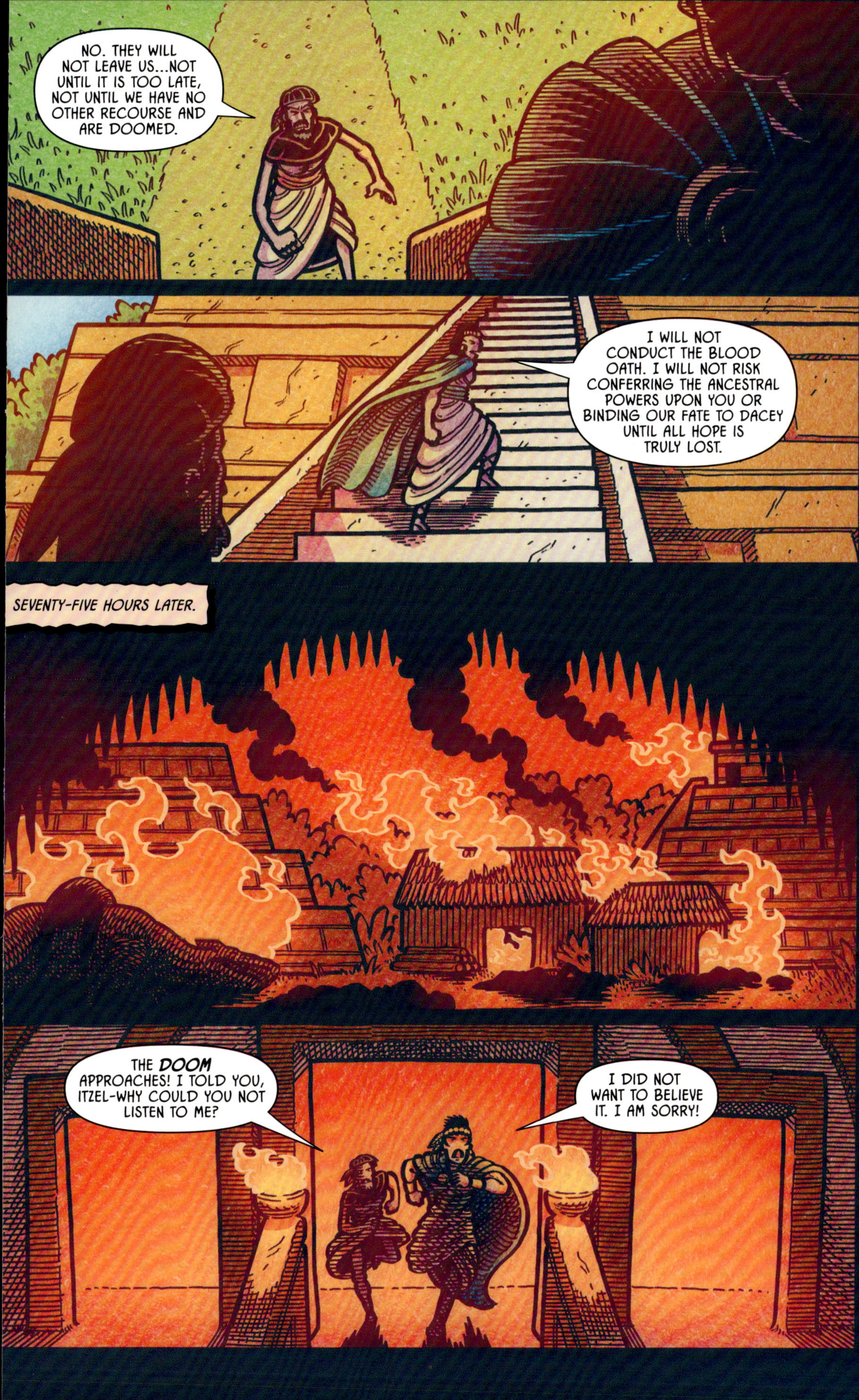
NO. THEY WILL NOT LEAVE US...NOT UNTIL IT IS TOO LATE, NOT UNTIL WE HAVE NO OTHER RECOURSE AND ARE DOOMED.
I WILL NOT CONDUCT THE BLOOD OATH. I WILL NOT RISK CONFERRING THE ANCESTRAL POWERS UPON YOU OR BINDING OUR FATE TO DACEY UNTIL ALL HOPE IS TRULY LOST.
SEVENTY-FIVE HOURS LATER.
THE DOOM APPROACHES! I TOLD YOU, ITZEL-WHY COULD YOU NOT LISTEN TO ME?
I DID NOT WANT TO BELIEVE IT. I AM SORRY!

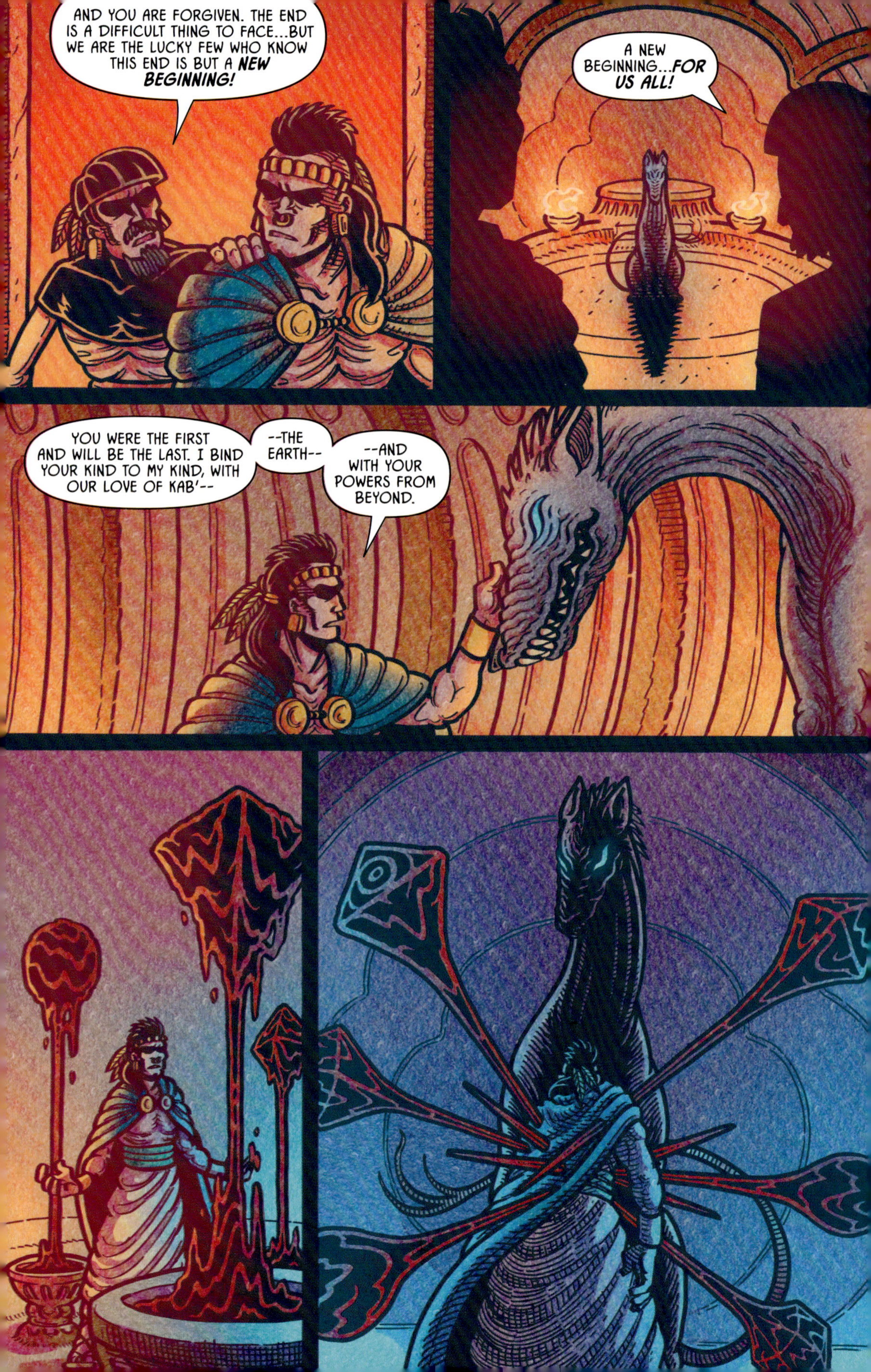
AND YOU ARE FORGIVEN. THE END IS A DIFFICULT THING TO FACE...BUT WE ARE THE LUCKY FEW WHO KNOW THIS END IS BUT A NEW BEGINNING!
A NEW BEGINNING...FOR US ALL!
YOU WERE THE FIRST AND WILL BE THE LAST. I BIND YOUR KIND TO MY KIND, WITH OUR LOVE OF KAB'--
--THE EARTH--
--AND WITH YOUR POWERS FROM BEYOND.

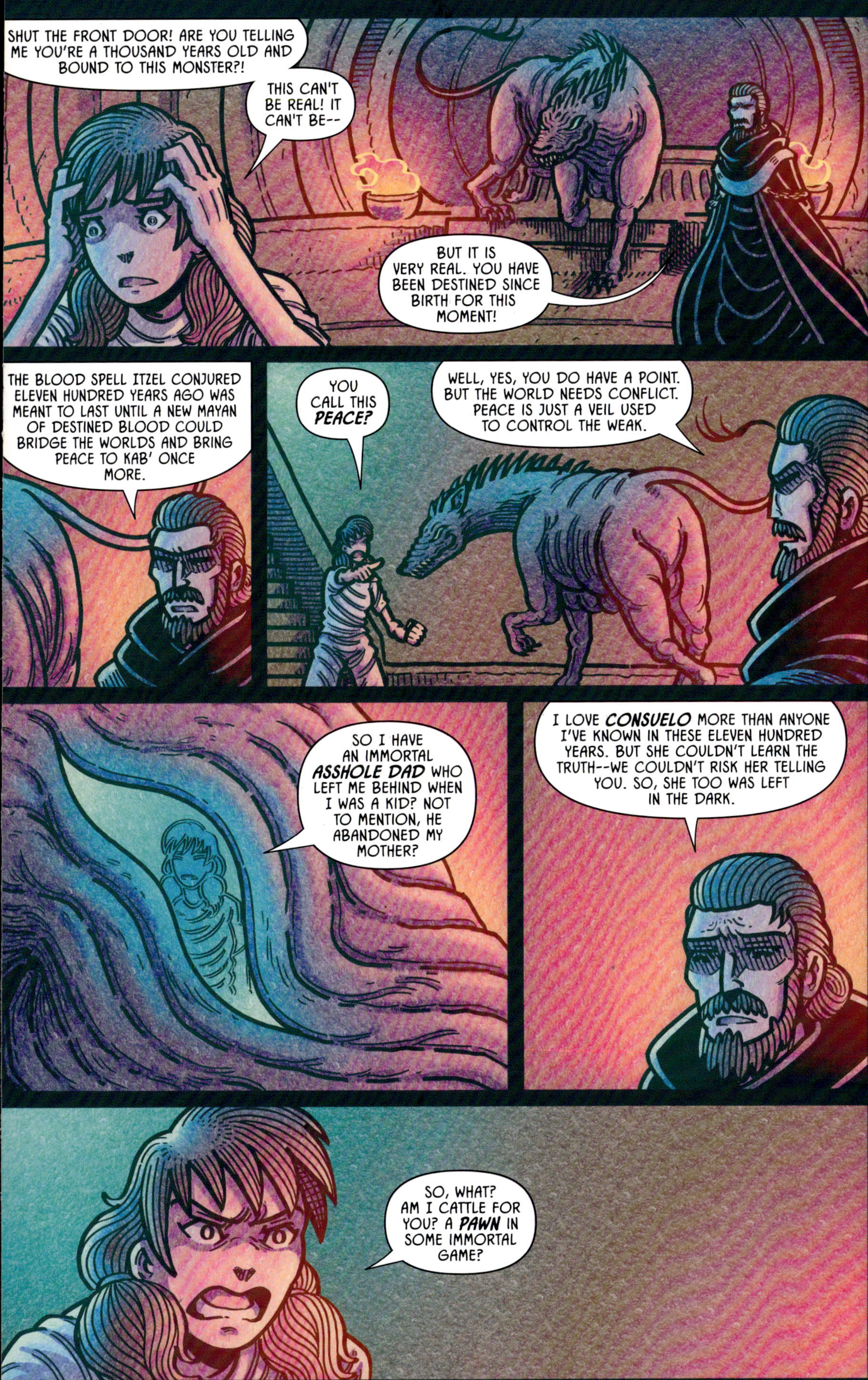
SHUT THE FRONT DOOR! ARE YOU TELLING ME YOU'RE A THOUSAND YEARS OLD AND BOUND TO THIS MONSTER?!
THIS CAN'T BE REAL! IT CAN'T BE--
BUT IT IS VERY REAL. YOU HAVE BEEN DESTINED SINCE BIRTH FOR THIS MOMENT!
THE BLOOD SPELL ITZEL CONJURED ELEVEN HUNDRED YEARS AGO WAS MEANT TO LAST UNTIL A NEW MAYAN OF DESTINED BLOOD COULD BRIDGE THE WORLDS AND BRING PEACE TO KAB' ONCE MORE.
YOU CALL THIS PEACE?
WELL, YES, YOU DO HAVE A POINT. BUT THE WORLD NEEDS CONFLICT. PEACE IS JUST A VEIL USED TO CONTROL THE WEAK.
SO I HAVE AN IMMORTAL ASSHOLE DAD WHO LEFT ME BEHIND WHEN I WAS A KID? NOT TO MENTION, HE ABANDONED MY MOTHER?
I LOVE CONSUELO MORE THAN ANYONE I'VE KNOWN IN THESE ELEVEN HUNDRED YEARS. BUT SHE COULDN'T LEARN THE TRUTH--WE COULDN'T RISK HER TELLING YOU. SO, SHE TOO WAS LEFT IN THE DARK.
SO, WHAT? AM I CATTLE FOR YOU? A PAWN IN SOME IMMORTAL GAME?

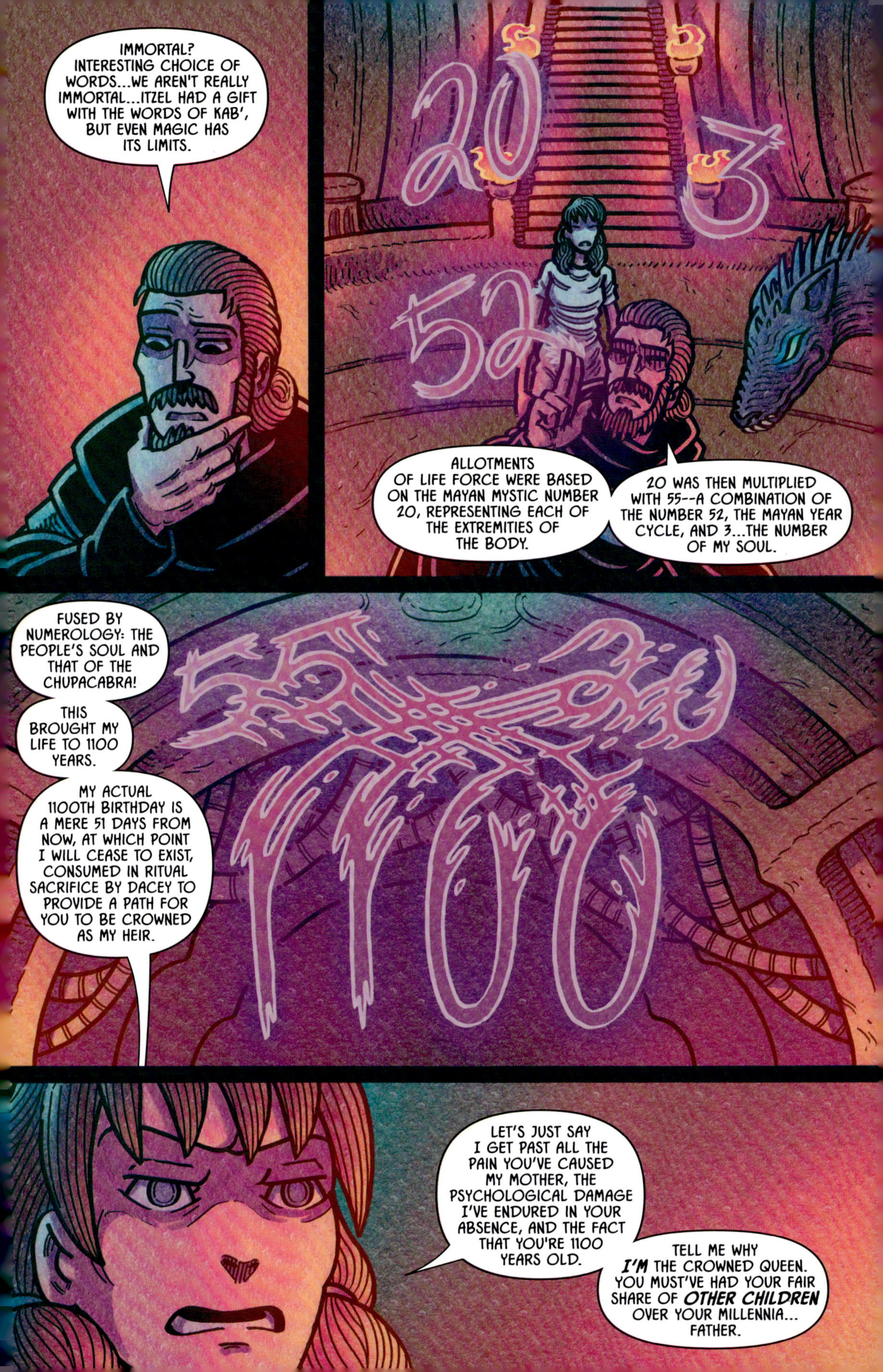
IMMORTAL? INTERESTING CHOICE OF WORDS...WE AREN'T REALLY IMMORTAL...ITZEL HAD A GIFT WITH THE WORDS OF KAB', BUT EVEN MAGIC HAS ITS LIMITS.
20
3
52
ALLOTMENTS OF LIFE FORCE WERE BASED ON THE MAYAN MYSTIC NUMBER 20, REPRESENTING EACH OF THE EXTREMITIES OF THE BODY.
20 WAS THEN MULTIPLIED WITH 55--A COMBINATION OF THE NUMBER 52, THE MAYAN YEAR CYCLE, AND 3...THE NUMBER OF MY SOUL.
FUSED BY NUMEROLOGY: THE PEOPLE'S SOUL AND THAT OF THE CHUPACABRA!
THIS BROUGHT MY LIFE TO 1100 YEARS.
MY ACTUAL 1100TH BIRTHDAY IS A MERE 51 DAYS FROM NOW, AT WHICH POINT I WILL CEASE TO EXIST, CONSUMED IN RITUAL SACRIFICE BY DACEY TO PROVIDE A PATH FOR YOU TO BE CROWNED AS MY HEIR.
55
1100
LET'S JUST SAY I GET PAST ALL THE PAIN YOU'VE CAUSED MY MOTHER, THE PSYCHOLOGICAL DAMAGE I'VE ENDURED IN YOUR ABSENCE, AND THE FACT THAT YOU'RE 1100 YEARS OLD.
TELL ME WHY ***I'M*** THE CROWNED QUEEN. YOU MUST'VE HAD YOUR FAIR SHARE OF ***OTHER CHILDREN*** OVER YOUR MILLENNIA... FATHER.

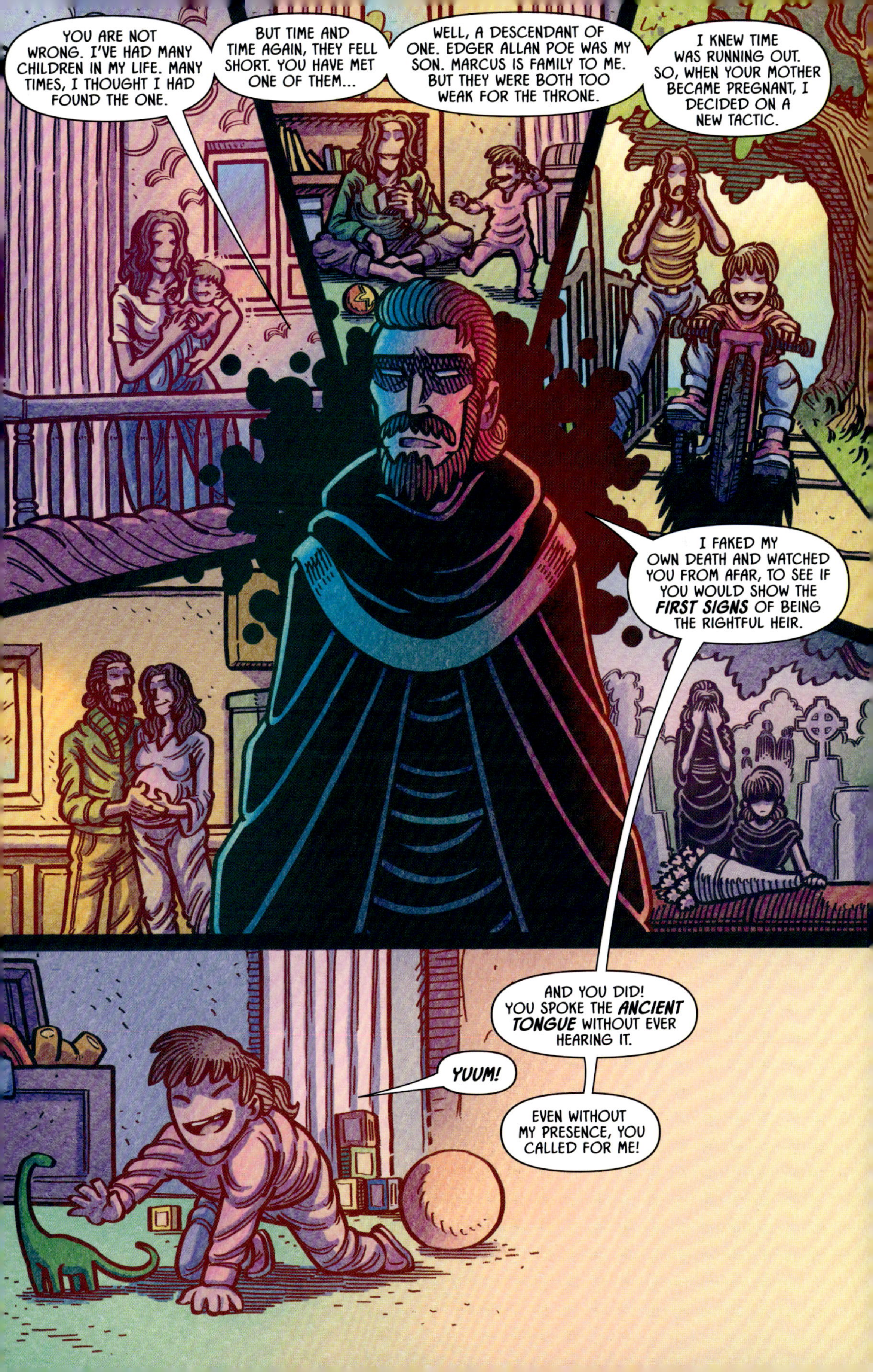
YOU ARE NOT WRONG. I'VE HAD MANY CHILDREN IN MY LIFE. MANY TIMES, I THOUGHT I HAD FOUND THE ONE.
BUT TIME AND TIME AGAIN, THEY FELL SHORT. YOU HAVE MET ONE OF THEM...
WELL, A DESCENDANT OF ONE. EDGER ALLAN POE WAS MY SON. MARCUS IS FAMILY TO ME. BUT THEY WERE BOTH TOO WEAK FOR THE THRONE.
I KNEW TIME WAS RUNNING OUT. SO, WHEN YOUR MOTHER BECAME PREGNANT, I DECIDED ON A NEW TACTIC.
I FAKED MY OWN DEATH AND WATCHED YOU FROM AFAR, TO SEE IF YOU WOULD SHOW THE FIRST SIGNS OF BEING THE RIGHTFUL HEIR.
AND YOU DID! YOU SPOKE THE ANCIENT TONGUE WITHOUT EVER HEARING IT.
YUUM!
EVEN WITHOUT MY PRESENCE, YOU CALLED FOR ME!

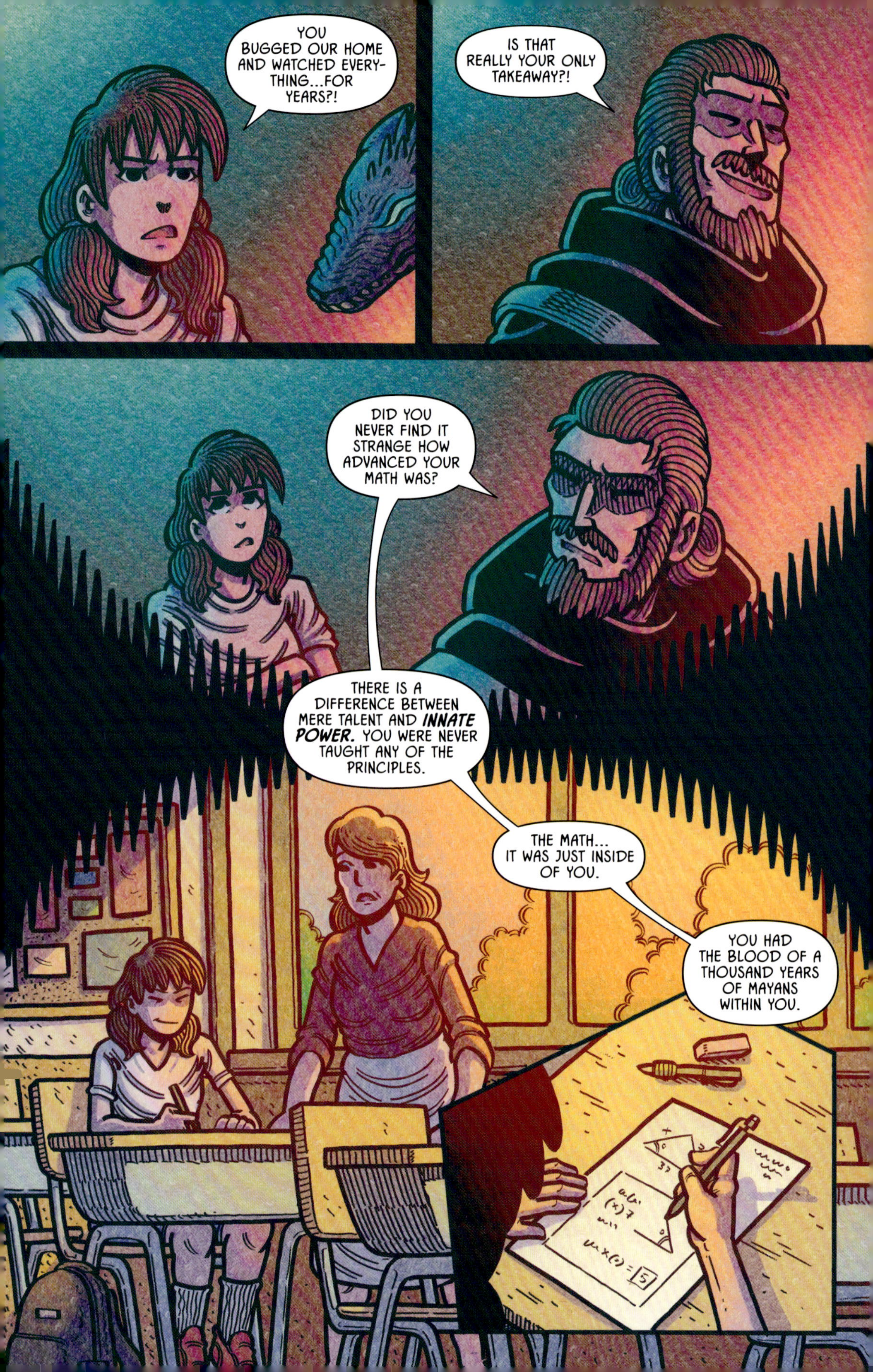
YOU BUGGED OUR HOME AND WATCHED EVERY-THING...FOR YEARS?!
IS THAT REALLY YOUR ONLY TAKEAWAY?!
DID YOU NEVER FIND IT STRANGE HOW ADVANCED YOUR MATH WAS?
THERE IS A DIFFERENCE BETWEEN MERE TALENT AND *INNATE POWER.* YOU WERE NEVER TAUGHT ANY OF THE PRINCIPLES.
THE MATH... IT WAS JUST INSIDE OF YOU.
YOU HAD THE BLOOD OF A THOUSAND YEARS OF MAYANS WITHIN YOU.

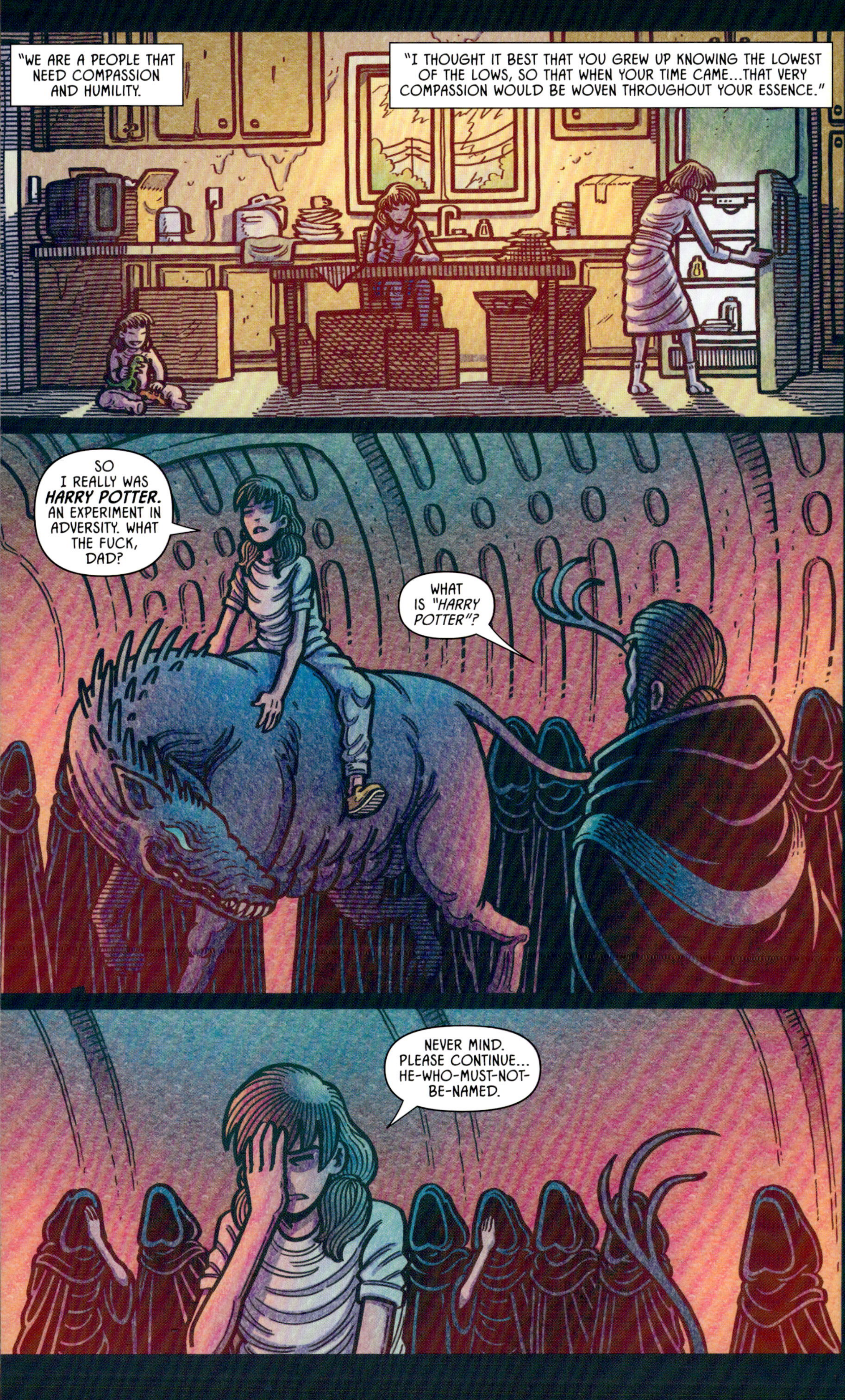
"WE ARE A PEOPLE THAT NEED COMPASSION AND HUMILITY.
"I THOUGHT IT BEST THAT YOU GREW UP KNOWING THE LOWEST OF THE LOWS, SO THAT WHEN YOUR TIME CAME...THAT VERY COMPASSION WOULD BE WOVEN THROUGHOUT YOUR ESSENCE."
SO I REALLY WAS ***HARRY POTTER.*** AN EXPERIMENT IN ADVERSITY. WHAT THE FUCK, DAD?
WHAT IS "*HARRY POTTER*"?
NEVER MIND. PLEASE CONTINUE... HE-WHO-MUST-NOT-BE-NAMED.

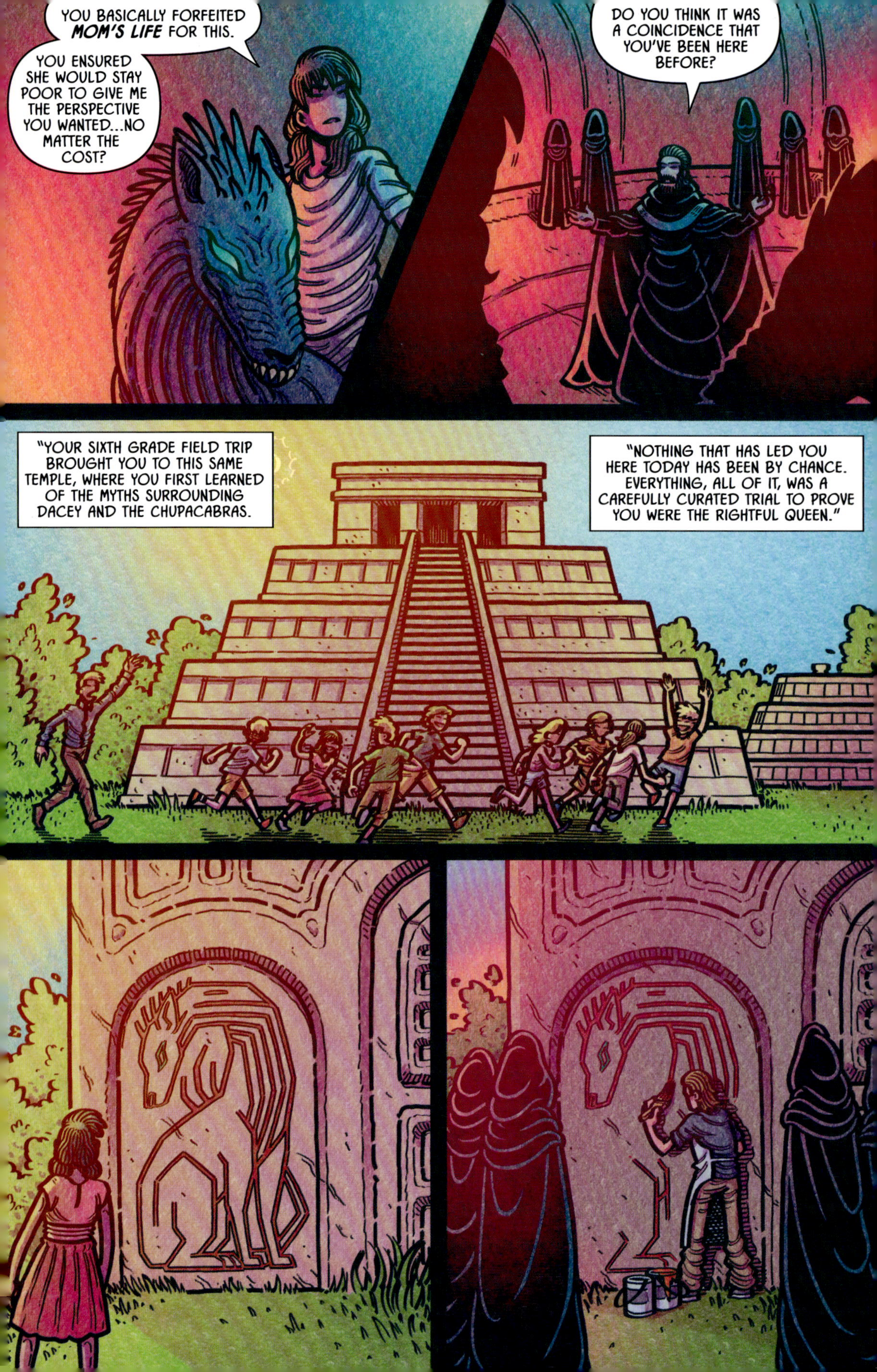

YOU BASICALLY FORFEITED ***MOM'S LIFE*** FOR THIS.
YOU ENSURED SHE WOULD STAY POOR TO GIVE ME THE PERSPECTIVE YOU WANTED...NO MATTER THE COST?
DO YOU THINK IT WAS A COINCIDENCE THAT YOU'VE BEEN HERE BEFORE?
"YOUR SIXTH GRADE FIELD TRIP BROUGHT YOU TO THIS SAME TEMPLE, WHERE YOU FIRST LEARNED OF THE MYTHS SURROUNDING DACEY AND THE CHUPACABRAS.
"NOTHING THAT HAS LED YOU HERE TODAY HAS BEEN BY CHANCE. EVERYTHING, ALL OF IT, WAS A CAREFULLY CURATED TRIAL TO PROVE YOU WERE THE RIGHTFUL QUEEN."

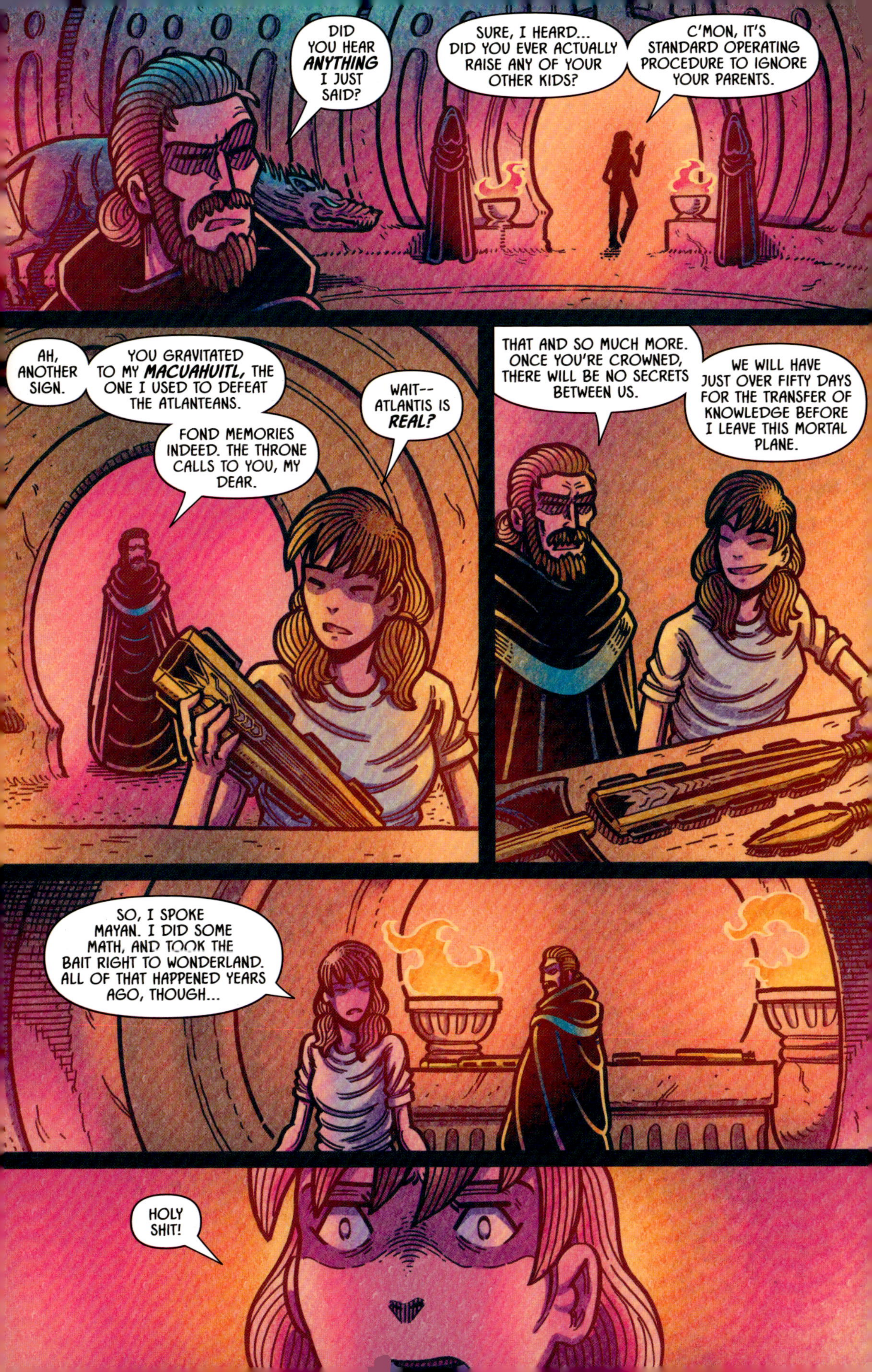
DID YOU HEAR **ANYTHING** I JUST SAID?
SURE, I HEARD... DID YOU EVER ACTUALLY RAISE ANY OF YOUR OTHER KIDS?
C'MON, IT'S STANDARD OPERATING PROCEDURE TO IGNORE YOUR PARENTS.
AH, ANOTHER SIGN.
YOU GRAVITATED TO MY **MACUAHUITL,** THE ONE I USED TO DEFEAT THE ATLANTEANS.
FOND MEMORIES INDEED. THE THRONE CALLS TO YOU, MY DEAR.
WAIT-- ATLANTIS IS **REAL?**
THAT AND SO MUCH MORE. ONCE YOU'RE CROWNED, THERE WILL BE NO SECRETS BETWEEN US.
WE WILL HAVE JUST OVER FIFTY DAYS FOR THE TRANSFER OF KNOWLEDGE BEFORE I LEAVE THIS MORTAL PLANE.
SO, I SPOKE MAYAN. I DID SOME MATH, AND TOOK THE BAIT RIGHT TO WONDERLAND. ALL OF THAT HAPPENED YEARS AGO, THOUGH...
HOLY SHIT!

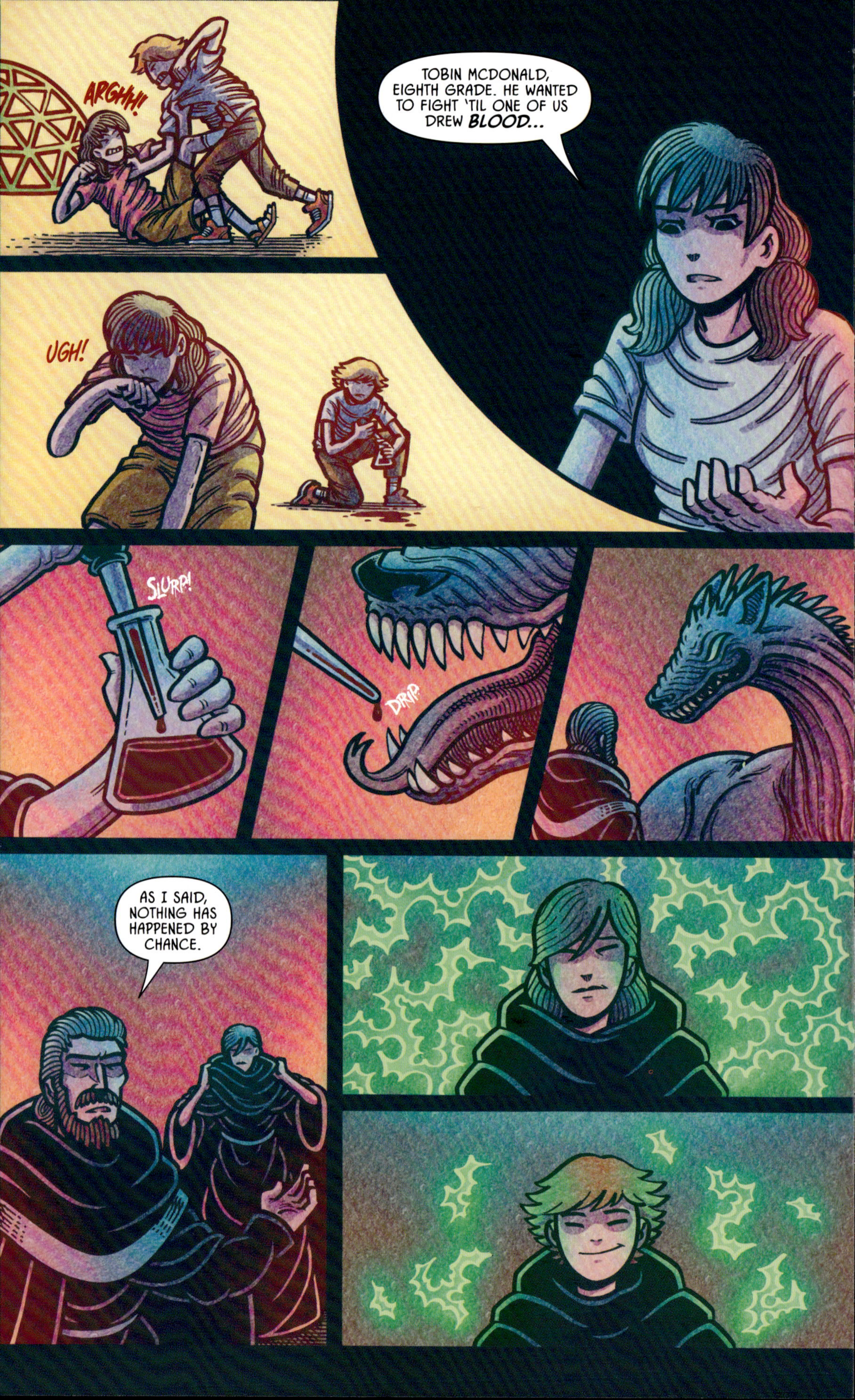
ARGHH!
TOBIN MCDONALD, EIGHTH GRADE. HE WANTED TO FIGHT 'TIL ONE OF US DREW BLOOD...
UGH!
SLURP!
DRIP.
AS I SAID, NOTHING HAS HAPPENED BY CHANCE.

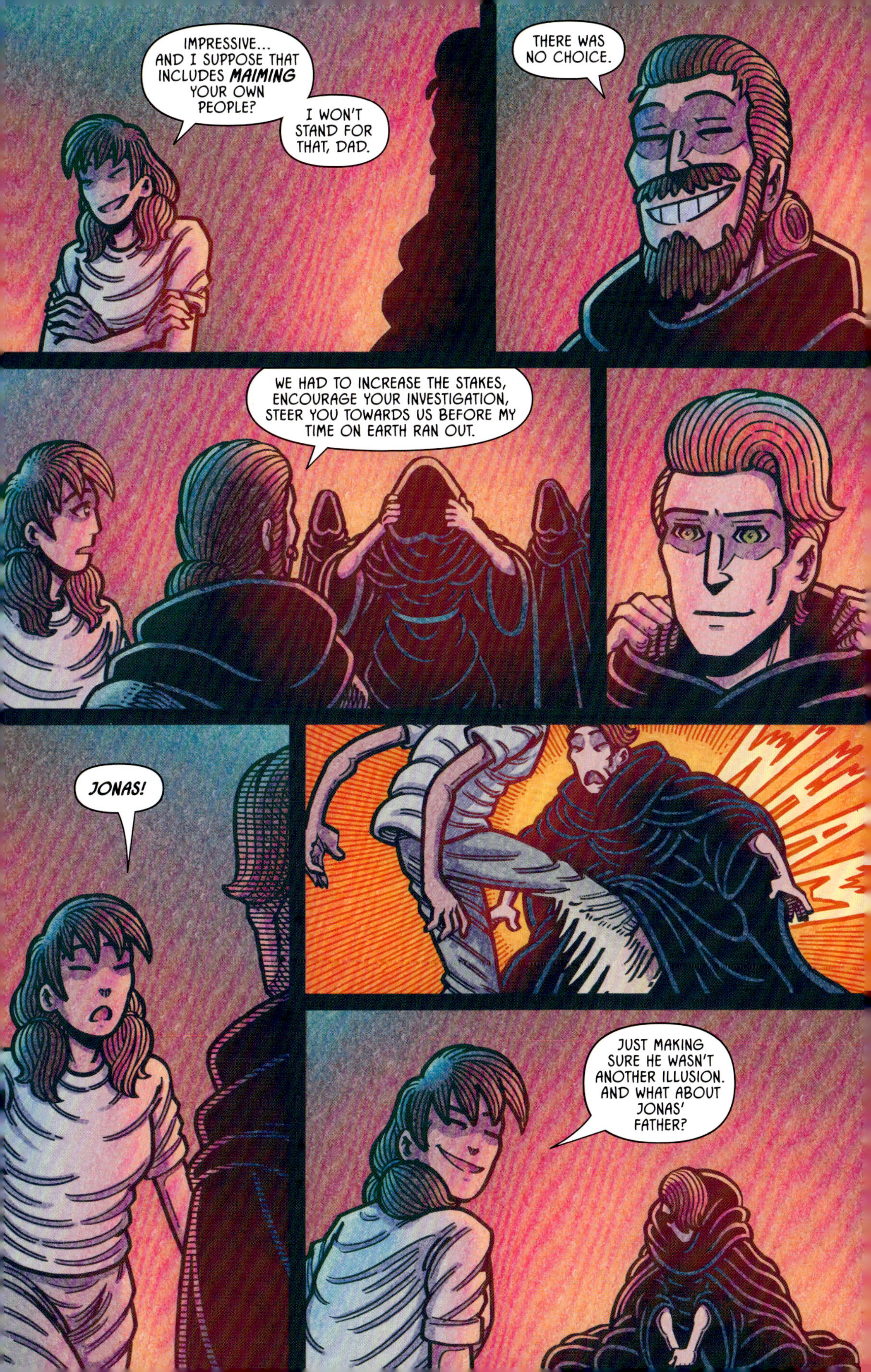
IMPRESSIVE... AND I SUPPOSE THAT INCLUDES MAIMING YOUR OWN PEOPLE?
I WON'T STAND FOR THAT, DAD.
THERE WAS NO CHOICE.
WE HAD TO INCREASE THE STAKES, ENCOURAGE YOUR INVESTIGATION, STEER YOU TOWARDS US BEFORE MY TIME ON EARTH RAN OUT.
JONAS!
JUST MAKING SURE HE WASN'T ANOTHER ILLUSION. AND WHAT ABOUT JONAS' FATHER?

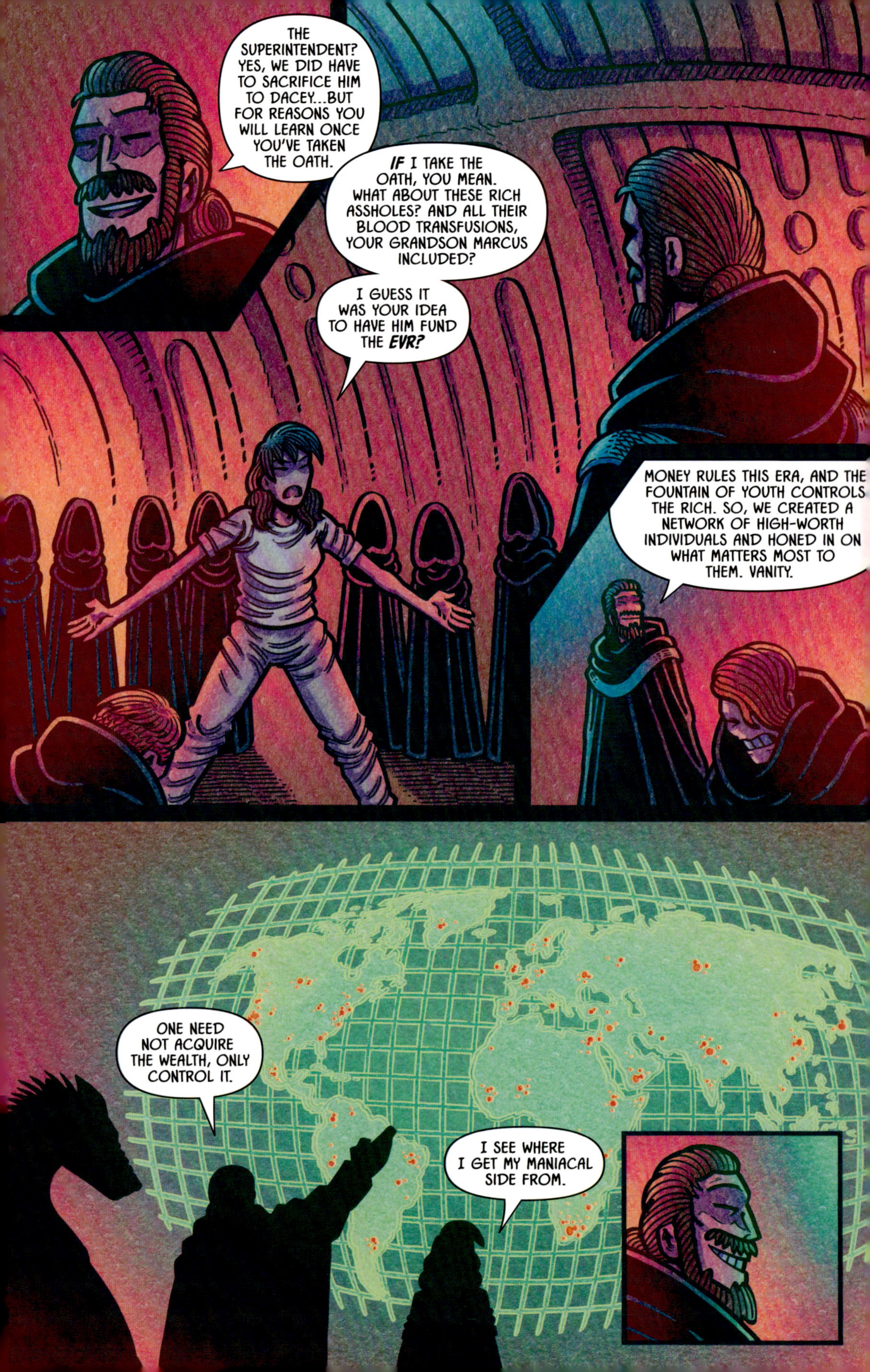
THE SUPERINTENDENT? YES, WE DID HAVE TO SACRIFICE HIM TO DACEY...BUT FOR REASONS YOU WILL LEARN ONCE YOU'VE TAKEN THE OATH.
IF I TAKE THE OATH, YOU MEAN. WHAT ABOUT THESE RICH ASSHOLES? AND ALL THEIR BLOOD TRANSFUSIONS, YOUR GRANDSON MARCUS INCLUDED?
I GUESS IT WAS YOUR IDEA TO HAVE HIM FUND THE *EVR?*
MONEY RULES THIS ERA, AND THE FOUNTAIN OF YOUTH CONTROLS THE RICH. SO, WE CREATED A NETWORK OF HIGH-WORTH INDIVIDUALS AND HONED IN ON WHAT MATTERS MOST TO THEM. VANITY.
ONE NEED NOT ACQUIRE THE WEALTH, ONLY CONTROL IT.
I SEE WHERE I GET MY MANIACAL SIDE FROM.

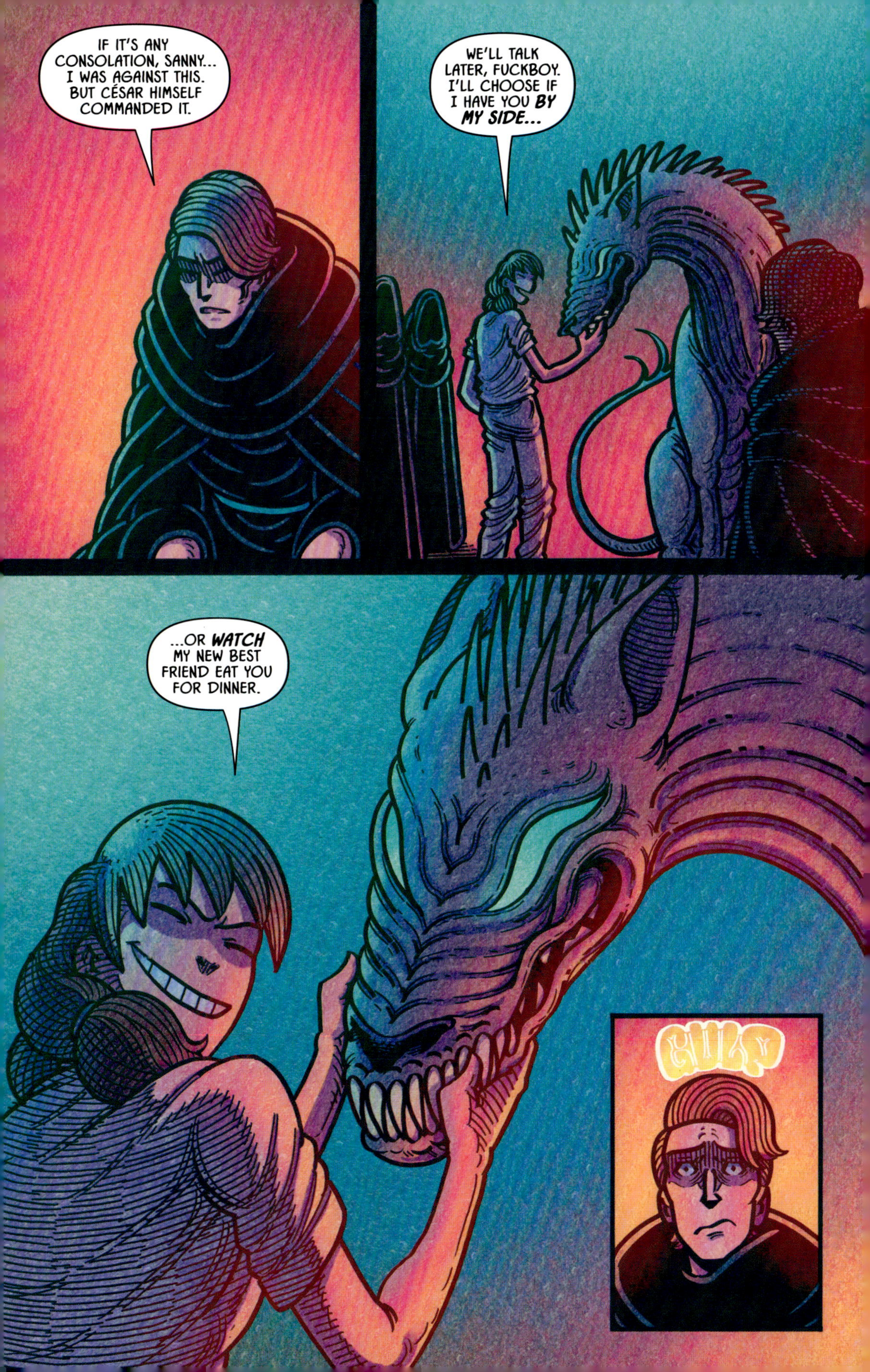
IF IT'S ANY CONSOLATION, SANNY... I WAS AGAINST THIS. BUT CÉSAR HIMSELF COMMANDED IT.
WE'LL TALK LATER, FUCKBOY. I'LL CHOOSE IF I HAVE YOU BY MY SIDE...
...OR WATCH MY NEW BEST FRIEND EAT YOU FOR DINNER.
GULP

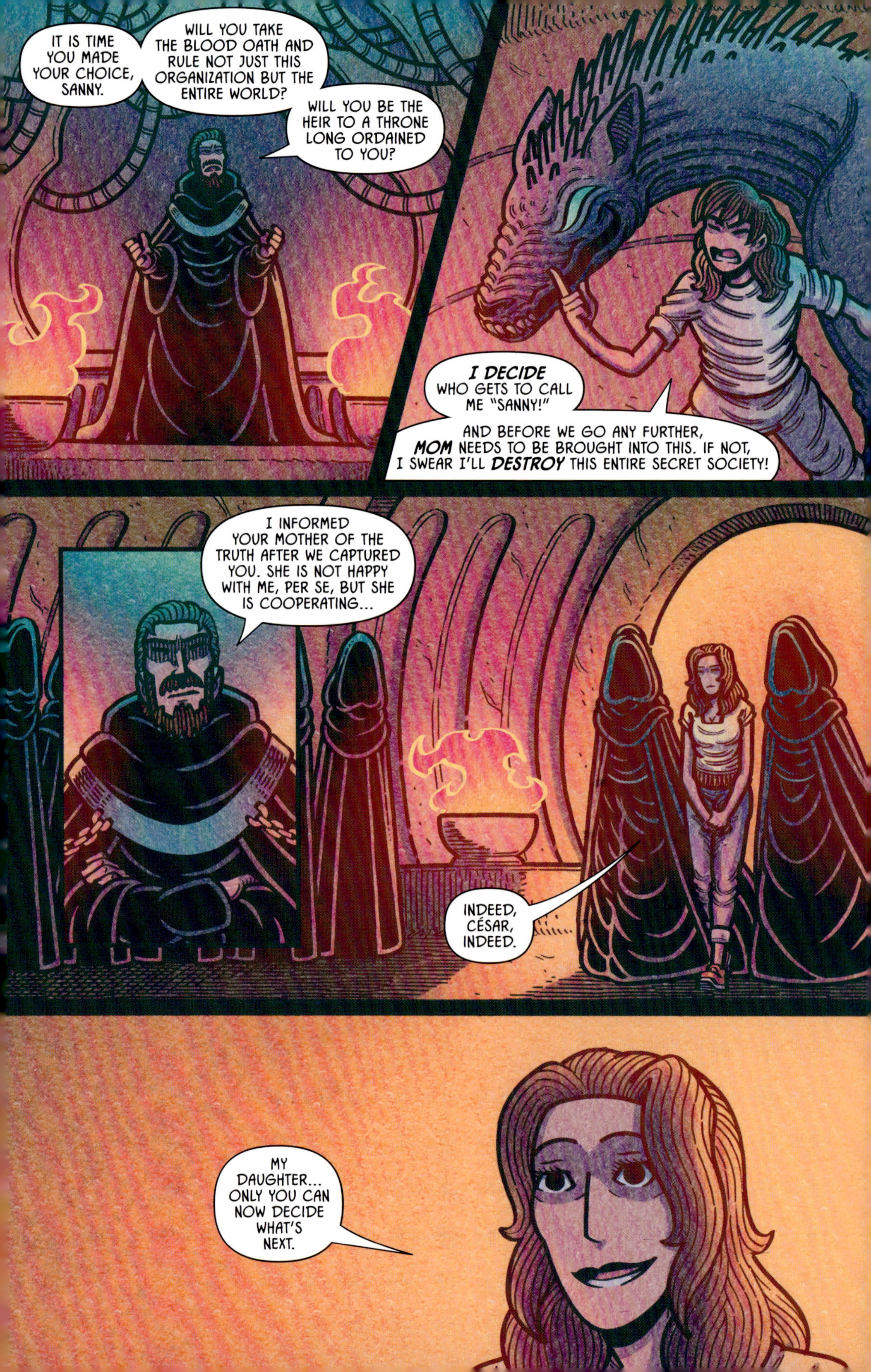
IT IS TIME YOU MADE YOUR CHOICE, SANNY.
WILL YOU TAKE THE BLOOD OATH AND RULE NOT JUST THIS ORGANIZATION BUT THE ENTIRE WORLD?
WILL YOU BE THE HEIR TO A THRONE LONG ORDAINED TO YOU?
I DECIDE WHO GETS TO CALL ME "SANNY!"
AND BEFORE WE GO ANY FURTHER, MOM NEEDS TO BE BROUGHT INTO THIS. IF NOT, I SWEAR I'LL DESTROY THIS ENTIRE SECRET SOCIETY!
I INFORMED YOUR MOTHER OF THE TRUTH AFTER WE CAPTURED YOU. SHE IS NOT HAPPY WITH ME, PER SE, BUT SHE IS COOPERATING...
INDEED, CÉSAR, INDEED.
MY DAUGHTER... ONLY YOU CAN NOW DECIDE WHAT'S NEXT.

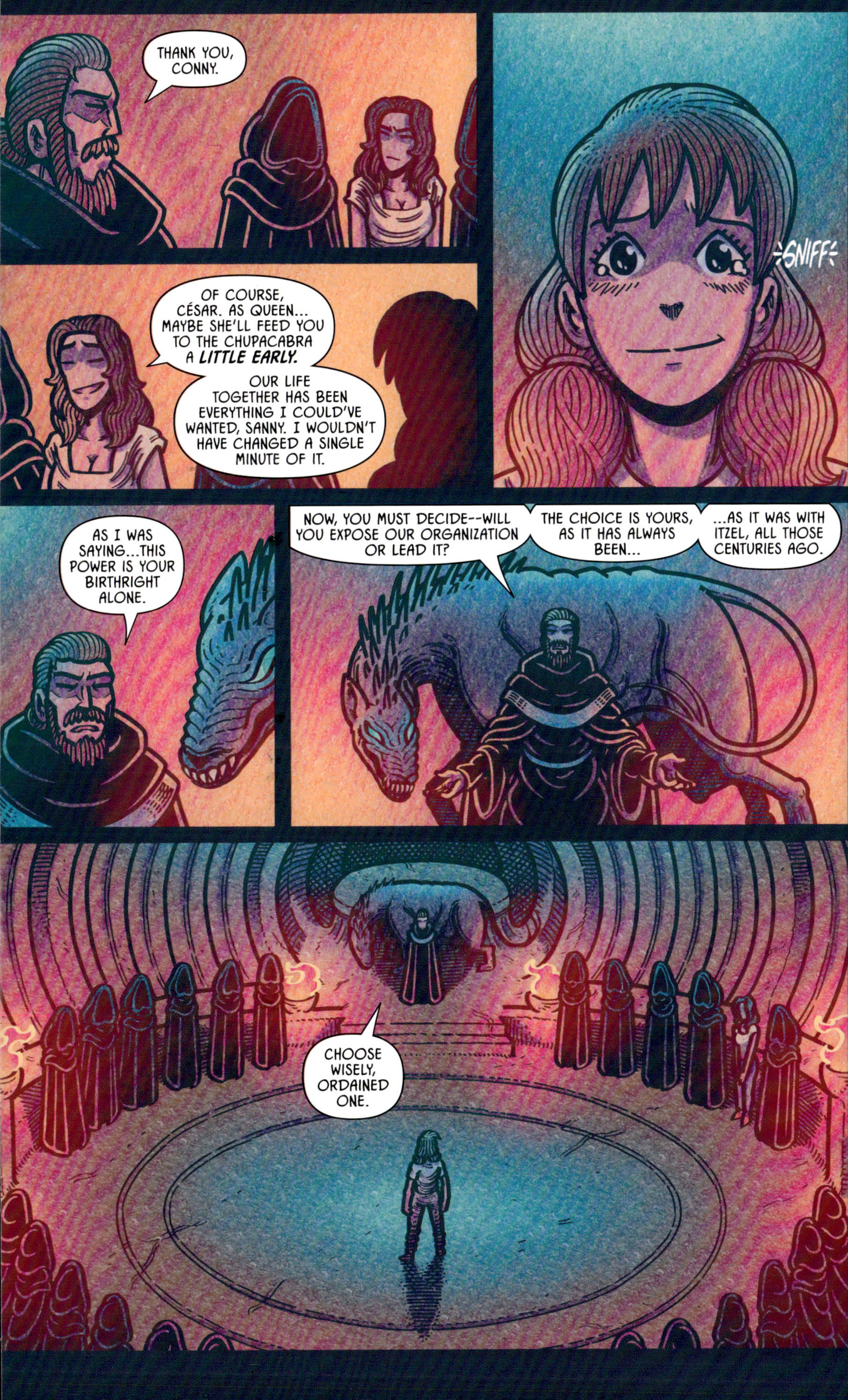
THANK YOU, CONNY.
OF COURSE, CÉSAR. AS QUEEN... MAYBE SHE'LL FEED YOU TO THE CHUPACABRA A *LITTLE EARLY.*
OUR LIFE TOGETHER HAS BEEN EVERYTHING I COULD'VE WANTED, SANNY. I WOULDN'T HAVE CHANGED A SINGLE MINUTE OF IT.
SNIFF
AS I WAS SAYING...THIS POWER IS YOUR BIRTHRIGHT ALONE.
NOW, YOU MUST DECIDE--WILL YOU EXPOSE OUR ORGANIZATION OR LEAD IT?
THE CHOICE IS YOURS, AS IT HAS ALWAYS BEEN...
...AS IT WAS WITH ITZEL, ALL THOSE CENTURIES AGO.
CHOOSE WISELY, ORDAINED ONE.

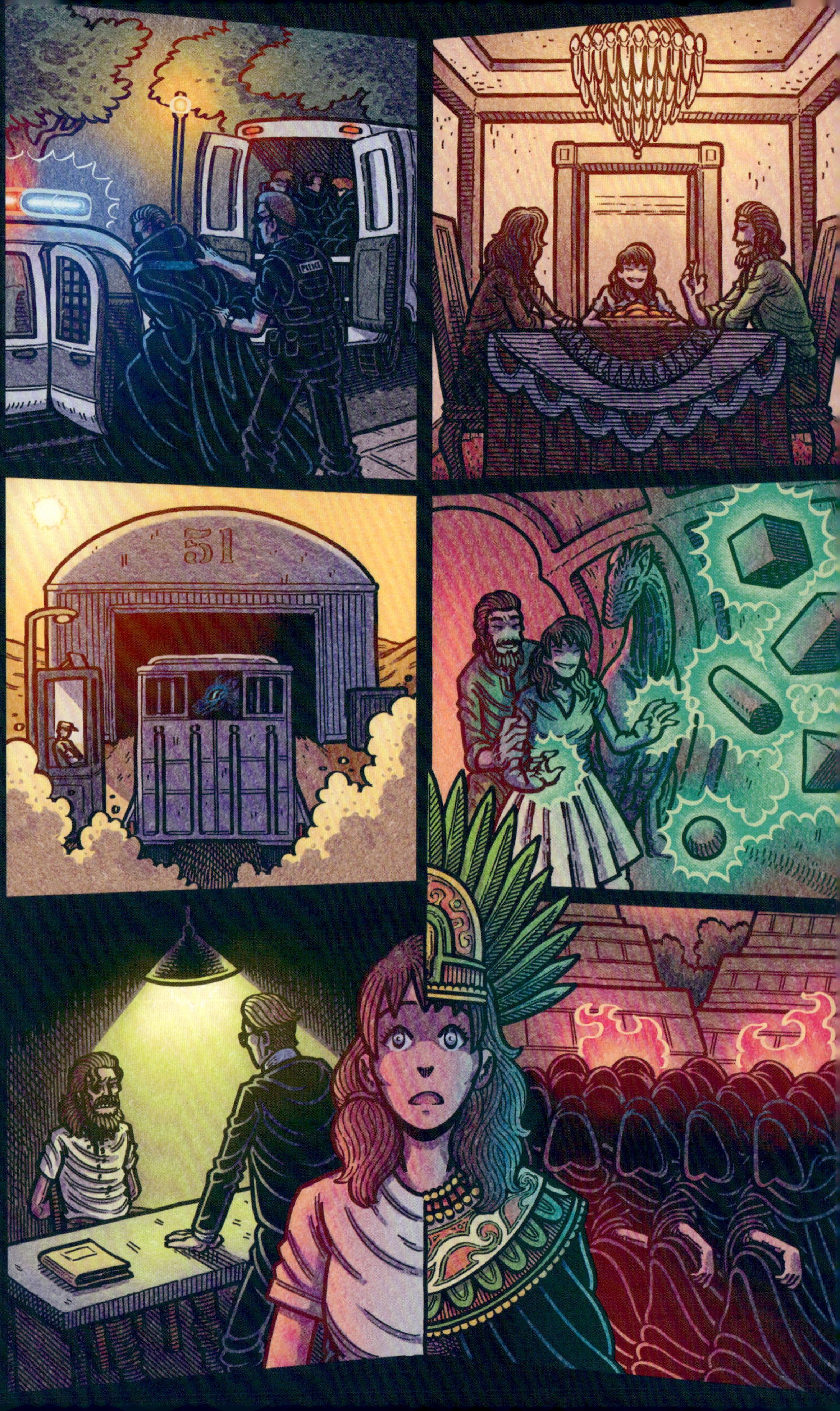
51

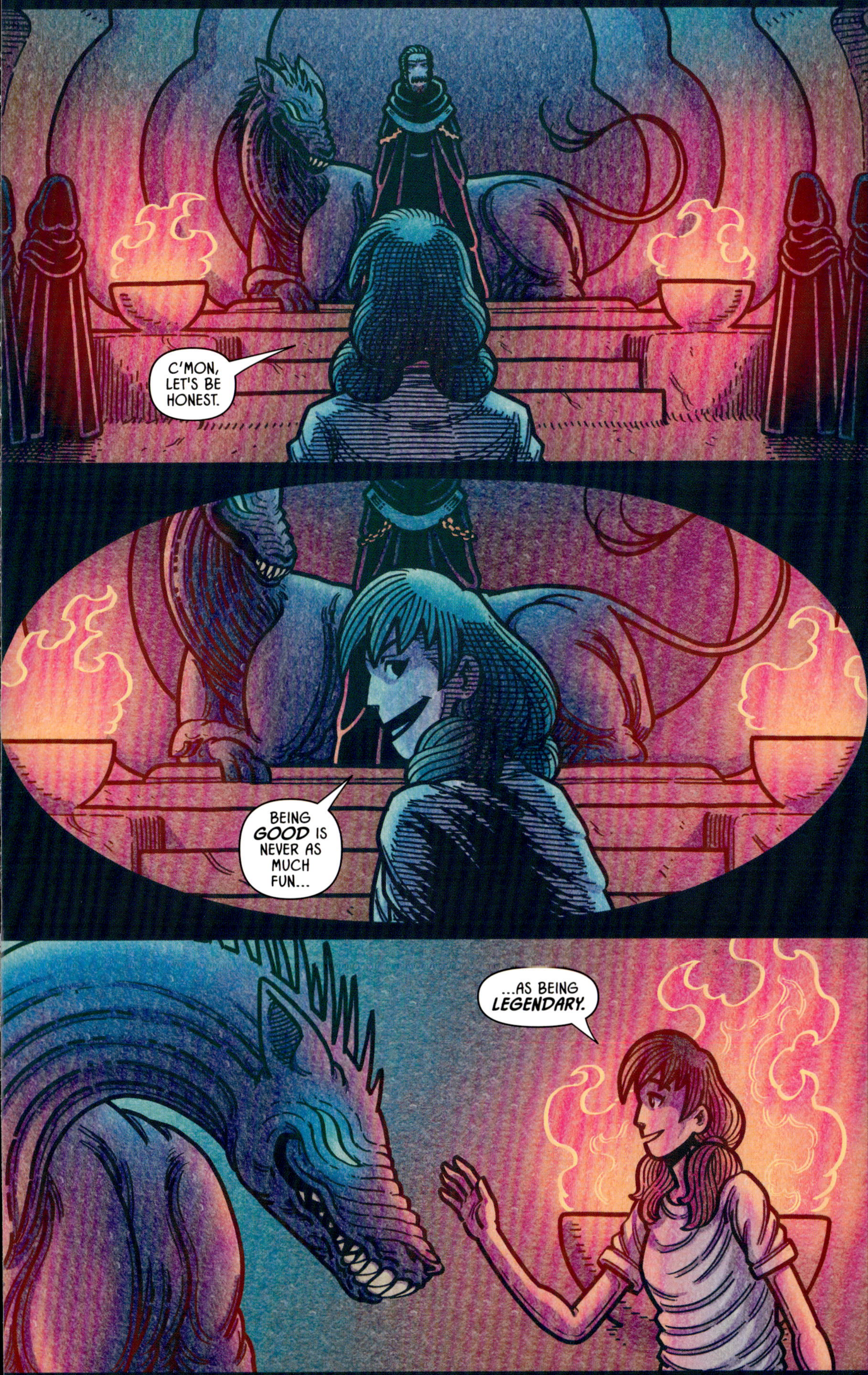
C'MON, LET'S BE HONEST.
BEING **GOOD** IS NEVER AS MUCH FUN...
...AS BEING ***LEGENDARY.***

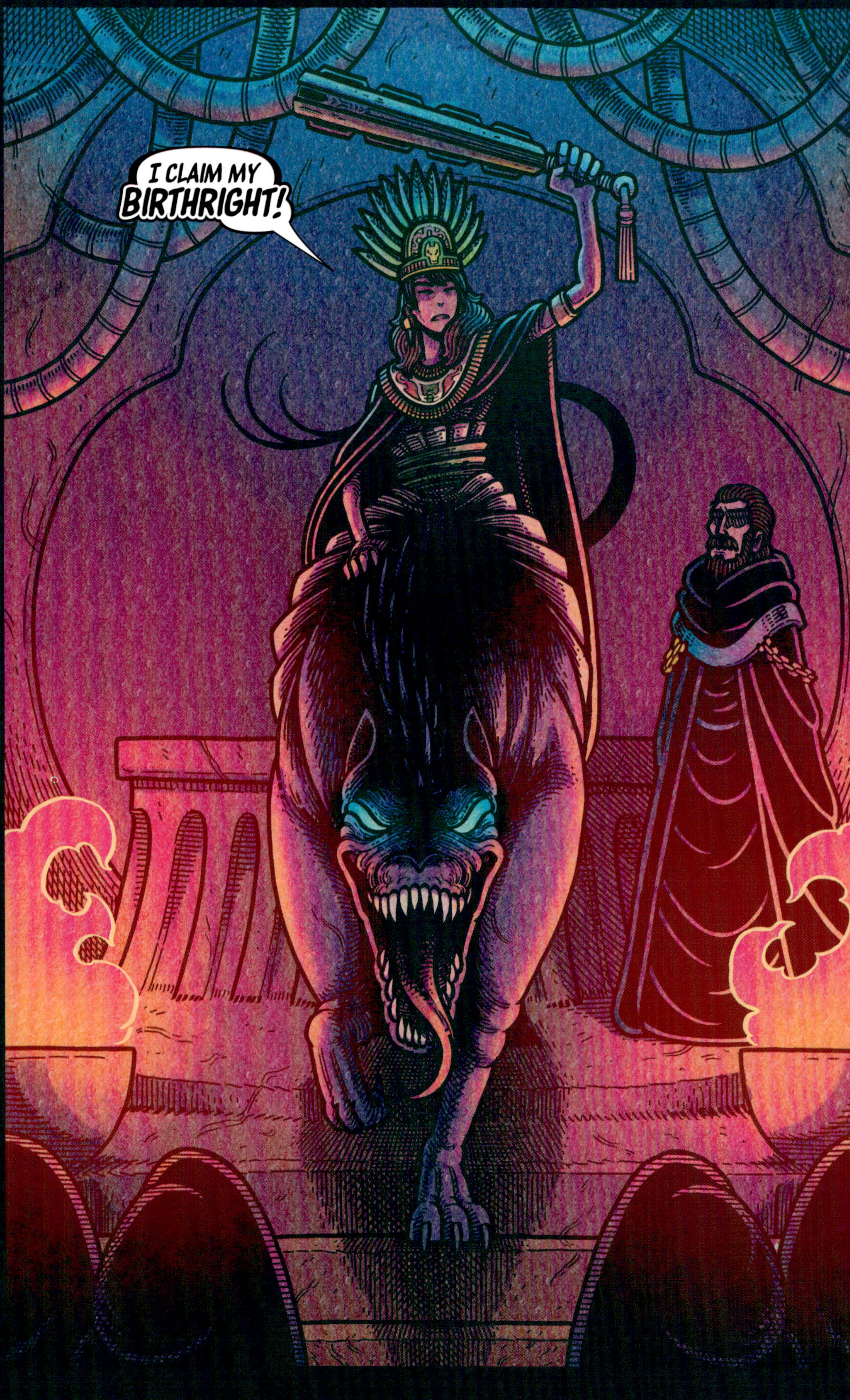
I CLAIM MY BIRTHRIGHT!

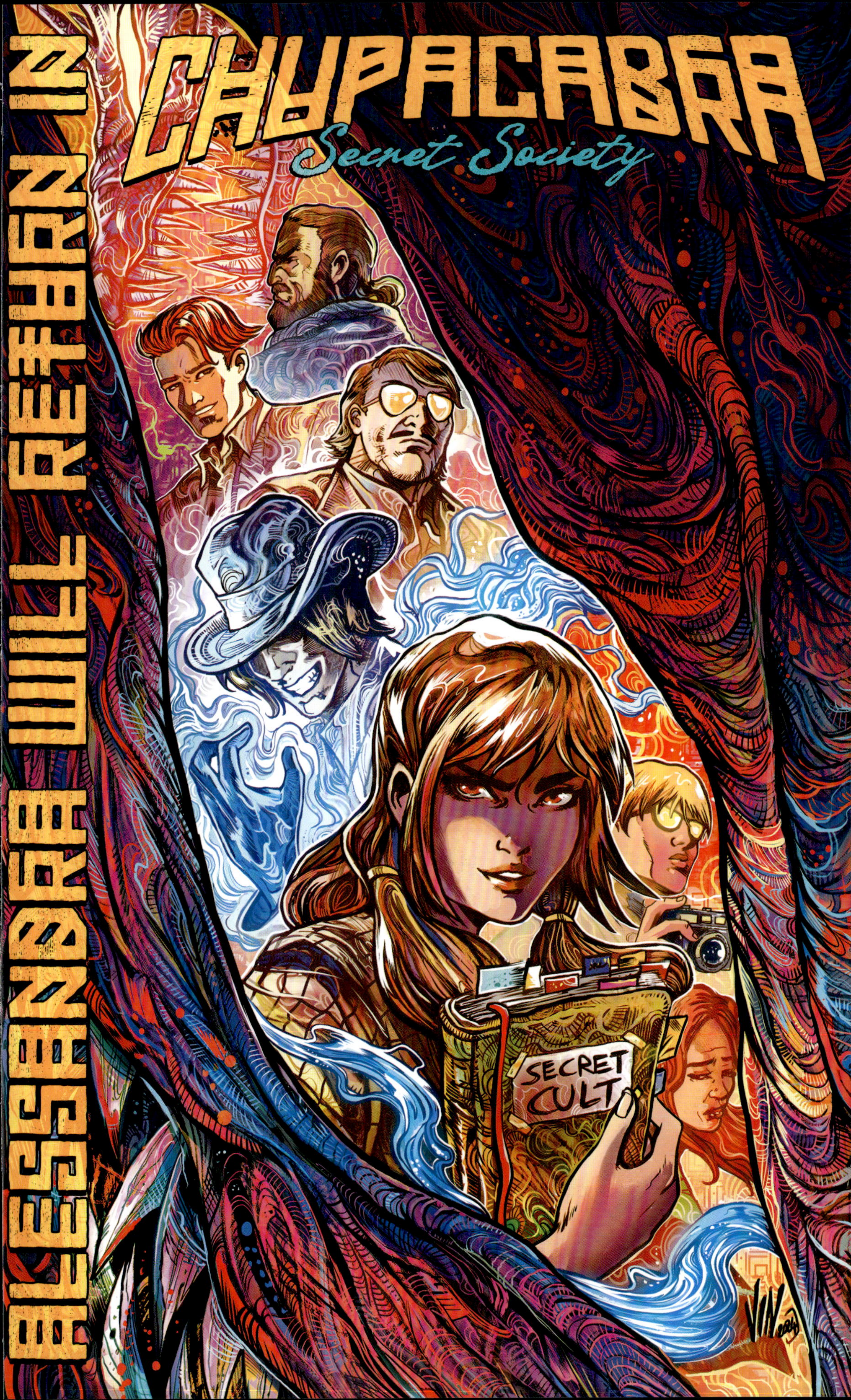
CHUPACABRA
Secret Society
ALESSANDRA WILL RETURN IN
SECRET CULT

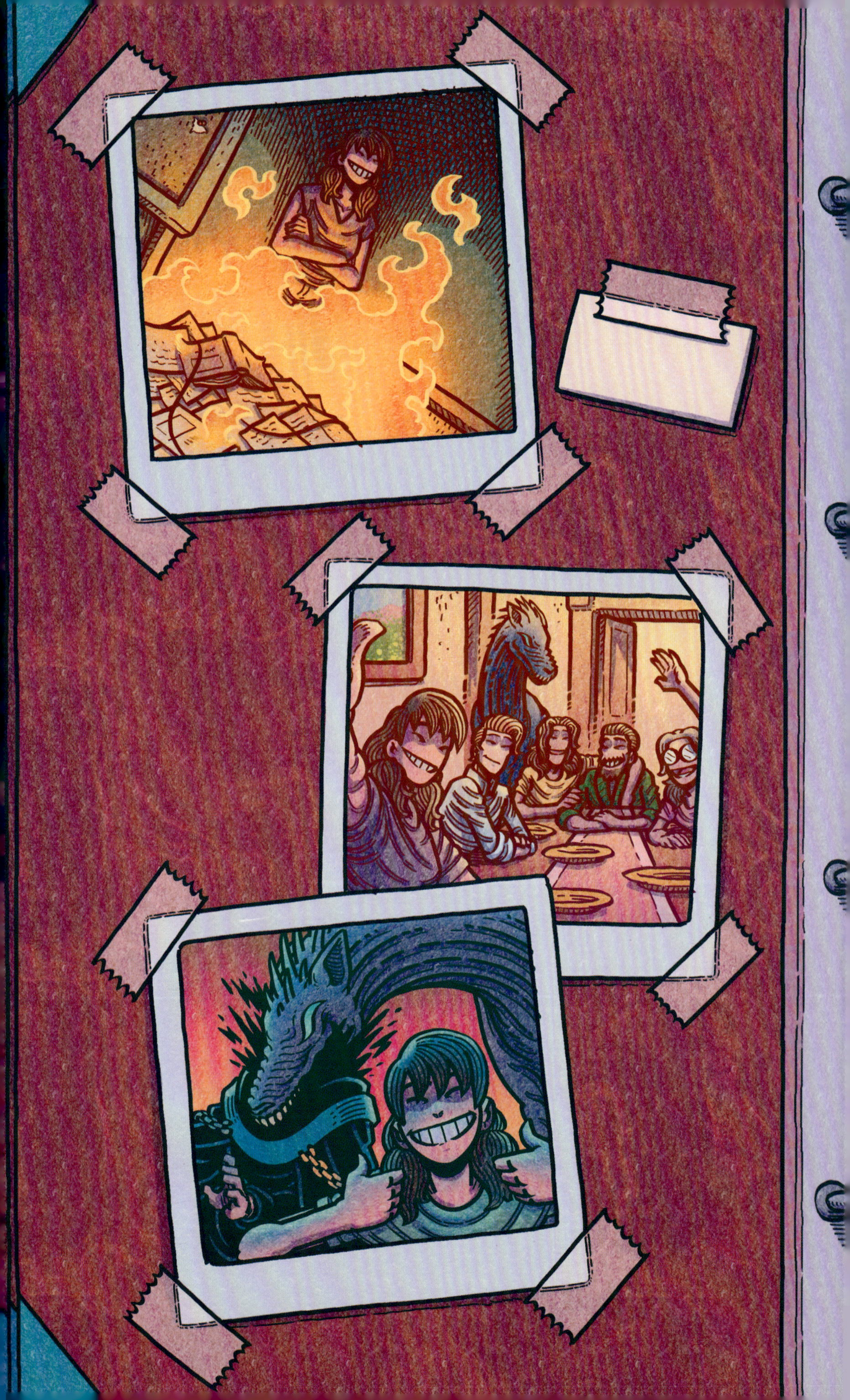

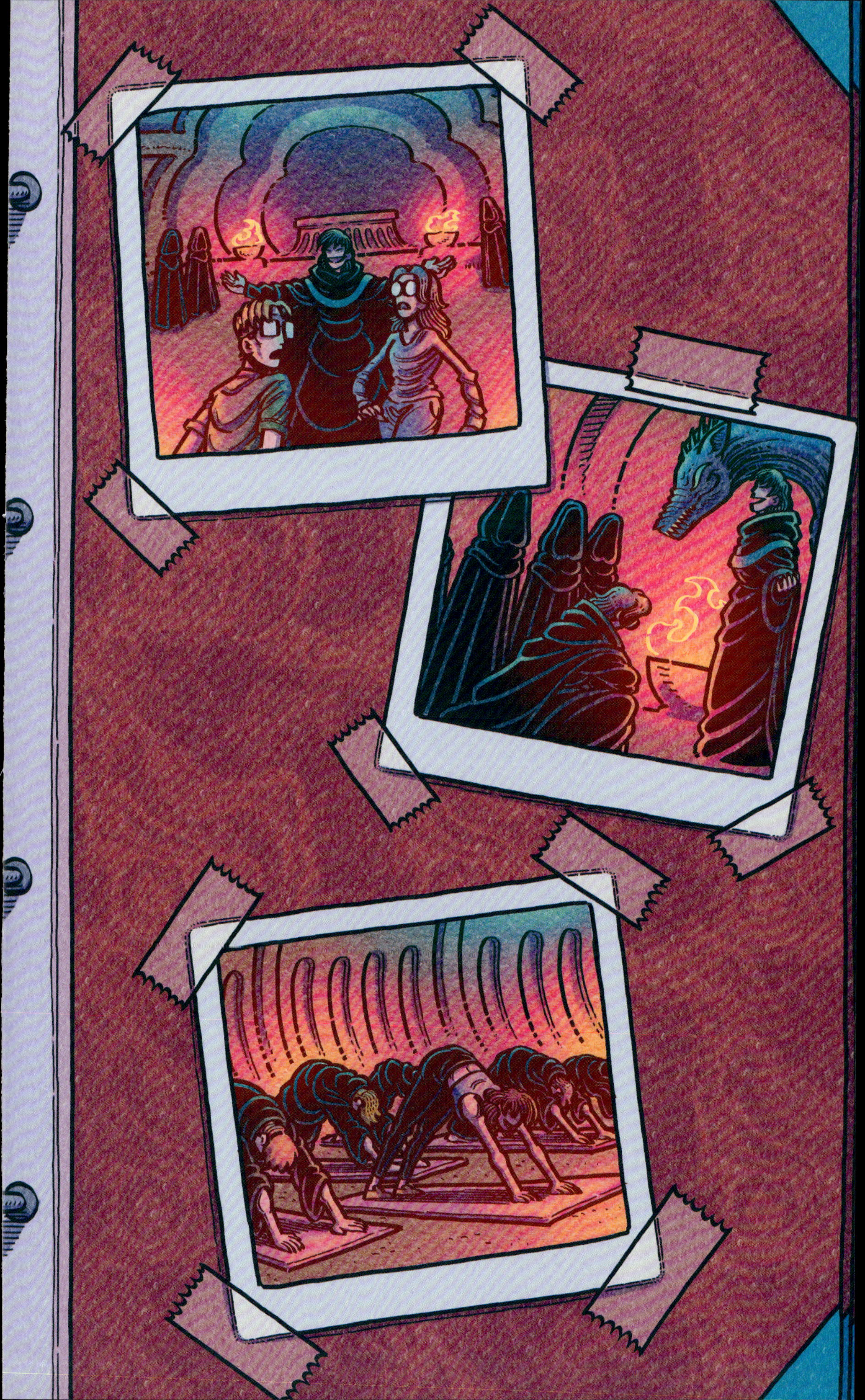

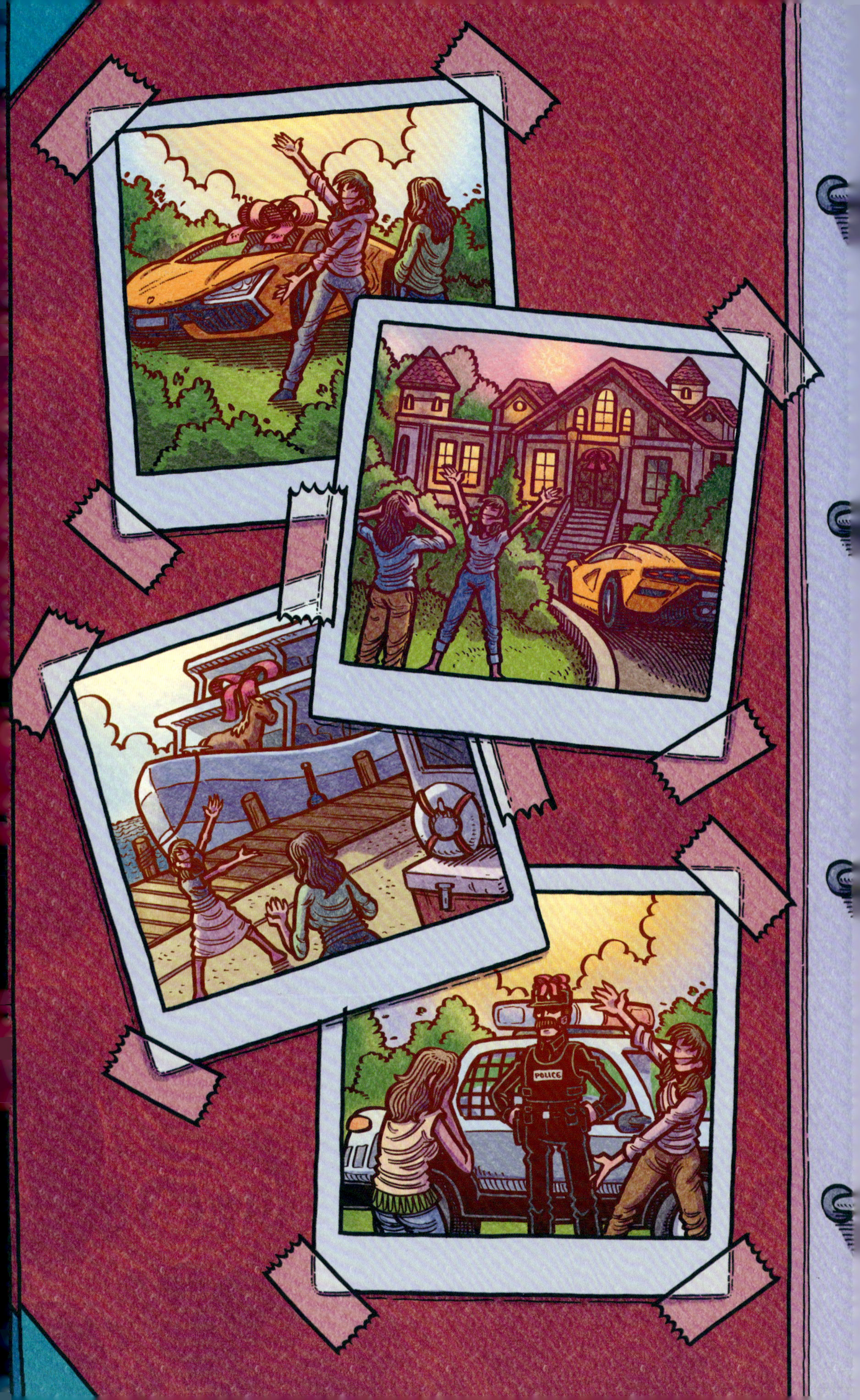
POLICE

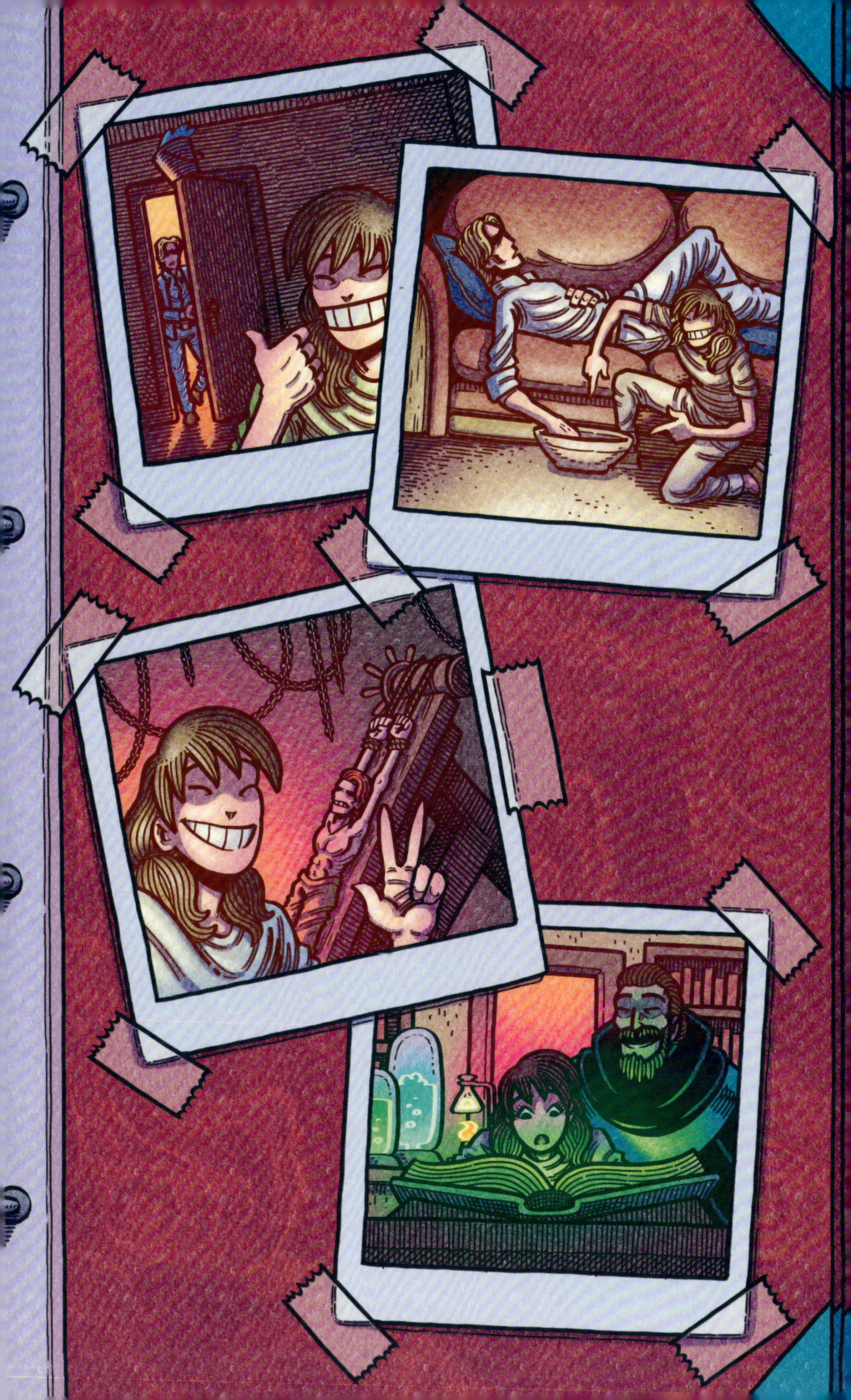

HERNENDEZ FAMILY

Shrouded in mystery, the Hernández family has resided in East Valley since they moved there when Alessandra was two years old. Even after César, the father, was killed in the tragic "accident," it seemed that little Alessandra, smart and ambitious, was on her way to great accomplishments. Little did she know, today her life is unfolding like a feel good story. Consuelo, her mother, works a minimum-wage job at the local coffee shop, never thinking twice about putting her daughter ahead of her own wants and desires.

This is a family brought together by unwavering love, divided by a grand secret, and reunited by the powerful truth.

EL CHUPACABRA

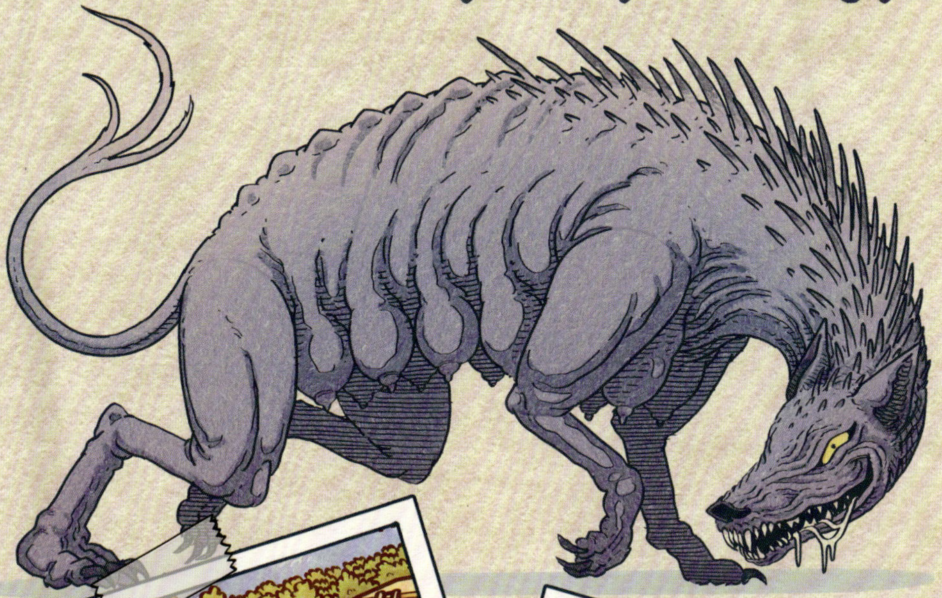

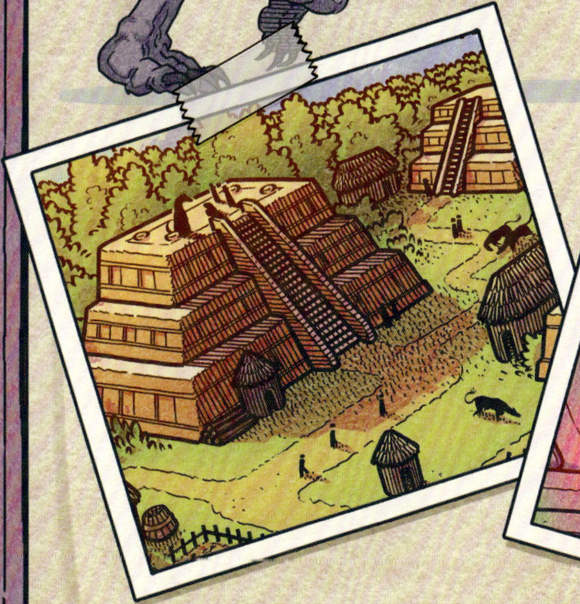

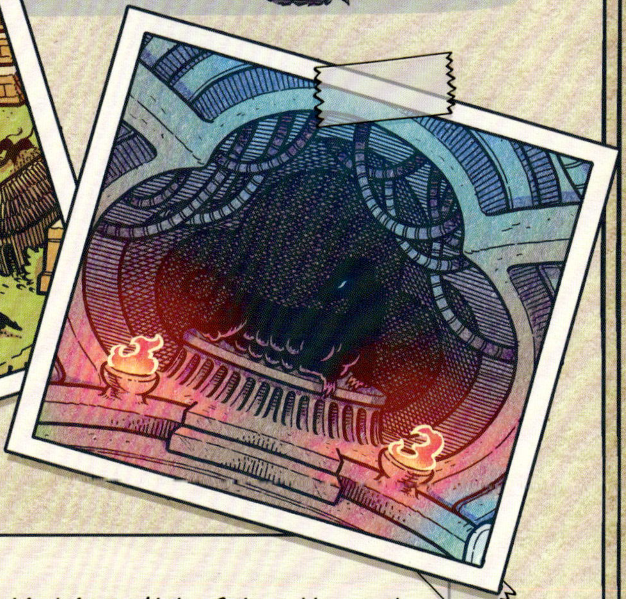

Dacey, the last of her kind, is an Alpha Cabra, the most ancient species of Chupacabra to have ever existed. Their existence is riddled with mystery, though during the ancient Mayan empires they reigned supreme. Their mystical powers are bestowed upon the entire race of Alpha Cabras and are not unique to Dacey herself. However, being the last of her kind does make Dacey rare and invaluable to the order of the Chupacabras.

Dacey, an ancient beast whose milk provides magical powers, whose hunger yearns for human flesh, and the sight of whom will terrorize even the most dangerous of men, will only follow those of Mayan ancestry.

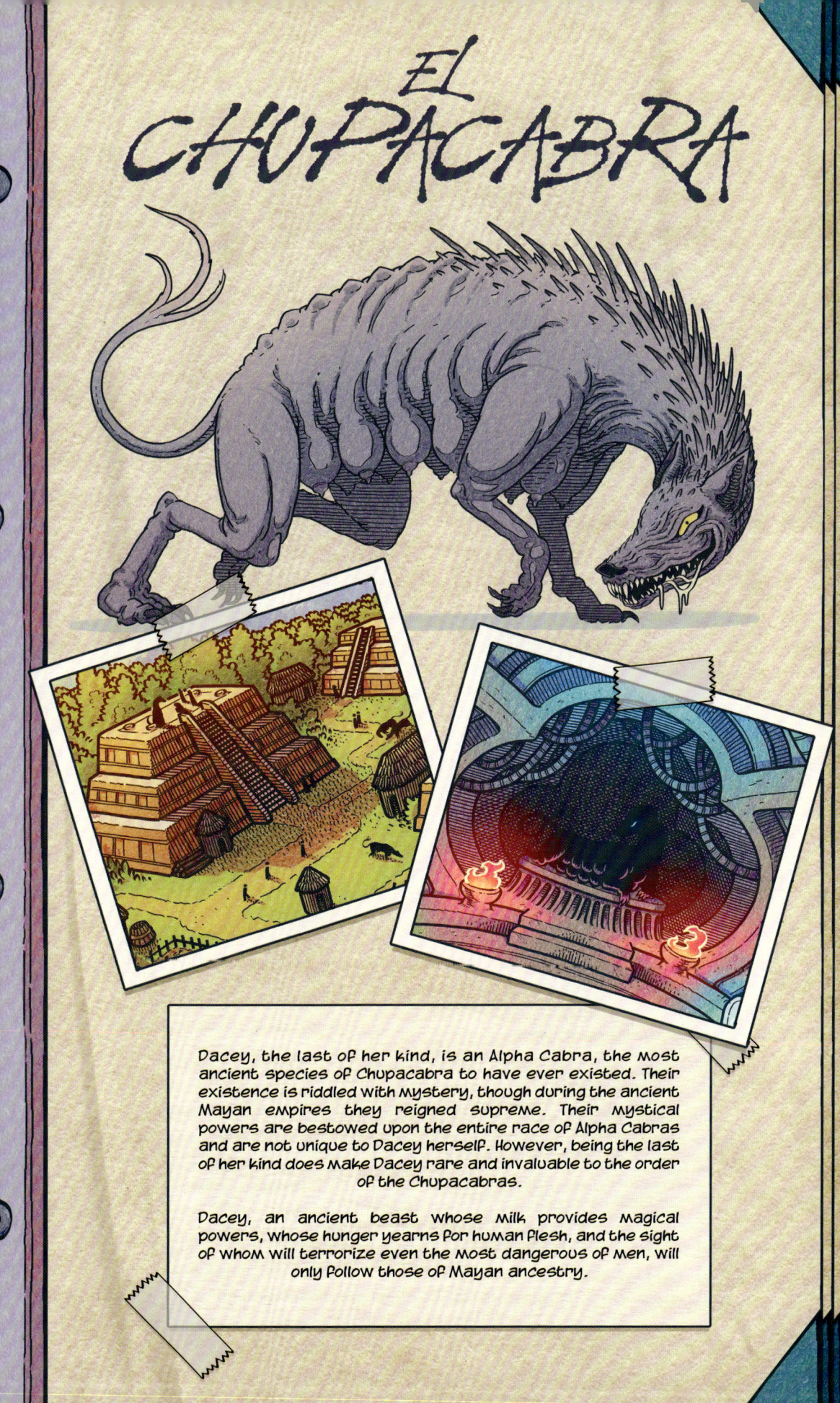

PHILLIP WRIGHT STONEHART

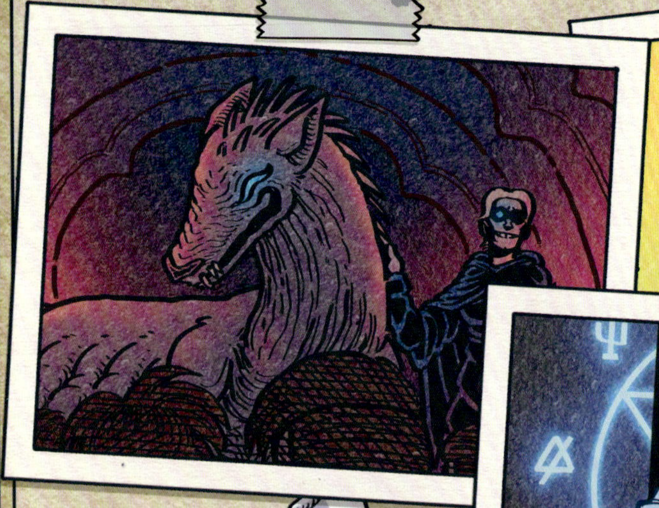

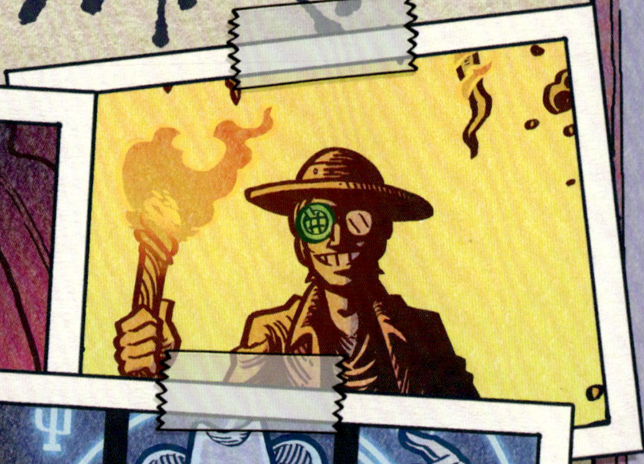

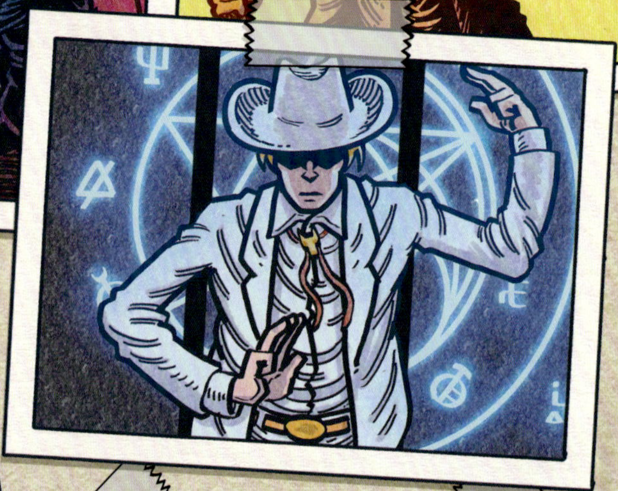

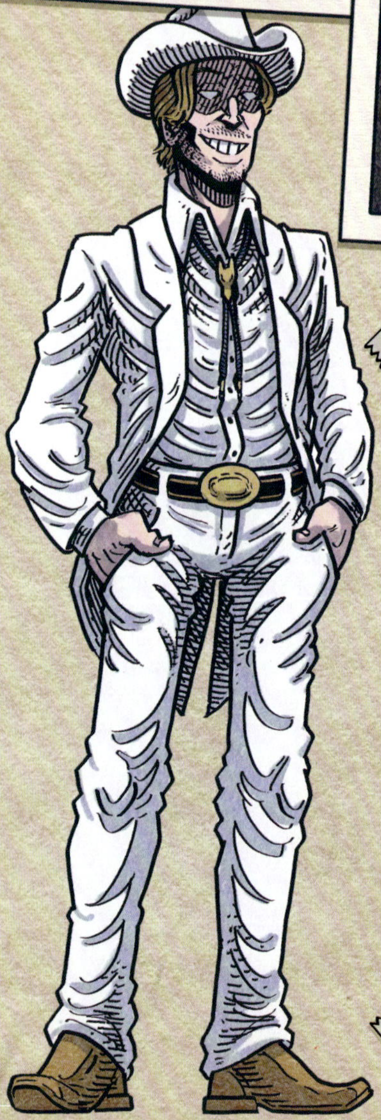

Phillip Wright Stonehart III has been the leader of the Order of the Chupacabras for nearly three centuries, thanks to the dark arts... and some babies' blood. The first white man to discover, find, and join the order, Stonehart serves a higher master... who remains unknown, at least for now.

Fierce, revolutionary, and bold, Stonehart has no problem with getting his hands dirty, but he also enjoys the extravagant soirees and riches that come with his position. Beloved, trusted, and admired, Stonehart is not just the leader of the Chupacabras, he's a beacon of light to all secret societies...that is, unless you get on his bad side and he feeds you to Dacey.

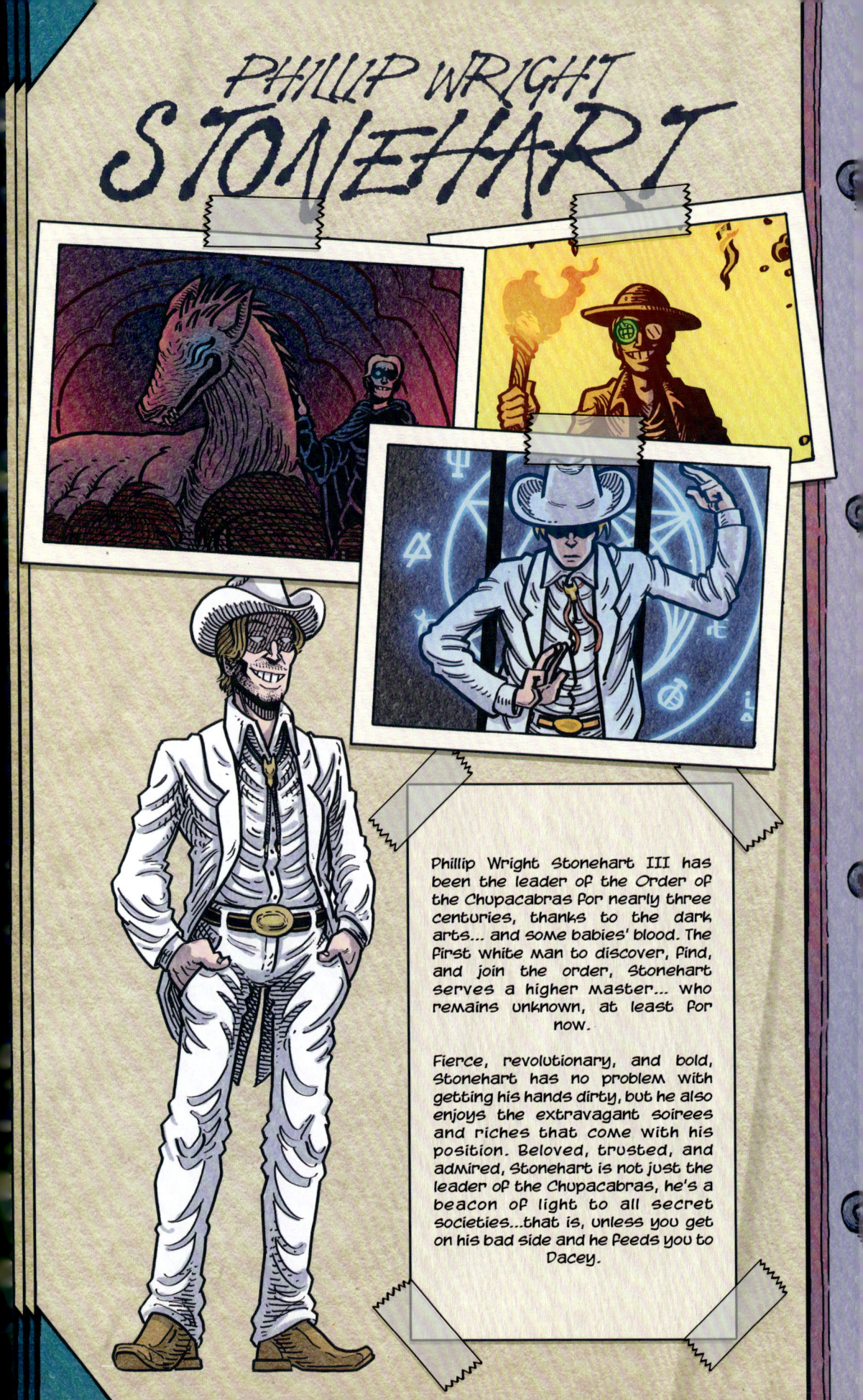

THE BILLIONAIRE MARCUS POE

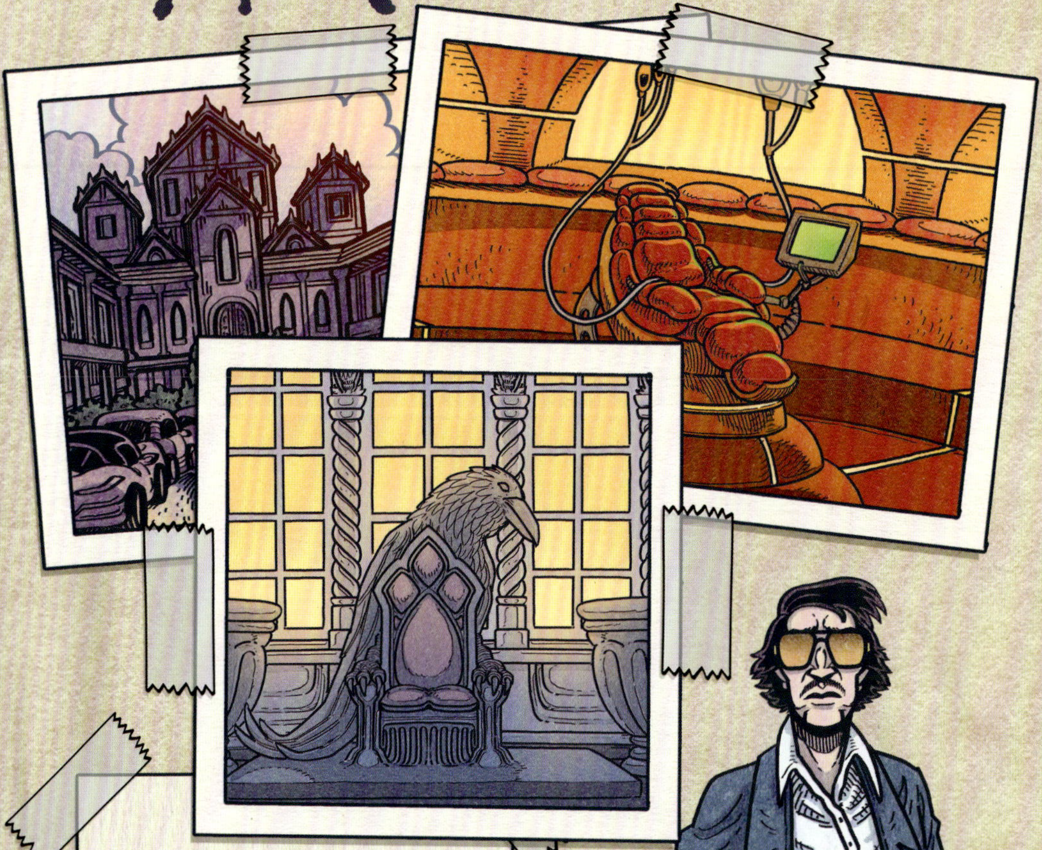

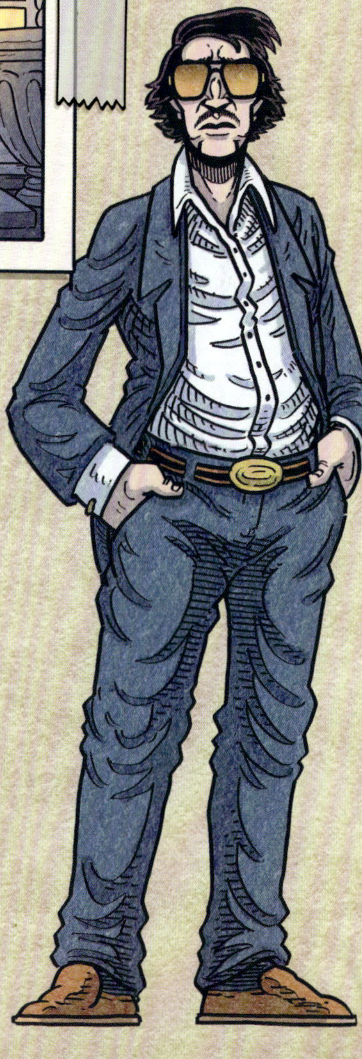

Descendant of Edgar Allan Poe and a prominent member of both the Freemasons and Illuminati, Marcus bridges the gap between the two great organizations for the Order of the Chupacabras. Marcus made his fortune through real estate and the family inheritance, like all respectable one-percenters. The archetype of the billionaire class, Marcus will stop at nothing to stay young, investing in blood transfusion therapy with the likes of Stonehart and others who can serve his insatiable hunger for power... but who is controlling Marcus?

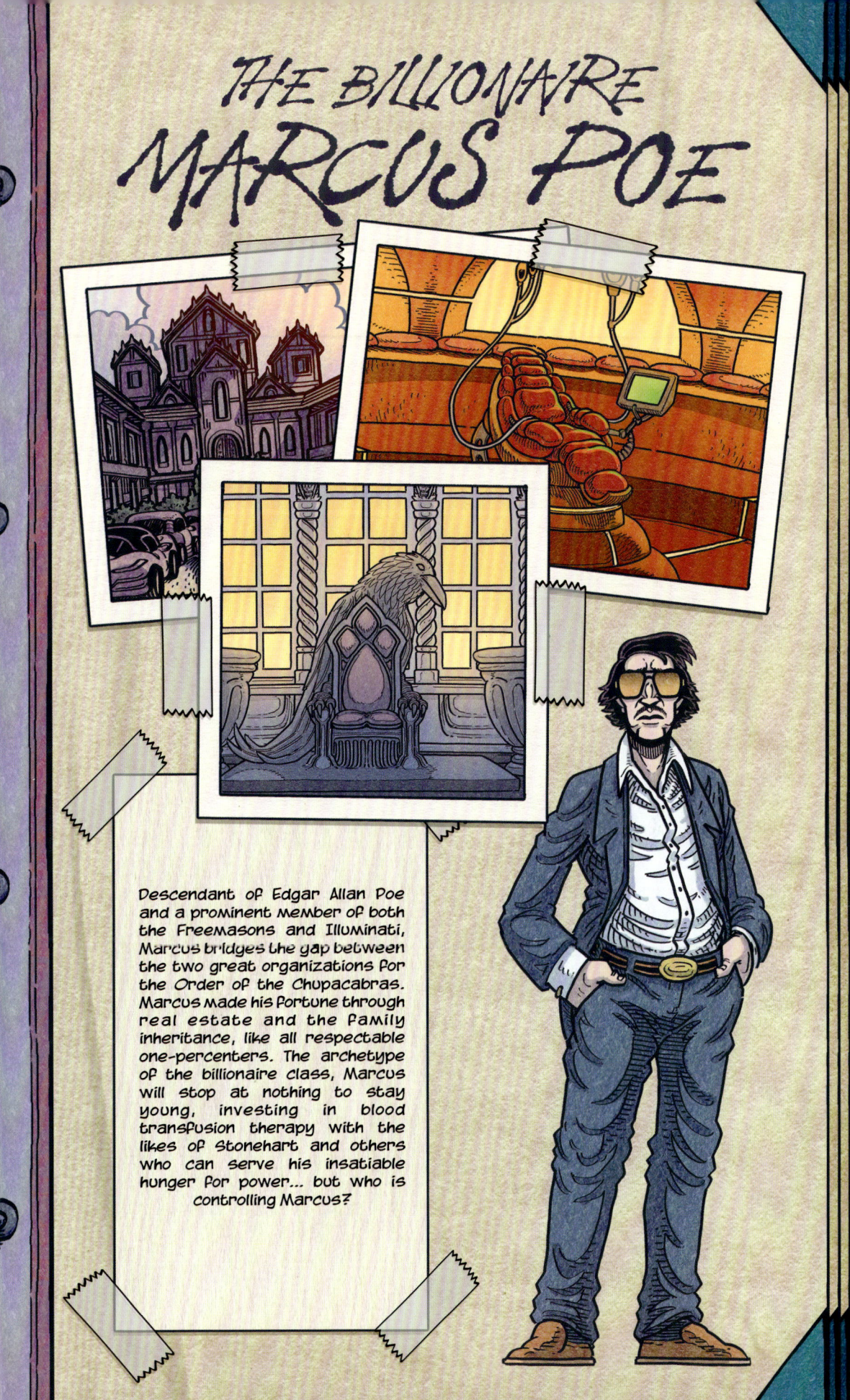

THE ORDER OF THE CHUPACABRA

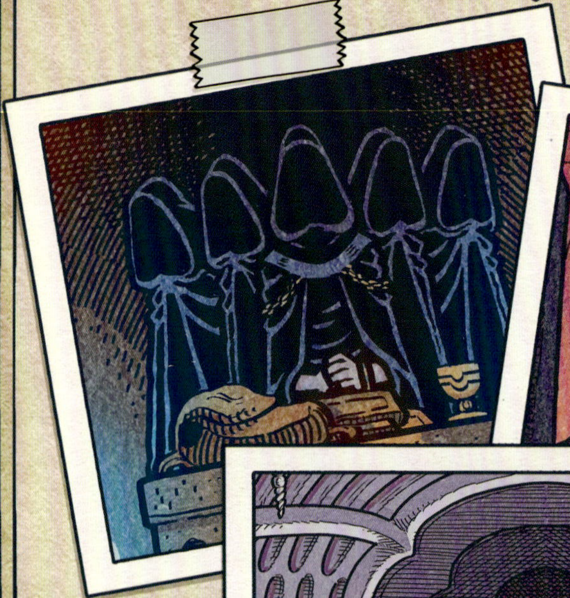

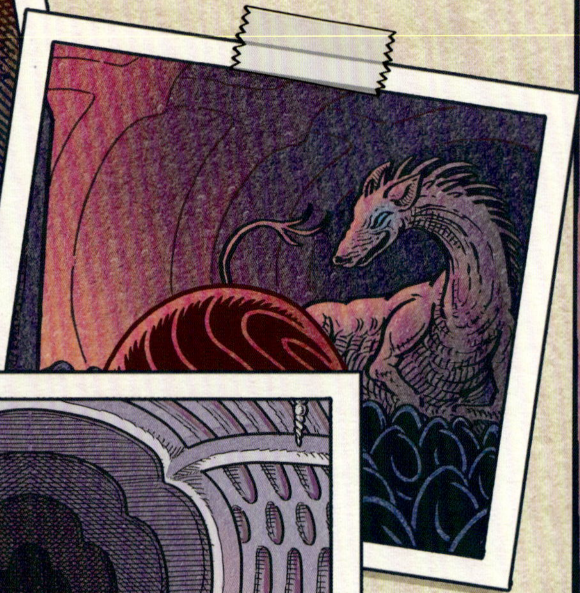

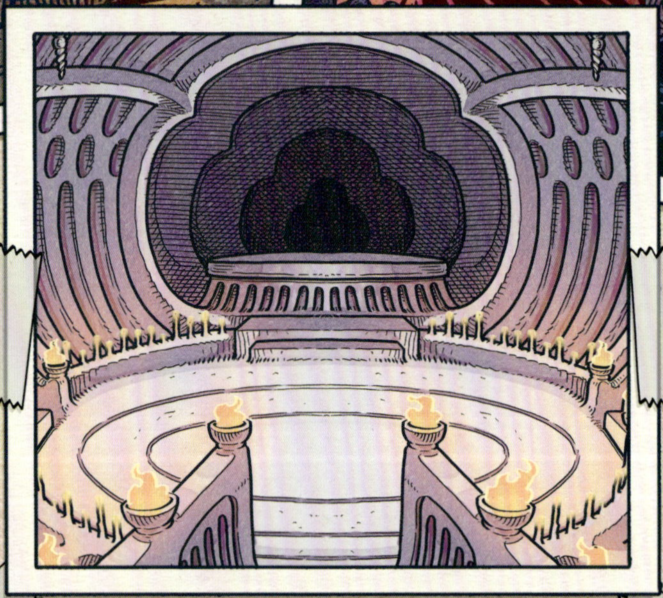

The secret organization to end all secret organizations. Members must first be a part of another secret society — any will do — before the opportunity to court the Chupacabras is even possible. They control the billionaires, they control the fountain of youth, they even control the weather.

The source of their power is a monstrous Chupacabra by the name of Dacey, who dates back to a time when her kind roamed the Mayan landscape and served no master but themselves. Between Dacey and the Order of the Chupacabra is an alliance honored until the end of time: blood oaths forged that cannot be undone. This union propels the Order to greatness no other organization could imagine.

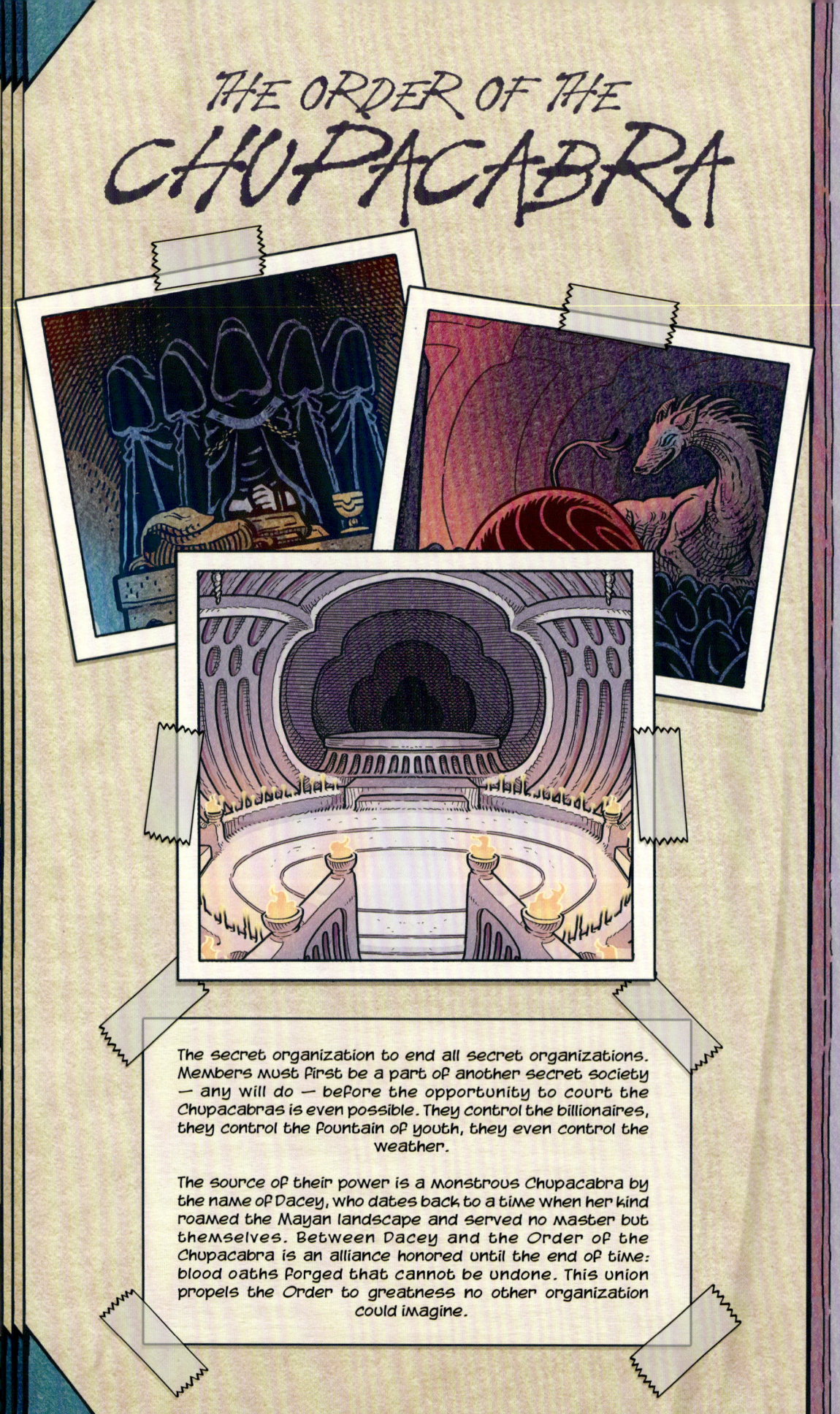

EVA DAILY

Vision is one thing, execution is another. Alessandra Dacey Hernández, like many students before her, knew her school needed a voice. But up until her, no one had done anything about it. But with the death of her father having precarious circumstances her thirst for the truth and having a vehicle to tell it felt almost preordained. Thanks to her unique drive and intelligence, she was able to bring forth a lasting school paper that would become an institution in the East Valley Ridge community. Like her father, Alessandra was much more than just a reporter, and the EVR Daily is much more than a school paper: it's a beacon for all students looking to find their way in the world of journalism.

In just a short four years, since its inception, the EVR Daily has transformed from a small school publication into a buzzing newspaper for the whole San Diego area. With Alessandra approaching her senior graduation, the paper is looking to find its next Editor-in-Chief who can crack the next award winning story, for which it has become accustomed to doing.